The Young in One Another's Arms

The Young in One

LITTLE SISTER'S CLASSICS

Another's Arms

JANE RULE

ARSENAL PULP PRESS
Vancouver

ARSENAL PULP PRESS
341 Water Street, Suite 200
Vancouver, BC V6B 1B8
arsenalpulp.com

The publisher gratefully acknowledges the support of the Canada Council for the Arts and the British Columbia Arts Council for its publishing program, and the Government of Canada through the Book Publishing Industry Development Program for its publishing activities.

Contemporary reviews, images of early draft manuscript pages, and the original Doubleday press release were provided by the University of British Columbia Archives.

Little Sister's Classics series editor: Mark Macdonald
Editors for the press: Robert Ballantyne and Brian Lam
Text and cover design: Shyla Seller
Little Sister's Classics logo design: Hermant Gohil

Printed and bound in Canada

Library and Archives Canada Cataloguing in Publication:

Rule, Jane, 1931-
         The young in one another's arms / Jane Rule.
(Little Sister's Classics)
Originally published: Garden City, N.Y. : Doubleday, 1977.
ISBN 1-55152-181-4
I. Title. II. Series.
PS8535.U77Y6 2005   C813'.54   C2005-900565-3

ISBN-13 978-1-55152-181-7

Contents

Preface

In the autumn of 1994, at the Supreme Court of British Columbia, a huge melodrama was unfolding. Vancouver's lesbian and gay bookstore was finally able – after a struggle that had already taken eight years – to set on record the abuses it had met at the hands of the clumsy and foolish would-be censors of Canada Customs. The books we imported from American publishers were routinely scrutinized by Customs officials as part of their dull-minded, perpetual witch-hunt for traces of what they themselves declared to be obscene. For Canadians who read, write, and sell books, the entire situation was obscene.

Testifying on behalf of the bookstore that year, Jane Rule said, in part:

> Now there are quite a number of people in Canada who do know that *The Young in One Another's Arms* won the Canadian Authors' Association Award for the best novel of 1978. There are a great many more people in Canada who know that *The Young in One Another's Arms* was detained by Customs. And that is what I have to carry. I have to carry a reputation created by this charge from which I have no way of defending myself. ... And I bitterly resent the attempt to marginalize, trivialize and even criminalize what I have to say because I happen to be a lesbian, I happen to be a novelist, I happen to have bookstores and publishers who are dedicated to producing my work. The assumption is, therefore, that there must be something pornographic because of my sexual orientation, and I think that is a shocking way to deal with my community.

These words, spoken in Rule's calm, precise tone in that hushed courtroom, with her uncommon mix of confidence and defiance, came to represent the condensed message that the bookstore would take to the Supreme Court of Canada in 2000, and into the new millennium as the court battles continued. Somehow Rule had managed to sum it all up: We are a community, and *we will not budge* – not to bigots, not to Canada Customs, not to anyone.

We are delighted and privileged to launch the Little Sister's Classics series with such an exceptional piece of literature. *The Young in One Another's Arms* is a complex and highly focused novel about the kinds of community that Rule spoke about that day in court. The book speaks to how we are as individuals, with all of our disparate backgrounds and causes, and how, when we come together, we are stronger as a community than on our own. This is a novel that speaks to the goodness of human relations without being giddily optimistic. We are all players on this delicate stage, and we are all responsible for our actions. And we are all, at the end of the day, "minorities" in one form or another.

As if the opportunity to present this beautiful novel in a new light were not enough, we take further joy in presenting an introduction by Katherine V. Forrest, a Canadian-born American writer introducing an American-born Canadian writer's book. Thanks to the diligent work of the archivists at the University of British Columbia (notably, Christopher Hives), this new edition of Rule's book features a complement of book reviews, manuscript details, and critical analysis.

We are very proud to be able to now part the curtains on this novel and this series. Our debt is to all who have come before us in this, our community.

Mark Macdonald, 2005

Introduction

KATHERINE V. FORREST

Like the best work of our best writers, Jane Rule's novels and short stories and essays remain germane to our contemporary lives and to the lives of the people we know. They portray nothing less than the intricacies of our existence, the profundities of birth and death, the complex internal contractions that inhabit all of us, the essential fluidity of our sexuality and identity – in short, the marvelous inventions so many of us who live on the margins have made of our lives.

Jane Rule's publishing history began four decades ago when her groundbreaking first novel, *Desert of the Heart* (1964), was initially published in England; it remains a world-wide classic of lesbian literature. It has now been sixteen years since she gave us her final novel, *After the Fire* (1989). In any one of the seven novels she published, the reader will find a writer concerned at some level with the workings of family and community, and an illumination of the realms of possibility open to those who no longer conveniently fit within the conventional, prosaic expectations of society. Her books explore life in transition, the connections all-too-human characters attempt and sometimes succeed in devising for themselves.

Today, Jane Rule stands tall as a visionary who held steadfast to a conviction considered iconoclastic by some contemporary lesbian critics and readers. As a minority community, it is we who have grown toward the themes freshly relevant to us in books that seem only burnished by time. Surely no recent development in our community of lesbians, gay men, bisexuals, and transgendered people exceeds in importance our redefinition and reconfiguration of family, the creation of our own communities that Jane Rule was writing about all those years ago.

No book of hers more represents and validates this view than *The Young in One Another's Arms*. Recognized and celebrated in its own time with the award of Best Novel of the Year in 1978 by the Canadian Authors Association, it is a book that is achingly, wrenchingly relevant to our times: no reader can help but superimpose the social upheaval, the political climate, and the headlines of war from today's newspapers on many aspects of its story.

The plot shimmers in its deceptive simplicity like the surface of a lake. It is set in Vancouver, the main character fifty-year-old Ruth Wheeler, who owns and runs a boardinghouse. In a kind of novelistic montage, we are presented with an ensemble cast of ten other characters who occupy the stage in significant degree. Loss and renewal form one of the central themes, and the house is a primary symbol throughout. In one sense it represents attempted replacement – Ruth bought the house with the insurance payoff from an accident two years ago in which she lost her daughter Claire, as well as her right arm. Ruth's husband, Hal, is yet another loss, having long since walked out on her after he remarked, "You're not the sort of woman to live with." But Hal is not quite an amputation; he turns up from time to time, as much to reclaim his husbandly place with Ruth as to resume his filial duties toward his mother, Clara. We soon learn that the house too has turned out to be a loss – it is about to be demolished, the land it sits on expropriated for use as a bridge onramp.

Amid this bleak landscape and isolation, Ruth's view of the world is reductive – blunt simplicity and practicality: "For her," the narrator tells us, "there was never any way out of a fact." She has taken on various degrees of care and responsibility for, as she considerably understates it, "six boarders and an ailing mother-in-law." Her boarders are of course far more than her rendition of them, and indeed of her perception of them; soon, they unfold themselves in ways that are disparate, intriguing, and unpredictable.

Clara Wheeler, the ailing mother-in-law, is closest by far to Ruth's heart, the depth of Ruth's feeling emerging in a powerful wonderment: "Did many women marry because they loved their mother-in-law?" The interdependence of Ruth and Clara, the choreography of their daily lives, their wordless understanding, and deep roots of emotional connection, exemplify a long-term lesbian relationship.

Willard Steele, mentally and emotionally stunted, a fourteen-year resident of the boardinghouse, is central to the narrative and turns out to be far less predictable than he seems. In a shocking turning point in the story, Ruth learns the true extent of his dependence on the routine that demarcates his life.

Other boarders are young men and women, misfits in their own idiosyncratic ways, and their interactions create turbulent undercurrents. Ruth has carefully not inquired about the history of any of her boarders, but knows full well that Tom Petross is an American military deserter, and that his job as a short order cook is beneath his abilities. Arthur, whose "military haircut has not had time to grow out," is another fugitive, the most recent arrival, who has taken sanctuary in the basement. Other boarders include Joanie Vaughn, a secretary dreaming and scheming to marry into wealth; Mavis Collingwood, who works on her PhD thesis in literature and has everyone reading Dickens; and Stewart Meadow, who plays the clarinet and passes much of the rest of his time stoned.

Gladys Ledger, a political firebrand and a teacher of handicapped children, is the contemporary cultural "twin" of Stewart – and the beating heart of this novel. Her generous, unselfconscious sensuality and largeness of spirit are a catalyst that draws Stewart, Arthur, Tom, and repressed lesbian Mavis into her orbit. As the story unfolds, she affects these four in particular in far-reaching, life-changing ways. When she shifts away from Stewart to the needy, emotionally damaged Arthur, it is a fateful act and another turning point in the narrative.

Later in the story, another catalytic and energizing character turns up: Boyd Wonder, an African-American of mysterious origins, who scandalizes the group with his self-parody and denigrating self-stereotyping – his insistence on being called Boy. All of his ingratiating Stepinfetchit behavior is designed both to highlight and mockingly undercut racial prejudice – an iteration of the behavior of many gay people who adopt similar protective coloration.

Comparing this novel to the one that preceded it, *Against the Season* (1971), we can see connective thematic strands. *Against the Season* takes place in America, but in this story a character named Cole, similar to Arthur and Tom, is also a Vietnam war resister. Amelia and Beatrice, like Ruth Wheeler with her boardinghouse of social misfits, take in unwed mothers, who in those days certainly belonged to the groups considered outlaws and deserving of societal repudiation. *The Young in One Another's Arms* is clearly a continuation of the working out of the theme of family and connection.

Against the Season and *The Young in One Another's Arms*, which were Jane's third and fourth novels, mark a distinct and permanent departure from the specific lesbian focus of her first two books, *Desert of the Heart* (1964) and *This Is Not For You* (1970). With *Against the Season* and *The Young in One Another's Arms*, she would begin to work with an ever-expanding fictional canvas, and if her lesbian and gay characters appear somewhat lesser, it is because they are portrayed in fuller context against the larger society and culture. Her fifth novel, *Contract with the World* (1980), set amid a segment of Canada's art world, is a particularly majestic work, powerfully written, richly textured, multi-faceted. The three-character novel *Memory Board* (1987) is,

I would argue (with prejudice), Jane Rule's finest and most mature work. *After the Fire* (1989), individually rewarding in its own right, seems an extension and augmentation of the brilliant delineation of character and long-term relationship first revealed in *Memory Board*.

Jane's portrayals of people breaking out of the isolation imposed on them by estrangement, and the complexities and confusions, the potential and the rewards involved in reaching out for human connection – these are among the great gifts of her work. *The Young in One Another's Arms* is by no means a utopian novel – Jane Rule is too wise and her perception too clear and grounded – but a sweetness inhabits the story, a hopefulness and the suggestion of sheer human potential as those in the small community revolving around Ruth, galvanized by the looming reality of losing its home, tentatively reach out to one another. When Clara's son drops in and asserts his filial sense of responsibility by moving his ill mother to a care facility in advance of the destruction of the boardinghouse, the emotional stakes ratchet up and the connections among the boarders, instead of fraying, develop and strengthen.

The arrival of Christmas – its meaning resisted in particular by Ruth who deadpans, "I don't keep birthdays of the dead" – provides a first tangible model of cooperation when Ruth's boarders elect to celebrate the day, and exercise an autonomy from Ruth that nevertheless carries her right along with it.

Emerging from beyond Ruth's matter-of-factness, beyond the bluntness only slightly leavened by drollness, lying barely under the surface of her every act, is the open wound of grief. Since the death of her daughter, Ruth's every choice has been in reaction to that inconceivable and cataclysmic loss.

Out of such a scenario and assortment of characters comes grace notes that echo in the mind well beyond the last pages of this relatively slender novel. Among these notes are the closing chapters that provide a vivid and altogether charming view of Galiano Island in British Columbia where Jane Rule has spent much of her life amid its close-knit community.

Beyond the relevance of the timing, I trust the reissue of this remarkable novel will lead readers to seek out Jane Rule's other work, where further rewards await. There is splendor in her prose, passages that lift off the page, like this description of the surrounds of Vancouver: "... roads cut higher and higher into the wooded mountainside, great wounds with scabs of houses forming on either side."

Readers will find themselves in the company of a singular, arresting, provocative, challenging mind not at all lacking in humor. Best of all they will always find a clear-eyed compassion, exemplified by the moment when Ruth Wheeler gazes at her boarders and reflects: "Later she would let them know that they could be let go, were free, but just for this time she held them in her dark eyes, in her quiet heart, for herself."

I remember a time I met with Jane Rule and Helen Sonthoff in the desert town of Borrego Springs, California during one of their winter sojourns away from their home on Galiano Island. I believe I was editing *Memory Board* at the time, the novel that remains my lasting pride as an editor. For those who don't know Jane beyond her name and her work, she has for decades suffered from crippling arthritis; nevertheless, she is a tall, handsome, indomitable woman. The warm, dry desert air had so dramatically eased her chronic pain that I could not help but selfishly ask this expatriate, who had, after all, been born in Plainfield, New Jersey: "Jane, why not come back and live here – in this much healthier climate?" Her immediate, flat response: "Because I can't deal with the politics." Some writers don't match up to their written words: she does.

The books of Jane Rule are not only groundbreaking in their historical context, they hold some of the wisest, most eloquent and passionate writing in our literature. In the face of such *prima facie* evidence, Jane Rule should finally be given her full due and the judgment she deserves: she is one of our finest writers – surely the most significant lesbian writer of the twentieth century.

The Young in One Another's Arms

for Helen

Chapter One

In the darkened street, Ruth Wheeler might have been mistaken for a boy of middle growth, sparebodied, light on her feet. She nearly always wore trousers, and the empty right sleeve of her windbreaker could seem a boy's quirk of style. But if she stepped under a street light, looked up and sharply beyond that illuminated space, her face redefined the first impression, the color of false pearl, dark eyes of remarkable size but limited by aging lids, anchored by taut lines to her temples: the face of a seventy-year-old woman. Ruth Wheeler was, in fact, just over fifty.

"I looked older than my mother when I was born," she claimed.

Most newborn do but outgrow it. She had not. She had lived with that birth face until age became the excuse for it or was beginning to be. Her body, ordinary enough in growing, had refused to age, small breasts still high, belly firm as if it had never given room to the one child she had borne.

"I'll die in pieces," she said, her right arm the first sacrifice to that process, an accident she didn't remember, though she'd lived with the fact of having one arm for fifteen years.

"I can only remember what's happened to other people."

Those accidents which she had not witnessed stayed vivid: her father crushed under a redwood tree (it didn't matter that the report blamed a bulldozer), her daughter falling like a sparrow out of the sky (the late news invented an automobile accident). Ruth still dreamed occasionally of the falling tree and the falling child (who was twenty-two when it happened). She dreamed as well of the great six-lane highway that flowed over the valley in which she had grown up, a river of cars spawning to impossible cities, to be seen as broken and battered as fish on its urban shores.

Ruth had been part of the debris, carried along like an uprooted bush or root – or so she dreamed it, snagged here and there by a job that didn't last, a man that didn't last.

"You're not a sort of woman to live with," her husband explained to her when he left. But not the sort to leave behind entirely either. A memory of her would catch him like the first cold air in the lungs, and he would come back to her for a day or a week.

"Like a tooth you don't get around to pulling right out. It flares up. You bite on it."

Aching root, uprooted stick, walking the night streets often because she did not much like to sleep in the dark, Ruth Wheeler would speak to strangers or not. A cigarette smoked in the middle of the bridge or down by the beach was as good a companion as any. She did not stay out long, no more than an hour or so. She had a house to go back to and a number of invented responsibilities: her mother-in-law, her six boarders, an ailing runaway boy in the basement. She could sit by an open fire and look through the bulb catalogue, her inventions asleep about her, morning as far off as spring.

If planting bulbs could have stopped the dread of spring, Ruth would have gardened in the middle of the night, but for her there was never any way out of a fact. This house, along with all the others on the block, was to be razed to make way for a new approach to the bridge. In March, she would not sit in a rocking chair with a shotgun across her lap as young Gladys Ledger would like her to do, nor would she let Gladys organize the other boarders into any kind of protest. For most of them losing the house meant no more than finding another room to live in. Mavis Collingwood had been about to move out when the expropriation notice arrived and was staying on now only out of loyalty, knowing Ruth couldn't easily rent her room again. The sick boy would be well and gone, in jail if Ruth couldn't prevent that either, or in working safety on a boat or in the trees.

The only two who worried her were Clara, her mother-in-law,

and Willard Steele, who had been in the house since Ruth bought it fourteen years ago, using as down payment the compensation money from her accident. Clara had decided that this was as good a winter as any to die, but she wouldn't. Willard did not think about it, incapable of living in any terms that included change. Whatever Ruth decided for herself would have to include both of them somehow.

"I thought you'd be a fighter," Gladys had said.

"What you lose is what you survive with," Ruth answered, her right arm for a house, her husband for her mother-in-law, two rooms in the basement from the insurance paid for a dead child, and now whatever she could get with this new compensation.

"You can't fight the expropriation itself," Mavis Collingwood had agreed, "but you can fight for a fair price."

Mavis, filling up her room with chapters of her Ph.D. thesis, which had everyone in the house reading Dickens, was good at the system and did not want to discover how little control one had over what happened, what a "fair price" for anything was.

"The government's always fair, isn't it?" Joanie Vaughan asked, her hair in curlers at breakfast and at dinner so that she always looked to Ruth like something to be opened later by a lusting boss or lusting boyfriend. For Joanie, with all her dependent daydreams, only people could be unfair, the men with big cars who either had wives or didn't want them.

"You're not going to try to buy another house, are you?" Tom Petross wanted to know. "Why don't you get into business? Why don't you go into business with me?"

"Doing what, Tom?" Ruth asked, her lined smile opening over handsome teeth, as young as her body.

Ten years younger, she could have been tempted not only because Tom Petross was an inventive and practical young man but because she would have liked to keep him near her. He had been with her longer than the others, except for Willard; he had been the first of the young Americans to come across the border for sanctuary. Tom had not needed her help after the first month, finding himself a job when no one could, in the middle of winter, as a short-order cook from six in the morning until two in the afternoon.

Ruth's husband, who had married her in a grand gesture just before he went gladly off to war, didn't like these young punks coming up across the border and curling up in Ruth's pocketbook and heart.

"They're my people," she said.

"You talk like Americans were a bloody tribe of Indians. You changed your citizenship when you married me, didn't you?"

She had and could therefore get a job sorting mail at Christmas, when she still had two hands, when she still had a daughter who would grow up Canadian, but a country for Ruth wasn't so much something to belong to as something more to lose, as these young men were losing theirs. She understood them as she understood herself, glad of whatever snag could hold her still awhile. She was also angry for them, as she was not for herself.

Sometimes she was angry for all of them, even for Joanie and Gladys. Anger was the one thing that could keep them all alive for her, even in her dreams, so that they didn't all come tumbling out of the sky at her like dying birds.

"I'm not fitting anyone with wings, Tom, especially you."

"Hey, that's cool, Ruth. You always stay in your space," Stew said, his eyes shining behind his long hair, in his own space always.

Stew Meadow would get himself carefully stoned and sit on a curb across the street to watch the house come down over no one's ears, a happening just for him, who would get past experience instead of going through it, taking nothing but new notes for his clarinet.

By the fire, late at night, with the bulb catalogue, Ruth listened to all their voices again, as another way of postponing her own dreams or listening to theirs, alive all around her in the sleeping house. Could she find an apartment somewhere? Might someone hire a fifty-year-old, one-armed caretaker with an arthritic mother-in-law and a three-quarter-witted man of forty? Two bedrooms – Ruth could sleep in the living room, when she slept, but how could she listen late at night to the sleep of all those other people from whom she might only collect rent and useless greetings? There had to be room for her own dreaming, the highway then flowing over this house as well, the sky falling.

"Ruth? Ruth? Can you hear the geese?"

Ruth got up, walked across the hall and into her mother-in-law's room. There was no light on, but she went up to the bed and reached for the hand she knew was there, frail-boned, painful.

"I never feel sorry for *them*," Clara said.

"All the pity's for the robins."

"And I don't even like *them*."

"Have you been asleep?" Ruth asked.

"It's hard to know, isn't it?"

Even after all these years it was difficult for Ruth not to offer Clara something more than her hand, but the old lady suffered being waited on only if she could give commands and stay unaware of how willing Ruth was, how willing they all were. She stood for a moment longer in case there was something Clara wanted. Then she put the hand back where she had found it and went out. Another thing they never did was say good night, perhaps because it would have closed off a time in which they often encountered each other briefly, like that, the two restless watchdogs of a house that was never locked. They were not afraid of burglars.

"No need to be while you've got all the thieves already living under your roof," Ruth's husband said.

Did many women marry because they loved their mothers-in-law? Ruth's own mother remarried when Ruth was ten, too old to learn to be the child of another man, too old to compete with the babies that came one after another. If there had been books, she would have read them. Instead she read the seasons in the south fork of the Eel River, in the meadows at the edge of the redwoods, until she was old enough – was it fourteen or thereabouts? – to work along the road, ladling up plates of gravied meat for the truckers, turning hamburgers for the tourists, listening to the locals' yearly doubt: "Where will the road go next year?" One straightened curve would take out a café, another a sawmill. "What the road doesn't take, the river will," people said, but they went on planting their gardens within reach of the spring floods and building their hopes along the twisting and straightening road. Nobody imagined in those days that it would finally simply take the valley, everything in it. Ruth went north to Portland with a trucker one night, then farther north to Seattle, and finally for no good reason across the border into Canada to discover Vancouver.

And met and loved Clara and married her son and gave her a granddaughter to be outlived, a house to be outlived. Why not pity the geese? Did Clara long simply for the regularity of the journey? Was that all she really minded, not ever being able to read the road?

"Haven't you gone to bed at all?" Tom asked, on his way to work at five in the morning, his young face still bland with sleep, no point in asking him if he'd heard the geese.

"Coffee?"

"No, I'll get it there. I like the walk on an empty stomach." Ruth thought of herself, walking to the same kind of job those years ago, down the forest track, blind in that dark, on accurate feet, out into the night light of the sky over the river, across the lumber bridge to the road. Sometimes it was raining, but she could never remember wind at that time of the morning. Tom's walk would take him across Burrard Bridge, which spanned the industrial confusion of False Creek, but in clear weather, even in the last darkness, he could look across the inlet to the mountains, lined against the open sky.

"Morning, Tom."

"Morning, old lady," he called in to Clara, a joke between them they didn't explain. He never called her anything else.

At the front door, he hesitated and turned back to Ruth. "An all-night café, why not?"

"With one arm?" Ruth asked.

"With three."

That sounded friendly. Nearly everything Tom said did, as if there were never broken things inside him, though Ruth knew better. As the door closed behind him, she began to set the table for breakfast, shoving the tea cart before her with one hip, quicker with one hand than a lot were with two, something Tom often pointed out to her.

"I use my head as well."

She had not liked being efficient before she lost her arm. There hadn't been any real point.

"Only solve the problems you have," she tried to tell them all.

"And if there's no solution?" Mavis had asked, baiting Ruth as she probably baited her students, with assumed detachment.

"Then don't call it a problem. It isn't one."

"Cool, Ruth, cool," Stew must always say.

"Cheating," Gladys contradicted, on Mavis' side for a change.

They couldn't ordinarily agree, those two, Gladys a street radical, Mavis a conservative. Gladys had a heart as big as her mouth and should have trusted it more. Mavis had a mind, though what good it would do her Ruth wasn't certain. So many gifts turn out to be obstacles, just by chance.

Willard was always the first up for breakfast, though he did not have to be at work until eight-thirty. The young people disturbed him in the morning. He preferred to begin the day quietly, neatly.

"You know, he even looks like a shoe," Gladys remarked one day, not in his hearing; they were all absentmindedly kind to Willard. "Would it happen to anyone?"

His black hair polished to his small head, his eyes as close together as tightly laced dress shoes, his mouth a short, straight line, Willard went off every morning to sell shoes, came home every evening at quarter to six, endured dinner, and then went off on Monday night to the movies, on Tuesday night to the laundromat (he would not let Ruth or anyone else touch his clothes), on Wednesday night to a card game in Chinatown, at which he lost a budgeted amount of his salary, to his room Thursday night to write to his mother in Kamloops, to the beer parlor on Friday. Saturday night he stayed home to watch television since there was usually no one else around. Sunday he went to church and then read a thriller until it was time for him to sleep. Week in, week out, year in, year out, Willard endured the griefs and changes of the house as if they had not occurred, and came to weight on Ruth like a negative habit. He was the only one in the house she was sometimes simply cranky with, nagging him about ashes on his butter plate, about the early hour he wanted breakfast. He was not meek so much as inattentive.

Willard had one odd, gentle mannerism. He always kissed Ruth goodbye in the morning, lips surprisingly soft and warm on her cheek. Then he knocked on Clara's door and called, "Have a day, Mrs. Wheeler." They had long ago stopped laughing about it or even using it themselves as a slogan. That persistent kiss and wish had lasted into minimal dignity. For the others, he behaved as if they weren't there and perhaps didn't notice when they had gone. Even Ruth's daughter? Willard obviously had not thought it proper to acknowledge her while she lived. He had no way, therefore, of acknowledging her death. Could a life be made so small as to keep all suffering and joy out of it? Perhaps, with help. Ruth would not leave Willard behind.

Between Willard's departure and the gang feeding at seven-thirty, Ruth took Clara her breakfast on the freshly cleared cart, an extra cup for herself for a companionable taste of tea until all sets of plumbing began their four-part morning harmony and it was time to cook the eggs.

Mavis was always on time, her short black curly hair wet and disciplined against her temples, her eyes shallow behind her glasses, refusing to focus a distance beyond her plate until she looked out over the podium at her first class. Because waking was always a bitter wrench for Mavis, in her dreams free of all that rational armor, she was extremely polite at breakfast.

Then Joanie, prattling about her dreams which were always vio-lently obvious, the ill-stacked curlers riding above her childish face, would appear in the kitchen to "help." Since she had never finished the buttoning and zipping when she arrived, Ruth simply herded her into the dining room in front of the cart, now carrying plates of eggs.

Gladys and Stew, cultural twins with their flowing hair and blue jeans, came in at the last minute, still sleepwalking into each other, disagreeable and affectionate. They both counted on a ride from Mavis, Gladys to the school for handicapped children where she taught a variety of uncertain skills, Stew to the university where he was slowly acquiring credits toward no degree.

Shortly after them came the boy from the basement, who had only the one name, Arthur. His military haircut had not had time to grow out and he wore an army shirt tucked into his jeans. After a week with them, he had begun to eat with less furtive greed, and, though the nerves in his face still didn't allow him to hold a smile, he risked quick ones now and then as a way of thanking. The others had learned not to ask these boys questions, waited for the tale to be told or not, and they didn't offer suggestions either until Ruth indicated that it was time to help. But each of them spoke to him, even those who had not bothered in the dark morning to speak to each other, and they called him by name, for he would need them as friends when he was well enough to have friends again.

Stew always wanted to give them hash as a way through the first painful time, but Ruth did not approve. She said, for these kids, it had to be a halfway house, not a far-out house. She wanted the police to have no secondary excuse to take anyone back across the border.

"If you want to be first clarinet in the pen band, Stew, that's your business."

"I can't see a narc getting through your front door, you know."

"Not only through my front door but into the living room for a cup of coffee," Ruth answered firmly. "I have no quarrel with them."

"No quarrel with the pigs?" Gladys demanded.

Ruth would not argue past practical point. She hadn't the patience. Mavis often did on principle. Gladys shouted out bits from *The Georgia Straight*, the local underground paper. Stew, even without aid of drug, floated out on his own smile, larking a whistle over the nose to counterpoint rather than harass.

"You're irresponsible," Gladys would shout after him. "A post-revolutionary state, achieved in isolation, isn't morally any better than capitalist exploitation."

"Oh, the poor language, the poor language," Mavis would sigh, giving up again.

Still, she not only went out of her way in the morning to see that Gladys got to work on time, but often waited for her in the late afternoon or went in to help with the last tying on of shoes and sand-bagging into wheelchairs.

"You wouldn't think Mavis had a way with kids," Gladys said one day, "but she does. Nothing she says to them. Not the way she looks at them. It must be her hands. She has very good hands."

Ruth had noticed that, too. When Clara needed help out of a chair, she did not turn to one of the men. She always ordered Mavis to her, who, not seeming to take more than ordinary care, could get Clara up without the briefest light of pain in her face. Ruth was at a disadvantage, but she and Clara together had developed a way for Ruth to get her out of bed fairly easily. It was Ruth's last chore of the morning, after the dishes were cleared away and Arthur settled to wash the pots and pans.

Clara sat in her room most of the morning, reading, sewing, dozing. Ruth usually stretched out on a living-room couch and slept.

This morning the foghorns had begun with the first gray light, and now that Ruth was not distracted by human noise she looked out to them, to the heavy sea fog, darkened and seasoned by the slash burning on the northern mountains, closed off from view. The only evidence of water out there just a few hundred yards away was the persistent and repetitive conversation of foghorns and ship whistles. Ruth could not see much beyond the two mountain-ash trees on the boulevard, whose orange berries signaled to irresolute and quarreling robins, in this northern and yet temperate climate never certain whether to stay or go. The debate in the branches grew inevitably raucous and unreasonable until one drunken bird sailed out over the lawn and into the plate glass of the living-room window, leaving blood and feathers like a signature on the misty view.

"Another one?" Clara called, having heard the thud.

"Another," Ruth confirmed and went to the back porch to find a shovel.

The fog-damp lawn soaked her sneakers, and she coughed against the taste of smoke, alerting the birds. They flopped out of the trees in disgruntled and alarmed pairs, racketing about Ruth and then shying off toward the house. She did not watch them, but her neck muscles stiffened to the dread of a mass suicide against the windows. They circled back into the trees instead, though a few remained in the large lilac by the house, under which Ruth would bury the dead bird. She did not know, as she dug awkwardly with one hand, whether the drops that fell wet on her back through her thin shirt were shit or rain.

The first bird Ruth had ever buried was one she had killed, by aggressive accident, shying a rock at it as it perched on her favorite river boulder. She had probably wanted to stone the small children who had edged her out of her room, the yard, and even the orchard, so that the river bar was the only place left for her to be alone, if she walked far enough. She could not remember feeling sorry, only surprised and then responsible. A hardhearted child, her mother had called her. Closed-hearted, more truly. If she had let grief in then, there would have been room for nothing else. It was Clara who had taught her this stupid pity. In March, when the bulldozers arrived, they would unearth all this planting of bulbs and birds.

Arthur had gone back to his room in the basement, leaving the kitchen in careful order. Clara was listening to her radio. Ruth went to her own room, changed her shoes and shirt, and stretched out on her bed, her arm over her eyes.

The day wore differently for each one. Tom was usually the first home, smelling faintly of cooking grease, tired and quiet. He went as directly as he was allowed to his room and didn't appear again until the others arrived, Mavis, Gladys, and Stew together, Joanie delivered to the door by one large American car or another, which would usually be back to collect her and the understood fare as shortly after dinner as she could get out of curlers again. Willard was last, carrying his head as he had all day, parallel to the floor. He did not straighten up until dinner was over and his evening routine was about to begin. Sibling rivals at the breakfast table, the young people courted each other at dinner or quarreled as lovers do for each other's attention. Gladys, whatever else people tried to pretend, was the sexual center. She always looked as if she were comfortably and wonderfully naked under her clothes.

"Rape is the only adequate answer to any of Gladdy's arguments," Stew announced.

"Our radical male chauvinist," Gladys replied, aware that Arthur was watching her, that Tom was refusing to.

Joanie shifted in her chair, restless with the attention Gladys always got, though she considered no one in the house eligible. Stew would be for Joanie the worst of the lot, with his hash and his clarinet and his long hair, never mind that he had lovely eyes. She did not know he had an allowance from his rich father. Tom, well, if Tom had been something other than a cook – say, a lawyer or a stockbroker or even just some sort of executive – he was attractive enough, even sanitary, but Joanie was a little afraid of him the way he was friendly for no good reason. Arthur was too new and illegal and sick to count. Once Ruth overheard Joanie asking Gladys why she would ever consider going to bed with Stew. "For the fun of it," Gladys had answered. Sad that Joanie could not believe even a particle of that reply. Or did her passion for large cars have at least something to do with the size and comfort of the back seat? No.

"I have an extra ticket to Cinema 16 tonight," Mavis said, apparently to the table at large, but Gladys immediately refused it. "Tom?"

"Sure, thanks."

"Could you drop me at the pub, though?" Gladys asked.

"It's not exactly between here and the university," Mavis answered.

"I know, but I ... "

"Yeah, I'll drop you at the pub."

Mavis was tired of being the household taxi, perhaps a reason she had decided to move out, though either Tom or Gladys was the important reason, Ruth couldn't decide which. Mavis did not ask silly questions or make silly remarks; so what went on in her silly heart Ruth had more difficulty guessing than with the others.

"You're not a keyhole peeper; you're a mind fucker," Gladys said to Ruth.

Not Clara herself, who usually joined them for dinner, could modify Gladys' language.

"If you have to be obscene, couldn't you at least be accurate?" Mavis asked. "I'm a mind fucker, if you like. Ruth's a mind reader."

No. Each of them had great areas of themselves which were closed off to Ruth. With Willard it might be because he was unaware of those areas himself. With Mavis, it was a matter of simple privacy. Ruth was not nosy. She felt required to know as much as each one of them wanted her to know, which was often more than they said. How else could she know unless she thought along with each one as far as she could?

The plot of Ruth's own life had ended two years ago with the death of her daughter, or she saw it that way. Perhaps there had never been much cause and effect, only accidents and whims, but having a child deceives one into believing in a future, the child's. Even birthdays are achievements. Then, afterwards, all those growing years seem random between the accidents of birth and death. She might have been, she might have had, she might have done anything ... even lived.

Now, watching Mavis believe enough in the value of her thesis to fear failing it, seeing Gladys out the door with one of her dozen outraged placards to demonstrate for a new world, waiting for Tom to heal enough inside to risk himself again, knowing that Stew courted a jail sentence to punish himself for all his unpaid-for joy, wondering when the final car would carry Joanie off to daydream domesticity, Ruth could hope only one thing, that each of them might live awhile anyway, even if in fear, protest, pain, guilt, need. She could be watchdog, cook, mind reader, cipher, whatever, from day to day a while longer herself.

In the evening paper, which Willard always brought home, were all the ads for houses, for apartments, for jobs. It was too soon to look, the move still nearly six months away. Ruth hesitated at the personals, safe and amused in the knowledge that no one would be advertising for her. Then she put the paper down and went in to Clara, who liked to be read to for an hour or so at that time of evening. Mavis sometimes read her Dickens, which Clara enjoyed with some critical confidence. Tom read her Loren Eiseley, whose ideas she often failed to grasp but whose language she thought so beautiful it didn't matter. With Stew, who read her concrete poems, and Gladys, who read her *The Georgia Straight* or *The Pedestal*, the local women's liberation paper, Clara was simply patient. Ruth was the only one who asked Clara what she would like. Lately she had wanted to listen to the novels of Ethel Wilson, who lived still, an old and ailing lady, not many blocks away in another world.

"How does she live in her world and write about ours?"

"Why do you think being married to a doctor and living in that kind of place makes so much difference?" Ruth asked.

"Because I like to," Clara admitted. "Still we all share the weather and the mountains. It is a bond."

Ruth would have liked to read a book about her own past weather and the trees. She never found one, and how could it exist? There had been so few to know it, and now it was gone. No one traveling seventy miles an hour had to suffer the smell of rotting eels, the wakening bear, the irritated skunk. Bridges were built high now, so that, even if there had been someone to listen through a night of swelling rains, there would be no sound of thrashing cable and splitting timber as the lumber bridge went out. But Ruth seemed to carry her weather with her: what could survive the winter was still broken by spring.

"You're tired tonight."

Ruth nodded, looking for her place to begin reading. Before she had found it, she had to get up to answer an assertive knocking at the door.

"Police," one of the two men said, neither in uniform.

"What can I do for you?"

"Answer a few questions."

"Come in."

Her age, her lack of arm, the family comfort of the large living room tempered their authority. She answered without hesitation questions about the ownership of the house, the number of occupants, the length of time she had lived there.

"Any Americans?"

"I was one once," Ruth answered, smiling.

"Any deserters?"

"Would you call me one?"

"Army deserters."

"I don't ask questions like that," Ruth said. "If the Canadian government has no objection to them, there's no reason why I should."

"Some of them aren't here legally."

"I wouldn't know," Ruth said.

"If you harbor … "

"This isn't a hideout; it's a boardinghouse. I don't harbor anyone. I do make a good cup of coffee."

They did not stay for it. The younger of the two hesitated at the door as if to explain himself, but before he had half a sentence out, his partner urged him away.

"Why are they coming here now?" Clara demanded. "They've never come before."

"Just routine, I suppose," Ruth answered, relieved that Arthur had gone to his room.

"Do you think he is illegal?"

"I don't know," Ruth answered, "and I'm not going to ask."

Some of the others surely had been, but legality for them was such a frail security that you couldn't read it in their behavior. The police, co-operating with American authorities, weren't always concerned with such niceties. In a world where even God, never mind Abraham, killed his only son as a loving gesture, how could the police understand a young Isaac or Jesus who wouldn't offer himself up to the slaughter? But they had not come to her house before. Something had happened.

In the morning, when Ruth saw the first moving van parked at the end of the block, she realized that the change was not to be put off until spring. One by one all the houses on the street would be emptied, waiting for demolition. As they were, the kids would begin to move in, paying a cheap rent by the month or even by the week. The police had anticipated that. They would be back, often.

Chapter Two

Ruth's restless insomnia had for years been a way for her to take the burdens of her own moods out of the house. Clara, who could not walk, needed space for the anxieties and griefs they shared, and the others in the house should not be infected by the seasons of bleak fright life could become. Ruth went out and returned at any hour, more like an animal than a human resident. She had always liked the friendly street she lived on, lined with mountain ash, open to the sky, its large old houses either converted into suites or used like her own as boardinghouses. There was more sociable traffic than in neighborhoods to the west, still zoned for single-family dwellings. But it was a street too close to the center of this young city to stay that way. The concrete canyon walls must inevitably rise against the hope of trees and sky. From wilderness to this edge where she was, Ruth had been moving closer and closer to that center. Was there any use in backing off now? The houses she walked by were for living in, high-rise apartments for jumping off, but where else was there to go?

On the beach that opened at the end of the street, Ruth sat on a great log, one of the many washed up from booms broken up in sudden storms. Often the students who stayed at the house got summer jobs on the tugboats, and they told stories of the slow-motion drama of that life, where there was no way to take quick shelter against unexpected weather. A cove in sight was still two hours' dragging weight away. The log boom she watched now, anchored in the sheltered bay, would soon be towed into one of the mills or around under Lion's Gate Bridge to the harbor, where ships waited for their cargo. Ruth knew men on the docks as well, those who balanced on the floating logs and dreamed of getting winch ratings in the winter weather. She had met several when they were clumped together for a time as industrial accidents of similar interest to hospital staffs, occupational-therapy clinics, and compensation boards. Five years ago she might have helped Arthur get a job either on the tugs or at the front, no awkward questions asked. Now there were too few jobs for such favors.

Ruth looked across the water to the north shore, which had been nearly wild coast when she first arrived in Vancouver in 1939. Now waterside apartment buildings blocked the view of smaller houses behind them, and roads cut higher and higher into the wooded mountainside, great wounds with scabs of houses forming on either side. She turned to look at the city itself, the west-end highrises a surprise growth of only ten years, where before there had been old wood frame houses, gradually abandoned by families but still creating arbitrary families like her own. Now it was one of the most densely populated areas in North America. She had heard her husband argue that such a concentration of people conserved land and fuel, cut down the need for transportation, and was a very civilized solution to population pressures. She had never heard anyone who lived in an apartment argue such virtues, probably because they did not sit down at large dinner tables to argue about anything. She saw a single TV dinner in the window of a toaster oven, a thin film of gravy bubbling on the surface of a dry slice of turkey.

She would not be alone, of course. There would be Willard and Clara. For Willard, if he noticed the difference at all, it would probably be a relief with no clutter of young people to evade or ignore. Clara would live more in books, and, if she wearied of the unaccustomed silence, she'd probably become one of those inveterate phoners of hot-line programs who occasionally amused or alarmed her now. Clara who had shaken her head in disbelief at a drunken old woman calling over the public airways, "My son's a homosexual and I need help to face this tragedy," might begin calling the world to say, "My son is a road builder ... "

Ruth felt a hand on her shoulder and turned to greet Tom, taking a detour onto the beach on his way home from work, the afternoon sun a pleasure after the days of fog. He sat down beside her, closed his hands over a book he was carrying, and rocked himself as if for comfort and warmth against some interior cold. There was no wind.

"Do you see it?" he asked after a moment, nodding at the view. "I forget to look."

"I see it," Ruth said, a reservation in her voice to suggest that she hadn't let it be a pleasure to her.

"I had a letter from my sister today."

Ruth had not known Tom had a sister, though she had assumed a family life for him as she watched him settle into her house.

"Funny, I've gone to General Delivery every week for months. Nearly forgotten what my name looked like, just written out in long-hand on an envelope like that. Made me feel ... oh ... odd."

As she often did with Tom, Ruth matched herself with him, wondering how she would feel to receive a letter from someone she was related to, but she had no idea where any of them were. She somehow doubted that her mother was still alive.

"Dad's had a heart attack. She says it's changed him. She and Mother wish I'd come home."

"To jail?"

"I don't know. She doesn't say."

"Are you going to go?"

"No," Tom said without hesitation.

They both watched a young man and a small boy playing with a Frisbee.

"When I think of them," Tom said, "'I think they have no way left to live.'" He thumbed through his book. Then he read aloud, "'The pond was a place of reek and corruption, of fetid smells and of oxygen-starved fish.'" He flipped a page and looked down it to another marked statement. "'It is here that the water failures, driven to desperation, make starts in a new element.'" He turned to Ruth. "He's talking about the lung-fish, the clumsy misfit who finally climbed out onto the shore. It probably didn't have much of a life, just learning how to breathe the air, but it did learn. I couldn't go back."

Ruth watched his face, the flesh finely and distinctively shaped over good bones, a strong, fair face, and tried to think of his family but was sorry for herself instead, knowing how much she would miss him when the move had to be made.

"I'm sorry about it, but there's no way to say that, even if my father is different. If I said I'd gone back to graduate school ..."

"Do you want to go back?"

"No."

They sat together in silence then, trying to see white gulls and sailboats, children, the high white snow the roads had not yet reached. When Ruth got up to go, needing to be home to fix dinner, Tom did not follow her.

She walked back along the street among crowds of schoolchildren, who had taken over the sidewalk in noisy bunches, shoals of them coming down the street on bicycles as well. Ruth was too old, and she was no lungfish to wallow out of the crowded shallows into a new kind of survival. Tom there on the beach might be, his breath hard and uncertain but his choice made. Ruth would be carried along instead to the next accident.

Gladys and Stew were just getting out of Mavis' Volkswagen as Ruth arrived at the house.

"Mavis says the narcs were at the house last night."

"I didn't say the narcs," Mavis protested, getting out of her side of the car. "I said the police."

"What happened?"

"Nothing," Ruth said.

"Jesus, when a house like this starts getting raided ..." Stew began.

"It wasn't raided," Ruth said. "It was just a routine check."

"They don't usually bring the dogs the first time."

"Oh, for God's sake, Gladdy, do we have to have political melodrama every time?" Mavis asked.

"What did you do, Ruth?"

"I answered their questions and offered them a cup of coffee."

"Can't you see?" Gladys demanded. "This is just the beginning. Once they decide to start hassling, there's no end to it."

"What was Ruth supposed to do, shoot them?"

"You don't let pigs into the house. You don't tell them anything. You don't make them a cup of coffee."

"So they come back with a warrant," Mavis said, "clean Stew out and take Arthur into custody."

"I'm clean. I'm clean," Stew protested. "I never keep anything at the house. Ruth knows that."

"Ruth did exactly what she should have done," Mavis said.

"How much do you have to see before you stop believing that? Do you really think they're going to go on playing by the rules? How much television do you have to watch?"

"You've told me yourself that cop-baiting in front of the cameras is standard guerilla theater. Why should I believe that?" Mavis asked.

"Because it's bloody well true! Somebody risks his head to show you how the pigs behave, and you still don't believe it."

"Leave all weapons and placards on the porch," Ruth said, opening the front door. "Hello, Clara. The troops are home."

They all went in to greet Clara, gentling themselves for her presence, and, while Ruth went off to put the meat loaf and potatoes into the oven, they settled, Gladys at Clara's feet, Mavis leaning against the bureau, Stew lounging on the bed in their custom of sharing the day with her. Ruth could hear Gladys giving reports on Shaky Sal, Two-Gun Charlie, Left-Wing Mike, some of the eight-year-olds she taught or, as her supervisor put it, terrorized with rough jokes, spontaneous games, and frank bullying. The children did get angry with her. Gladys brought home proof of their rage in grotesque pictures of herself, afflicted with all their ailments and frustrations. She put the best of them up on the bulletin board in her classroom. Of course, a child struggling to say a simple word could hate her easy tongue. A child strapped into a wheelchair could wish her running legs broken. Ruth suspected that the bruises Gladys actually suffered were almost always the result of burrowing or clutching love. When Joanie once asked, "How can you teach children like that?" Gladys had answered furiously, "I've been given permission by the authorities to love them." Gladys did love them for the gang of little realists and revolutionaries she could teach them to be. They *should* be angry about the bodies they had been born or hurt into, angry enough to learn what they could, change what they could, and insist that the people teaching them come up with miracles.

Ruth was stacking cutlery and glasses on the cart when Arthur came up out of the basement.

"Let me do that."

"No, I only want done what I can't do myself."

"It would only take a minute."

"It takes me exactly four minutes," Ruth said, smiling at him. "Pour Clara her sherry and take it in to her, but leave her door open. I like to listen to Gladdy."

They both heard her voice, rising in energy to her story. "I said, 'Don't sit there and cry because your pencil's broken. I'd sooner you threw it at me. That would get you another one fast enough.' In a rain of misaimed pencils, in walks Supe, and everyone has to listen to a lecture about how eyes could be put out. 'The step from self-pity is to self-control, not to bursts of indulgent temper.' Fuck! The only thing wrong with my teaching methods is that I can't get them to work better around here. My eight-year-olds would no more let the pigs intimidate them, the city bulldoze them …"

"I think the school board would take a dim view of your leading a wheelchair march of eight-year-olds into the city hall," Stew said.

"Fascist politics are being practiced in every classroom in this city. The school board never raises an eyebrow about that!"

Arthur and Ruth exchanged smiles as he left the kitchen with Clara's sherry.

"How was Roger today?" Clara asked. "Oh, thank you, Arthur. Sit down. Join us."

"Oh, Roger, he's such a little faker. I said, 'Roger, how come, when you know how to spell a word, I can understand you perfectly, and when you don't, you talk like you had a mouth full of marbles?' Supe says, 'Never cast doubt on a child's honesty. Never threaten a child's self-esteem.' Roger's self-esteem is the best bubble gum in town. He can blow it twice the size of his head."

Ruth hoped Clara could keep Gladys on the subject of school and off the subject of the police while Arthur was there. He could do without her fantasies, given the number of his own he must have. But Ruth had learned long since that there was no way to protect people from each other if they lived under the same roof.

Joanie came in and went straight to her room for her curlers. Then Willard nodded in at the kitchen before he went to his habitual chair in the living room, set apart under a good light, to finish reading his paper. The final shutting of the front door was Tom, who didn't join the others in Clara's room. He would instead take quieter time with her after dinner, reading to her about the lungfish. Instead of going to his room, he came to Ruth in the kitchen and began slicing the meat loaf. She didn't order him out as she had Arthur or would have any of the others. He was comfortable for her, nearly as easy as her daughter had been.

"I'm going over to the Gulf Islands this weekend. A friend of mine says there's a café for sale on Galiano right near the ferry dock, good business in the summer, possible business in the winter if you could encourage the locals."

"How many people live on Galiano?" Ruth asked.

"I don't know, maybe five or six hundred in the winter."

"Mostly pensioners without money to eat out," Ruth suggested.

"Well, I thought I'd look around."

"Do you have money to buy a café?"

"No," Tom said, and he grinned. "I still think I can persuade you to buy it."

"Clara on an island? Where would Willard sell shoes?"

"Couldn't Willard garden and chop wood and fish?"

"He'd get pretty discouraged with his shoehorn, and it's the only tool he's ever mastered."

Tom picked up the platter of meat, carried it into the dining room, and called the others. Clara came, Mavis on one side, Gladys on the other, Stew and Arthur behind them. Then Willard came in, his eyes to the floor, and finally Joanie, breathless.

"What make and year tonight, Joanie?"

"Oh, Stew!"

"For your sins you're going to marry an antique car-freak and have to ride around in a Model T."

"What's the top of the news tonight, Willard?" Tom asked.

"More bad weather on the way," Willard said, which was one of his two stock responses. The other was, "It's a troubled world."

Ruth's hand trembled a little as she tried to help herself to meat. She had for years been able to live with those simple gloomy truths, and there was no point in feeling fainthearted about them now. Tom didn't need her. Clara and Willard did. Their presence in other crises had kept her sane and responsible. Losing a house was not, after all, like losing an arm or a child, if only she did not have to give up as well this large unlikely family who even now could distract her from her distress.

"Are we all pubbing tonight?" Gladys asked.

Stew had a club date. Mavis had work to do.

"Well, Arthur, your hair's long enough by now to risk the pub," Gladys said.

"Don't you get Arthur involved in any of your demonstrations, Gladdy," Ruth said.

"Not right away, all right, but deserting is only a negative political act. There's got to be positive political pressure as well. This isn't lotus land."

"Making it into lotus land might not be a bad idea," Tom said.

"You think you can save the world just by giving it indigestion day after day?"

"The world's been saved by odder means. Once a fish had to learn to breathe."

"Loren Eiseley," Mavis said impatiently, "wants the world to go to the dogs. He even dedicated a book to his. He doesn't really like people."

"Do you?" Tom asked.

"I think on the whole, I prefer birds," Clara said.

"Far out," Stew said. "My best friend when I was a kid was a lizard."

"I bet," Joanie said.

"And I bet you always wanted a pony," Stew said, not unkindly, "and still do."

"Do you, Mavis?" Tom repeated.

"Oh, well enough," Mavis said. "I don't think there's really much choice. We're social animals after all."

"Maybe we shouldn't be resigned to that," Tom said.

"It's not a matter of being resigned," Gladys said. "We have to do something positive about it."

"Well, you could help me clean up the kitchen," Arthur suggested in the first glimmer of ease he'd shown.

"A practical man in our midst," Mavis said with approval.

"With sinister male chauvinist tendencies," Tom said.

"Sure, I'll help you," Gladys said, surprising them all as she often did, good humor overtaking her in the middle of the fiercest arguments.

"Would you like to go to the movies?" Willard asked Ruth.

"Why, it's Monday night, isn't it? Yes, I would. What a good idea."

Ancient-faced, Ruth had always been taken for Willard's mother when they were out in public together. She did not mind. One did not choose one's children, either those born to one or those come upon by accident. Ruth had been given this odd man to love, who could bring her just such simple distraction and comfort as a movie she didn't have will enough to go to on her own. She took his arm on the way to the bus stop.

"How many movies do you suppose we've gone to, Willard?"

"Never thought to count."

He was instead secretly counting the change in his pocket. Ruth could feel the muscles in his arm working. Would he have enough to offer her a beer after the show? Ruth could have told him that he did. But he needed to get to his decisions by his own route.

"Have you ever done any fishing, Willard?"

"Fishing?"

"Catching fish."

"No."

No, he'd never caught anything but feet in his life, and he never would. Ruth had no business to confuse him with such questions. She had to prepare him for the simple move he could make.

"I want you to move with Clara and me into an apartment when the time comes. You know that, don't you?"

"The future takes care of itself," he said, evasive rather than comfortable in his tone.

"But you're coming with Clara and me."

He signaled a bus and, once they were settled in their seats, there was no point in talking with Willard. He would not make minimal conversation again until they sat down for their beer, and Ruth knew she wouldn't have the heart to bring the subject up again. The narrow limits of his life did give him the virtue of being able to live from day to day, if he were let alone to do so. There was probably no virtue in being prepared for pain.

It was after eleven when they got home. Willard had to go right to bed to keep the variation in his schedule to reasonable limits. Ruth went in to chat with Clara, who had spent her evening with Tom and then been settled in bed by Mavis.

"Nature is a metaphor," Clara said decisively. "It's just that there seems to be less and less of it."

"You're not convinced by the lungfish?" Ruth asked, smiling.

"The lungfish came ashore millions of years ago when life was crowded only in the shallows. It chose light and air. I said to Tom, 'What about those who chose to go deep, to take the pressure and the dark instead? If the whole sea is dying, how do we know what will come lumbering up out of it this time?' Mavis says I sound like one of those Doomsday cranks. The end of the world isn't any longer such a crankish notion, though, is it?"

"I don't suppose so," Ruth said. "But it doesn't seem near enough to solve any personal problems."

"You and Mavis, always so practical."

"Did Tom talk about a café on Galiano?"

"Yes," Clara said.

"We couldn't live on an island."

"I suppose not, not with Willard."

Clara sighed and turned a little in her bed. Her age and her pain set her against the future, and why not? Ruth straightened the sheet a little as a way to apologize and then left Clara.

Mavis was in the kitchen, looking for ice.

"Too geared up to sleep?" Ruth asked.

"Not for long. A good stiff drink will do it. Join me?"

"Thanks."

"Imagine Tom trying to turn himself into a new species," Mavis said impatiently, venting her irritation on the ice tray. "This house is full of cranks, do you know that? Stew with his acid alteration of consciousness, Gladys cleaning up the world with blood instead of soap and water, Tom with some kind of Aquaman complex. Why is it so hard for them all to live in the real world?"

"Tom isn't really impractical."

"Oh yes he is. He should go back to school, and he knows it, but it's easier to be a fry cook and a lungfish than a responsible sociologist trying to help sort out the mess. He's worse than the others. He's got more to waste."

"You're a good puritan, Mavis."

"All it takes is will and tranquilizers and a bit of this," Mavis said, holding up her glass. "Why should I apologize?"

"No reason I can think of."

"But it's *Tom* you love …"

Ruth looked sharply at Mavis, but her remark was guarded with an ironic smile. Mavis debated; she did not plead.

"I've sometimes thought you loved him."

"Creatures of different species don't breed," Mavis said, and she stood up. "That should do it. Good night, Ruth."

Mavis had a heavy walk, a middle-aged way with her shoulders, though she had not yet turned twenty-five. Maybe she needed to be that defensive. For her it was obviously not a good idea to love Tom, or any of them. But she did.

The front door opened. It was Stew, carrying his clarinet.

"Is that Gladdy just going up?"

"Mavis."

"Oh. Is she home?"

"Don't know. I haven't been in long myself."

He went up the stairs two at a time, grasshopper-legged, happy. You had to be a night owl or a heavy sleeper like Willard to survive in this house of blatant living. Nobody was really noisy. People closed doors, but, since Ruth didn't lay down rules and regulations except about drugs, there was nothing to sneak about, neither a drink nor a lovemaking. That set moods loose in the halls and stairway, Mavis refusing her own loneliness, Stew leaping up toward simple appetite.

He was clattering down again within two minutes.

"Not there?"

"Damn," he said, then grinned at Ruth. "Well, there's a party I can go to."

After the door had closed behind him, Clara said in her light yet carrying voice, "She's downstairs with Arthur."

Ruth stood in the living room thinking about that, but to be young was not to measure the strains as she did. You didn't use one arm well until you had only one. Stew did have a party to go to, and

Ruth didn't have the prejudice against sex that she did against drugs. If Gladys could stop the flickering of Arthur's smile, steady it into a grin, perhaps not much harm would be done.

When Ruth heard the front door open again, she moved quietly into the darkened dining room. Joanie at that time of night was too used to lay eyes on. She needed to take herself off to her room for repairs to her clothes and her person among her threads and needles, creams and lotions, finally to crown herself with curlers and sleep. Was she so different from what Ruth had been herself at that age? Softer, sillier, more childish, she would have chosen the traveling salesmen rather than the truckers. Ruth had liked the aloofness of the truckers from what they hauled. Their friendliness was simpler, but Joanie would have been tempted instead by the briefcases of samples, the company cars, the cheap, travel-polished suits, the salesmen's banter. It made very little difference really whether you lay on packing blankets in the back of a truck or on sample cases in the back seat of a car, as long as you thought you were being taken somewhere away from your own stagnant life. Ruth was afraid it took a war for women like herself and Joanie to marry, only being married made you see what little difference it made for most, anyway, who hadn't the wit or even the will to hold a man for long. Life was easier without one.

At that moment Ruth missed her husband, not really because he would have been any help. He could bluster as noisily and ineffectively as Gladys in his own unionized jargon or berate Ruth for stupidity of buying a house in a neighborhood bound to be torn down, anyone could see it, could have seen it years ago. No, what she missed, wanted, was to be reduced momentarily to his simple need, urgent enough to arouse her own, to be part of his rutting pleasure. She was too old now to be able to give herself such comfort often, and alone an orgasm was more like the relief of tears, which brought with it the rain of children out of the sky. Even Mavis, not yet twenty-five, usually chose to drink herself to sleep instead.

Ruth turned on the dining-room light and began to set the

breakfast table. Gladys came sleepily up the basement stairs, a sight to envy if you hadn't learned the deep lesson of vicarious pleasure. Ruth smiled at her.

"Arthur's going to be all right," Gladys said, stretching and yawning. "We had a long talk."

Ruth tilted her head.

"Oh, and a lovely screw," Gladys admitted and laughed. "Good night, Ruth."

Not willing to sleep but even less willing to intercept any more traffic of this restless night, Ruth finished her chores, spoke softly to Clara, and went out among the mousing cats to walk away her need of anything at all, even to draw a picture of Gladys without one arm and with a face of weathered stone.

Chapter Three

"Gladys said, 'Stew doesn't own me,' and then Mavis said, 'You don't own the house either, and you're making everyone uncomfortable.' Do you think you should speak to Gladys?"

Ruth sighed. Sometimes she and Clara were like a pair of ancient parrots, passing the time by repeating everything they had heard and overheard in the house. It had been an increasingly uneasy place in the days since Gladys had shifted her attention from Stew to Arthur. Jealousy hung in the house like the smell of cabbage, and, if it was strongest in Stew's presence, it had begun to permeate other people as well. Arthur was too nice a boy to be lordly about his good fortune, but he was also too needy to let Gladys alone long enough for her to negotiate any comfort for Stew, which however much against her principles might not be against her good nature. Tom, who maintained the same friendly distance from Gladys that he did from Joanie and Mavis, had begun to make ironic comments about Gladys which were not entirely kind and discovered him in unacknowledged needs of his own, harder to keep in check when they were being acted out nightly under his own roof. While Gladys was Stew's girl, there was a settled erotic climate about the house. Now appetites were riled. Mavis, practically moral, was right: the quarters were too close. But her judgment was too charged with anger for Ruth to be comfortable about agreeing with it.

"Mavis wants Gladdy punished with good Dickensian clarity. I can't quite see what that punishment would be, never mind the justice of it."

"Do you think she has any idea what trouble she may be stirring up?" Clara asked. "Stew's making himself quite sick."

"Perhaps I should talk to him."

"Have you tried to lately ... about anything?"

"If we could find Arthur a job far enough away from Vancouver ..."

"He's a dear boy," Clara said.

"Not to be banished?"

"I just don't know."

Ruth would have liked to put the circumstance into the category without solution, therefore not a problem, but something to be lived with, like the occasional stench of the pulp mills when there was an easterly wind, but her own level of tolerance had not been reached by anyone else in the house. If she didn't try to do something, someone else would. Stew was so stoned most of the time that the only real danger from him was to himself. It was not in him to be violent. And he would agree that he did not own Gladys, but you did not have to own to suffer loss. Gladys could be made aware of that, but what real good would her sympathy do? It was no substitute for her presence in Stew's bed. Seeing to it that Gladys felt guilty would satisfy no one but Mavis, and it would have no happy effect on Arthur, whose well-being had so recently been the generous concern of them all.

It was stupid of Ruth not to have known at the start. If she had been detached enough herself, not so busy stemming her own envy, she might have frowned instead of smiled. At that time her disapproval might have accomplished something. Ruth was not averse to asserting herself, but she had more faith in keeping the bathrooms clean and the ownership of towels straight than she did in insisting on the tidiness of relationships to keep everyone comfortable.

Breakfast, even relieved of Tom's increasing haughtiness, was nearly unendurable. Mavis was now forcing Stew to get up in the morning. He sat at the table, his long hair uncombed, his usually expressive eyes with the deceptive shine of wet pebbles in an acid wash, his mouth a bad imitation of the Mona Lisa. Mavis shoved food at him like an aggressive bird, but he ate nothing.

"Stew, you've got egg in your hair," Joanie reported with disgust. He did not register her complaint. Arthur had to do it for him.

"You've got curlers in yours."

"*I* have to go to work, unlike some people around here."

"Gladdy, if you don't go up and get your clothes on in a hurry, we're all going to be late," Mavis said.

"Just this last piece of toast," Gladys said cheerfully, a robe wrapped around nakedness only she was unmindful of. "I'm starving this morning."

Arthur smiled, still too recently satisfied to take her nearing departure and his empty day seriously. Now that he had Gladys to wait for, even his idleness could be a pleasure, lying on his back remembering how he had been wakened with her teasing fingers, her tongue at his ear, his lust lazy, his hands playful at her breasts until he slid a hand down into the soft, swelling wetness of her ...

Ruth willed herself out of Arthur's idle day, but, if even she could dally there, her own hand guiding Arthur's, what violence was being committed in Stew's imagination? The rational censor in Mavis must be strained to breaking.

"There's no point in asking Gladys to dress before breakfast," Ruth said to Clara. "It wouldn't make any difference."

"I enjoy her," Clara said. "I'm afraid we all do."

"She enjoys herself," Ruth said, remembering again that yawning stretch, Gladdy's young breasts, free and up-tilting under her blouse, which came untucked at her hips, revealing the soft skin of her back, her trousers so low that they did not completely cover the shadowed cleavage of her buttocks, a sight to make one almost cannibal-joyful about human flesh. Joanie had always been jealous of her. No imitation of style or contrivance of cosmetics could ever produce for Joanie an erotic moment to touch Gladys, who didn't even try.

"Perhaps, if Arthur got a job night shift somewhere ..."

There was a hard knock at the door. Ruth and Clara looked at each other.

"Oh, I hope not ..." Clara said.

They were in uniform this time, and they knew Arthur's name.

"I'm not sure he's in," Ruth began.

She had never thought to plan out what she would do in this circumstance; she had not even, after their first visit, taken Gladys' warnings seriously.

"Arthur?" she called at the basement door.

They all heard his door open.

"Yes?"

Run, she wanted to shout, but she saw their guns.

"Has he done anything? Do you have to take him?"

"We want to talk with him, that's all."

What were Arthur's rights? Did he have any? Ruth felt stupidly ignorant and helpless as she watched Arthur walk meekly down the path with the two men in uniform. They all got into the car. Before a minute had passed, the engine started, and the police car moved away from the curb and was gone.

"Can they do that?" Clara demanded. "Can they just take him off like that? Did they have a warrant, or whatever it is?"

"I don't know," Ruth said, and she wished she had paid some attention to Gladys' lectures on civil rights, however inaccurate they might have been. "Maybe I didn't even have to let them in."

Ruth knew no lawyers. They were attendants for criminals and the rich. If she had a problem with the city hall or the telephone company or a department store, she dealt with whoever answered the phone. She did not even know the groups organized to help deserters and draft dodgers. Hers had always come to her because a lot of people happened to know that Ruth Wheeler would take in such young men without asking questions. They simply arrived at her door, and she let them in, just as she had let the police in.

"He mustn't be taken off," Clara protested. "That's not right."

They waited, watching the street for the car to return. In that hour, neither of them put the obvious question to the other: how had the police got Arthur's name? Neither of them wanted to suffer the obvious answer. Stew might have had nothing to do with it.

The police were checking before Stew had any reason to be rid of Arthur. Arthur had begun to go out with Gladys in the evening. He had probably met dozens of people, one of whom might sell bits of information to the police. Ruth's reputation for housing Americans could have come to police attention in any number of ways. Their source didn't really matter.

"I could just phone the police," Ruth finally decided, "and tell them what happened. I could say I'm worried about him and would like to help him if he's in trouble."

"Yes, do that," Clara said. "We could hire a lawyer."

The police had no information. Arthur had not been booked.

"But they can't just drive off with him and then pretend they don't know what's happened to him. If he hasn't been booked, why haven't they brought him home?" Clara demanded.

"I suppose they could simply have driven him to the border," Ruth said, "and turned him over to the military police."

"But that's wrong!"

"I've got to order the groceries," Ruth said.

The phone hunched to her ear by her right shoulder, Ruth modified weights and numbers as she read her list, canceling Arthur's rations from bread to liver, her voice as aged as her face, a nearly deaf resonance in it, cut off periodically by the stinging sweetness of the bile in her throat.

She did not want to be angry with Stew. She never wanted to be angry with any of them. Arthur, so newly made sane with the joys of his body, was being humiliated again now, his clothes taken from him, his head shaved, a cell door locked against him. She was angry *for* Arthur. It shouldn't have been a problem, his loving Gladys. Why couldn't they all understand that and learn to live with it? She was angry for Mavis, who had to live in her own prison of morality, and, yes, she was even angry for Tom, the ungenerous price he had to pay to stay aloof from so many of his own needs. Poor Stew, if he had this on his conscience, how much more he'd have to abuse himself to deny knowledge of himself, to become, as he put it on a happier evening, "Just a melody."

It had begun to rain. By the time Tom arrived home without his rain gear, he was soaked and cursing this damned rain forest that was healthy enough for trees except that they were all being cut down.

"Tom, the police came and got Arthur this morning. They haven't booked him and he hasn't come back."

"Then they've taken him home," Tom said, unconscious of that irony.

"I don't know how to find out. Is there any way we can find out?"

"Maybe," Tom said.

His wet shoes in his hand, he went up to his room.

"Could it happen to Tom?" Clara asked.

"I don't know," Ruth said. "He's a landed immigrant. I suppose it could happen to anyone. If that is what's happened to Arthur."

In a dry shirt and trousers, carrying a pair of socks, Tom came back downstairs with a mimeographed list of telephone numbers.

"The Unitarian Church is the best bet," he said. "Arthur wasn't registered with them, but I don't think that matters. They've got good lawyers working for them."

Three phone calls later, there was again nothing to do but wait.

"He should have been careful," Tom said angrily. "He didn't have any sense."

"There's no point in being angry with Arthur," Ruth said.

"There's no point in a lot of the things I feel," Tom replied and went off to his room.

For a moment Ruth was relieved to see Gladys and Mavis coming up the walk without Stew. Mavis would have given her no sign; she always trudged, shoving herself forward a shoulder at a time as if the air were as heavy as water; but Gladys, who enjoyed the sun, who enjoyed the rain, was usually as skittish and playful as a pup. Her steps up the porch stairs were nearly as heavy as Mavis'. They must somehow already know.

"We've put Stew in the university hospital," Mavis said.

"I've been telling him for months," Gladys said, pleading with Ruth, "one of these days he was bound to have a bad trip. You can't drop that much acid; you just can't."

"Take off your raincoat before you flood the hall," Mavis said, but her gruffness was affectionate and concerned.

"Is he all right?" Ruth asked.

"Oh, we got a bloody great comforting lecture from the doctor about the number of permanent psychoses he's seen lately. Only two more and he ought to be able to write a definitive article."

"He'll probably be all right," Mavis said to Ruth. "He's in a pretty bad state now. He thinks he can fly. He thinks he has to fly."

"Silly bugger!" Gladys muttered, her voice threatened with tears.

The phone rang. Ruth answered it and called to Tom.

"Where's Arthur?" Gladys asked suddenly.

"We don't know," Ruth said. "Tom may be finding out now."

"What happened?"

"The police came this morning and took him away to question him. He hasn't come back. He hasn't been booked. We just don't know where he is."

The great burst of political violence Ruth had expected from Gladys didn't occur. She walked over to Tom and stood by him, watching his face until he said, "Yes, thanks," and put the receiver down.

"They did take him back. They turned him over to the American military police at Blaine. It's cheaper than a deportation order, of course."

"What can we do?" Gladys asked quietly.

"Make a great, fine, principled stink, get lots of media time for the next two or three days, maybe even finally an investigation of police action to scare them enough so that they won't do it again for several months."

"What about Arthur?"

"There's not a damned thing we can do for Arthur," Tom said, and then his tense anger broke, and he put an arm around Gladys' shoulders. "I'm sorry, Gladdy, but that's the way it is."

Ruth, Tom, Mavis, and Clara in her room all waited for Gladys to rage into action, but she only turned quietly out of the shelter of Tom's arm and went to her room.

"How did the police find out?" Mavis asked.

Neither Tom nor Ruth offered to answer, and the silence from Clara's room was complete.

The news of Stew's bad trip and Arthur's deportation, "two bad trips" as Mavis put it, seemed to have more effect on Joanie than on anyone else. She cried, an embarrassment to the others who could not get beyond stupid silences and bursts of nervous irritation. They all needed something useful to do, but even the publicity and pressure for police investigation was out of their hands. There was an experienced and efficient committee for that.

"Should someone go to the hospital to see Stew tonight?" Ruth suggested.

Tom and Mavis, for the moment, wanted no part of him, and Gladys had stayed in her room.

"I could go myself," Ruth said.

"Leave it until tomorrow night," Mavis said.

"I could go tomorrow night," Joanie offered.

Gladys did not appear for dinner, which was a sorry affair of their diminished numbers, nothing to talk about that could be talked about except the weather, which interested no one but Willard, oblivious to the tension.

"Do use the ashtray, Willard!" Ruth snapped.

"Shall I take something up for Gladys?" Mavis asked.

"Do," Clara said.

"I'll take care of the dishes, Ruth," Tom offered.

They were clearing the table when Mavis came back with the plate of food she'd taken up.

"She's not hungry."

"That's decent of her."

"Oh, Tom, let's not blame Gladdy," Mavis pleaded in real distress.

"Or anyone," Ruth added, "except the police."

"Which won't do much good," Tom said.

Ruth wanted to speak to the bitterness in him, but she had nothing to say, and Mavis, who could usually moralize anyone into a frenzy, was obviously too unhappy herself to try. Tom bristled with his own vulnerability. They worked together without more attempt at conversation until the kitchen was set to rights.

"Will you read to Clara tonight, Mavis?"

"Of course."

Ruth left the kitchen and went upstairs. Gladys was sitting at her desk, a confusion of papers, books, old coffee cups, and underwear, like every other surface in her room. Normally she spent very little time here even to sleep, and her resolute pose now was unconvincing.

"This isn't a good idea, Gladdy," Ruth said.

"What isn't?"

"Shutting yourself up."

"Ranting around about things is pretty much a waste of time, though, isn't it? I thought you always thought so."

"It's not my way, that's all."

"It's not mine either. I'd rather bust heads," Gladys said, but sullenly, softly.

Ruth cleared a space on Gladys' unmade bed and sat down.

"Why do you want me to talk about it?" Gladys demanded. "You're not a fucking shrink! You're only my landlady."

Ruth shrugged and lit a cigarette.

"Well, what do you want me to say? That I've screwed things up for everybody? I've already had that lecture, before the fact. I'm a prick collector, as Mavis says, with a cunt for a brain."

"That doesn't really sound like Mavis ... or Dickens," Ruth said, smiling.

"No, I've got the only foul mouth in the house."

It was, actually, a very sweet mouth, soft with sympathy and humor and pleasure most of the time, trembling now to refuse tears.

"What's happened isn't your fault, Gladdy."

"How can you say that?"

"Because it's true."

"But it's so obvious what happened. How else could the police have found him if Stew hadn't reported him?"

"Do you know that?"

"I might as well know it," Gladys said. "Stew's really freaked, Ruth. He's in terrible shape."

The tears did begin then, but Gladys put a fist against her mouth and closed her eyes to stop them.

"Why can you eat or drink or work or argue or just about anything else with people, but not ... screw? Why is it such a big deal?"

"I don't know."

"So, since there's no solution, it isn't a problem, right?"

"That's what I like to think," Ruth admitted.

She went to Gladys then, offering the holding arm she had. Gladys turned into the gesture, pressed her face against Ruth's spare body, and wept. Ruth stroked her hair, a shining, lively tangle, and stared down with intent eyes to keep this particular girl before her who still needed comfort, never mind how little real good it could do.

In the morning the young were variously contrite and ready to forgive each other if not themselves. Tom had information about what they might do to help the protest committee. He, Mavis, and Gladys would go to a meeting together that night.

"Is it safe for you, Tom?" Gladys asked, in concern she would have been scornful of a day before.

"Safe enough," Tom said. "Something's got to be done."

"What about Stew?" Joanie asked.

"I phoned this morning," Gladys said. "He's under such heavy sedatives he won't know whether he has visitors or not for the next day or two."

"Just the same," Joanie persisted. "Shouldn't somebody ... ?"

"Shall you and I go?" Ruth suggested. "We could just look in."

Ruth was not accustomed to Joanie's company anywhere but in the house. As they walked along the street toward the bus stop, Ruth was aware of a furtive attention from knots of teenaged boys. She wondered if a street so friendly to her could, at the same time, be this kind of uncomfortable, undeclared contest for Joanie or Gladys. Perhaps the street itself was beginning to change. Ruth liked neither possibility. Purposefully she spoke to people as she passed them, her eyes insisting on being met.

"Do you know everyone in the neighborhood?" Joanie asked.

"I like them to think I do."

"I guess I'm not very friendly."

"I guess I wasn't at your age either."

But walking alone had never frightened Ruth, whether through night woods or along the docksides of the cities of Portland and Seattle. Something in her face, as if she's suffered her whole life from the beginning of it, warned people against interfering. If she did not make contact, none was made. She had to ask for trouble, and she often had, usually finding it at the hands of a man who did not enjoy being abusive but felt a masculine suspicion of the small kindness Ruth could read in his face. Joanie read pocketbooks instead, which were even more carefully guarded from commitment than a kind nature.

"I thought at least Mavis would come to see Stew," Joanie said when they had settled themselves on the bus. "She doesn't usually go to those sorts of meetings."

"No, I never thought I'd see Mavis involved in that sort of thing either."

"I'd be afraid to go," Joanie said.

"Would you?"

"Tom said it wouldn't help Arthur anyway."

"No, but it might still help Tom and all the others up here."

"Lots of people I know think they shouldn't be allowed into Canada. I guess I thought that too, but then, when you think about Arthur or Tom ..."

Ruth watched Joanie's puzzled face, unexamined categories of judgment breaking down before the simple experience of eating breakfast and dinner with particular people day after day. And she could offer this kindness to Stew though she didn't approve of him either or what he suffered from.

"Will you go?" Joanie asked.

"Where?"

"On the protest march they're planning."

"It hadn't occurred to me," Ruth said.

They arrived at the hospital and were directed by an officious nurse who made it seem a reluctant personal favor to tell them where Stew was.

"I'm afraid of hospitals, too," Joanie confessed.

"We all are; it's natural."

Stew was in a room by himself. As they went in, he seemed asleep, but then he turned toward them, and his eyes were open.

"Hello, Stew," Ruth said.

He looked at her, but she knew he did not see her, his mind blind with whatever sedative he had been given.

"Hi, Stew," Joanie said, nervously cheerful. "We came to see you."

"Gladys and Mavis are at a meeting tonight. They sent their love."

"Can you hear, Stew?" Joanie asked.

Nothing disturbed the surface of his face. Ruth brushed the hair back on his forehead, so like Gladdy's own hair. Twins they'd seemed, more than lovers, and should probably have observed the taboos of kinship.

You don't have to fly, Stew. None of you do. There isn't any way out of the maze that's human.

"We'll come back soon."

"Has he lost his mind?" Joanie asked once they were out of doors again.

That sounded to Ruth violently physical, like losing an arm, the wrong way to put what was happening behind Stew's serene eyes.

Going out of his mind was a better cliché, a journey he had been taking intermittently for a couple of years, lifting up out of himself on the notes from his clarinet to escape all the inadequate complexity of thought, even of feeling, wanting to be neither troubled nor touched.

"He's a sick boy," Ruth admitted, "a very sick boy."

The next day, before any of them had an opportunity to see him again, Stew was transferred to Riverview, the mental hospital, where only his family was allowed to visit him.

Tom, Mavis, and Gladys painted placards, made telephone calls, and marched in the streets with dogged energy, which left them muted at home. Nothing any of them could do would bring Arthur back, an unhoped-for miracle they had irrelevantly linked with Stew, whose sentence now seemed as harsh. When, after a few days, the television cameras could no longer be attracted, Tom and Gladys kept on going to meetings, but Mavis went back to her thesis, brooding on the morality of plot. Joanie had a new and hopefully developing relationship with a blue convertible. Willard, who had not missed a step in his routine, still kissed Ruth goodbye in the morning and called, "Have a day, Mrs. Wheeler," but he could not restore Clara. She felt the grief in her bones and could not make the effort to join them at dinner any longer. Nor was she much interested in Dickens or Eiseley, and Gladys didn't even offer to read articles from the radical press. Clara ebbed into the winter in which she intended to die.

The house next door, as well as the house on the corner, was vacant now. They no longer listened for geese but instead for the shattering of glass. One rock was heaved into Stew's empty bedroom. After that, Ruth made sure to leave a number of lights burning. She sat with Clara through longer periods of the night when it would be easiest for Clara to slip away for good from her pain. Ruth did not venture out now except to patrol the block, her face under the street-light stern, her eyes sharp with dark, glittering watchfulness. If she had lived by herself, the current of change would already have caught her up and carried her elsewhere. But there was Willard, there was

Clara, and even the others seemed increasingly dependent on the house and each other, survivors together of lost battles.

A week before Christmas, like a premature nightmare of Santa Claus, Ruth's husband suddenly arrived, chucked his hat and coat in the hall closet, went in to greet his mother, then carried his suitcase back into Ruth's bedroom, calling to her in the kitchen, "I could use a drink."

Joanie, standing puzzled in the living room, said, "Who is he?"

Willard looked up from his paper and made one of his rare offerings: "Mr. Wheeler."

Chapter Four

Hal Wheeler should have been a physically big man. Long-torsoed, heavy-shouldered, he looked at least six feet tall when he was sitting down, but when he stood up he strained to reach five feet six inches: bandy-legged, the only detail about his father Clara could clearly remember. A short-legged man, like a short-legged dog, has to make a lot of noise around the house. If he's a bastard as well, his father a myth instead of a restraint, he will need to be a hero among men, a bully with women, an authority on everything from septic tanks to international finance. Clara would not, even so, have found her son so difficult to like if she had not felt guilty about him. She had given in to the short-legged bully, his father, but then she had been too proud to force him into marriage. Clara loved her son and felt sorry for him.

He did not feel sorry for himself. He was a hero on the road gang, riding tall on his great earth-moving machines which could shove around boulders and tree stumps the size of a house and take the cheek out of a mountain. For twenty-five years he had worked pushing roads deeper and deeper into the British Columbia wilderness, preparing the way for other men to mine and lumber off, to build working towns, mills, foundries, to make B.C. the richest goddamned province in the country. And he made enough money at it to come into town a hero as well, a roll of bank notes in his pocket large enough to impress any kind of drinking partner and buy the sweetest pair of tits in the place if he felt like it. That's how he spent a weekend in Prince George or Kamloops.

In Vancouver, on his rare visits, he had to be that harder thing: a family man, a son, a husband, for twenty-two years a father. Though he blamed Ruth for his long absences, she suspected a basic decency in him kept him away from that role for long periods because he was so bad at it. But she and his mother and even his daughter had been bad at teaching him how or letting him be. Each had wanted something from him that he simply couldn't give, a space of her own in his presence. Hal was not an ungenerous man, but he couldn't give space to anyone easily and to women, never.

Aside from Willard, Tom was the only one in the household who had experienced one of Hal's visits before.

"Gladdy will kill him," he said quietly to Ruth.

"No one has over the years," Ruth said. "I don't imagine she will, but maybe you'd better all go to the pub tonight."

"Did you know he was coming?"

"I never do, but he won't stay long, two or three days maybe."

She took the drink he had ordered in to her husband. He was just coming out of the bathroom, naked to his waist, the grizzled hair on his chest damp from washing, a toothpick in the side of his mouth, a habit he'd acquired when he gave up smoking.

"It was a shame to put money into fixing up that bathroom," he said, hoisting his trousers a little self-consciously, probably because he'd put on a bit of weight.

"I suppose so," Ruth said.

"Mother's poorly."

"She has a lot of pain."

"You're keeping about the same."

"Yes, I'm all right."

He took a clean shirt out of his suitcases and put it on. Then he picked up his drink from the dresser and tilted it at her before he took his first swallow. She liked the shape of his head, but it reminded her of the sharp pleasure she had taken in seeing it repeated in the infant head of their daughter. She'd had his smile, too, lopsided, with one deep dimple, not matched on the other side of his mouth. It was like a movie running backwards, the face of a dead child living on in her father's.

Tom had set a place at the other end of the table, left empty since Clara had given up the effort of eating dinner with them. Hal took it as if he had been sitting there every evening for years. Then he looked at Joanie.

"There will be no curlers at my table," he said.

"I'm sorry," Joanie said, startled. "I'm … I'm going out tonight."

"I said, there will be no curlers at my table."

Joanie looked at Ruth, who said nothing, and then excused herself from the table.

"When I first saw the news, I thought it was you they got," Hal said then to Tom.

"Did you?"

"Don't know why Canadians have to put up with so much American bellyaching."

"I was bellyaching," Gladys said, "and I was bellyaching because I'm a Canadian."

"Nobody's ever going to send you to war. Women don't know what a country is. It's a crime they should vote. Look at Ruth here. She's supposed to be a Canadian. There's a housing shortage in this country, did you know that? There's a job shortage. She'd give the whole damned country, never mind her house, to the Yanks if she had her way."

"The house is being torn down," Gladys said. "If women could vote where it counted, if women ran the city, somebody might fucking well pay some attention to the housing shortage."

"If there's one thing worse than a woman in curlers," Hal said slowly, "it's a woman with a foul mouth."

"We've already tried washing it out with soap," Mavis said good-humoredly, "and it doesn't work; so there's no point in suggesting it. Gladdy does have a point, though, don't you think?"

"This house should have been torn down years ago," Hal said, uncertainly deflected. "The whole neighborhood should be highrises by now."

"Would you live in one?" Ruth asked.

"Why the hell should I live in one?" Hal asked.

"That's the way I feel," Ruth said. "It's the way Clara feels too, but there doesn't seem to be much choice."

"You could live anywhere you wanted," Hal said. "Move to the country if you want space. As for Mother, she's going into a home as soon as I can find one."

"A home?" Ruth repeated. "It would kill her."

"She needs to be looked after," Hal said. "I've made up my mind."

There was no point in arguing with him before an audience, particularly one where he had no allies, which had always been the circumstance in this house, but the silence Ruth kept was tense with unspoken protest around the table.

"She is being looked after," Mavis finally said in a low tone.

"I don't need advice at my own table."

"It fucking well isn't your table!" Gladys burst out.

Hal got to his feet, dwarfing himself in fury. Willard, who sat between him and Gladys, went right on eating. Tom stood up, too, comfortably tall.

"Come on, Gladdy," Tom said quietly. "It just makes it unpleasant for Ruth."

Gladys gave Ruth a look of disbelief, got up, and left the room with Tom. Mavis followed them.

"I sometimes wonder where you find them," Hal said.

"Sit down and eat your dinner," Ruth said. "Have some more chicken, Willard, now that there's plenty."

"Still selling shoes, Willard?"

"That's about it," Willard said.

"Where are you going to go when they pull this old barn down?"

"The future looks after itself."

"I suppose it can," Hal said, settling again to his dinner, "but now and then it needs a little help."

Hal and Ruth took coffee in to have it with Clara, who had made an effort to look comfortable and cheerful in her bed.

"Ruth here thinks is would kill you to go into a home; so you'd better set her straight."

"I want to go, Ruth," Clara said. "I asked Hal to look after it for me."

"Now is that clear?" Hal asked.

Ruth looked at Clara, her companion through all these years. They both knew a home would kill her. That was why she could not have asked Ruth as she could her son, who seemed to Ruth ironically at that moment the unselfish one, ready to do his mother's bidding at some cost to himself. Ruth, given the opportunity, would have fought. She had been fighting through all those unspeaking nights, keeping her need before Clara, refusing to measure the pain. *Do you have to?* Ruth wanted to ask. Clara had had low points before and recovered her little strength and large spirit. Surely she could again.

"Let me go, Ruth."

"It's not up to Ruth. You want to go. I said you could go. That's all there is to settle."

"Yes," Ruth said.

"Ruth?"

"I understand."

Hal was forcefully cheerful, full of tales of his exploits, a ready line of new jokes, old in their intention to set men up and put women down. The classic pose is Mrs. Murphy with her tit caught in a wringer, Mr. Murphy with an eager wrench in his hand. As Ruth brought Hal his third drink, he cupped a hand under her buttocks and squeezed, the sureness of ownership in his gesture. Ruth had never denied him in that as she had in every other manly essential from his wallet to his politics. She was always mildly surprised that he still wanted her.

"You're such a woman in bed," he said. "I don't forget that."

I don't forget you either, she might have said, but one of the things he enjoyed in bed was that he did all the talking, telling her what he wanted, what she wanted, with such candid eagerness that she did want and want badly to come to him and did, but, as he slept heavily beside her, she wondered if she could endure his other needs for more than another day without laughing at him or throwing something at him. Poor bastard … he'd come home to help her as well as his mother.

Ruth heard the young people come in, being unusually quiet for that, or any hour. You didn't explain a man like Hal to anyone. It didn't do any good. Tolerance was not what he wanted. They'd all have to cope as they could.

Ruth tried to sleep, but, like a drunk, she could not close her eyes for long before the bed began to fall away into space, and her own mother's face would loom large, then recede, saying over and over again what Clara had said: "Let me go, Ruth." There had never been any way to bargain, even when she had had that proverbial right arm. Her losses rained down on her from the great space of the night. What little comfort there was, she had had.

Ruth got up quietly, put on a robe, and went out into the hall. It wasn't fair now to take her wakefulness to Clara. It wasn't any longer loving to do so.

"Ruth?" that light voice inquired. "Ruth?"

A rock crashed through one of the high remaining windows next door.

I hear the geese, Clara, and I do feel sorry for them. Ruth wiped tears from her face and went back to Hal, who slept like a monument to himself, no flying thing, rock or bird, disturbing his faith in the future.

Joanie was timidly presentable at breakfast, the only one to appear. Tom and Willard had gone off early as usual, and Mavis and Gladys had left without eating. Ruth fixed Hal a proper trucker's breakfast, and he was glad to occupy himself with that until he refused a second piece of pie.

"Got to watch it." He said ruefully. "Let me tell you something,

Joanie. Looking like that at breakfast is a real improvement, gives a man a good appetite."

Joanie smiled uncertainly at him and excused herself.

"Girl like that," he said to Ruth, "doesn't have much going for her and has to make the most of it."

He helped clear the table, disturbing the efficiency necessary to Ruth to accomplish the tidying, but she did not correct him. She could manage for a day or two, even if he went on being helpful.

"That was good pie," he said, and again his hand reached down for her and squeezed. "Good piece of ass, too." The dimple at the corner of his mouth was deep. "Wouldn't mind seconds of that."

"I'm not interested in that toothpick," Ruth said.

He laughed, pleased with her, pleased with himself.

If being his wife were just this, she could have managed, oh, very well. His appetite had always been good. She liked to feed him. His sexual vanity was something he could share with her, make her feel for herself, but she could not live with the bullying vanity of his mind.

"Minds don't come like cunts!" she had once shouted at him. "Leave me alone!"

"A woman's mind is a cunt, and don't forget it!"

She had a frigid mind then as well as a closed heart. His need to be obeyed and believed, when it went unmet, was as painful to him as it was to her, but she could not meet it and had to watch instead his normal intelligence go stupid with power. He did have a prick for a brain, and Ruth didn't think it natural, except in bed, where he could tell her what she wanted and give it to her, even now after all these years of separateness, of bitterness, of loss.

Taking a shower afterwards, she could hear snatches of his self-satisfied whistle as he shaved. Having been a good husband, he must now set off to be a good son. He would not ask her to go with him, and she was glad of that. She did not want to be a good daughter to Clara if it meant finding a clean and comfortable place for her to die.

Clara and Ruth did not try to explain to or comfort each other through the day. They carried on their usual, open-ended conversation, the hesitant duet of voices they had accomplished over the years, and they were both relieved when Tom came home in the middle of the afternoon.

"Hi, old lady," he called.

"Hello, son," she answered, the lightest brush of love in the term which she'd never used to address Hal.

"I'm taking the harem out to dinner tonight, Ruth," he announced, "even Joanie. Gladys says my generosity is a mark of profound cowardice, but she's accepted the invitation; so has Mavis."

"You should let me pay for it," Ruth said.

"I wouldn't think of it. Where we're going they nearly pay you to eat the food anyway, and I may have help. Who do you think dropped by to see me today? ... Stew. I didn't recognize him, his hair all cut off. He even had on a tie."

"How is he?" Clara asked, a hopeful urgency in her voice Ruth hadn't heard in weeks.

"He seems really fine. Oh, a bit nervous at first, a bit thin. He's staying with his folks over on the north shore. He's going to apply to law school for the fall."

"Stew?"

"That's right," Tom said. "I invited him for dinner. He wasn't sure he could make it. I told him everybody'd love to see him. I told him he should drop by here to see both of you."

"He doesn't think we're angry with him, does he?" Clara asked.

"I told him Joanie and Ruth had been to see him at the hospital. He didn't remember that, but I think it made him feel better, easier about coming over."

"Oh, Tom, I'm glad," Ruth said.

"Yeah, it was good to see him."

"Did he ask about Arthur?"

"No, we didn't mention Arthur." Tom paused and shook his head. "He may not even remember Arthur."

What was remembering? The flickering smile like a light about to go out for good? Some children lasted only a few days and then were washed away by one current or another. Though Ruth still sometimes dreamed of her lost hand, she could not even remember clearly what it had looked like. Categories of concern break down. She let memory fail her, the only kind of dreaming she could sometimes avoid.

"Here's Hal," Clara said, having turned to the window at the slamming of a car door.

He came in jaunty, hat tilted back on his head, toothpick riding high. Tom nodded and turned past him in Clara's doorway.

"The professional dodger," Hal said, laughing at his own wit. "Well, it's settled: private room and bath, color TV, in Queen's Court, and I can move you in tomorrow."

"Tomorrow!" Ruth exclaimed.

"A job needs to be done, get it done. We can pack you up tonight, Mother, and we'll be ready to go in the morning."

"But Christmas is only five days away," Ruth protested. "She could move after the New Year."

"I haven't got 'til after the New Year. I've got to be out of here tomorrow night."

"You don't have to move her," Ruth pleaded. "Tom could do it, he and Mavis."

"She moves tomorrow, and I do it. That's settled."

"It is not settled!" Ruth shouted.

Clara put her face in her frail hands.

"Oh, Clara, I'm sorry. I'm so sorry," Ruth said, going to her.

"Let him get it over with," she said, quietly, "please."

Hal stood, fury in his face at the scene before him. *You are a good son*, Ruth wanted to say to him. *It's just that you're such a bastard.* She turned away from Clara, walked past him out of the room, out of the house into the strong taste of snow that had begun to fall. Why wasn't *she* old enough to be able to go off and die? What point was there now in anything?

At quarter to six she was, nevertheless, in the kitchen, cooking for Hal and Clara and Willard, who smiled in at her before he went to finish his paper.

"Willard, Clara's going into a nursing home tomorrow," Ruth said.

"She's getting on, Mrs. Wheeler is," he observed.

There was no point in imagining, after all this time, that she could teach Willard to talk. The unnatural quiet in the house was prelude to what living would come to be. Without Clara, without the buffer of young people between them, Ruth wondered if she had the charity for Willard. His refusal to take any space at all had been convenient in the clutter of living this house had contained, but he'd be less company than a dog when they were alone together, stored tidily in a highrise for the rest of their arbitrary lives.

Ruth only half listened to Hal's monologue through dinner. He was talking about investments, a duplex or a small apartment building that could pay for itself out in the valley somewhere maybe or on Vancouver Island. His plans for her did not include Willard, whose welfare concerned Hal as little as it concerned Willard himself.

"I haven't decided," Ruth said evasively.

"You've got two months at the most," Hal insisted. "There's nothing to hang on for now that Mother's settled. You'll have the money to move next week."

"I'm not ready to move."

"You want to wait until the kids break every window in the house?"

"Kids aren't going to scare me out of my own house."

"Ruth, you've got to make things happen. You can't just wait around and let them happen to you. Women!" he said, shaking his head at Willard, who, simple as he was, would be expected to understand better than Ruth.

"It's not your problem," Ruth said.

"Listen, any problem you've got is my problem."

Ruth yawned. It was nerves more than weariness, though she knew she must be very tired. Hal pounded so on the doors she had shut and locked against him years and years ago.

"I'm going to shovel the walk," Willard announced.

Packing Clara's belongings was not a major undertaking. She had only a few clothes. Aside from her sewing box and her radio, there was nothing else she wanted. Clara did not like cluttered surfaces, and she did not keep reminders, like photographs. The baggage of the past she carried in her head.

"Books? No, dear," she said in answer to Hal's question about the contents of her bookcase. "I don't read much to myself any more."

"There'd be room for your chair if you want it," Hal offered.

"Take it," Ruth urged, bewildered by the meagerness of Clara's possessions.

Clara consented to please them both, but she was essentially indifferent to what left the house with her, not born into a culture accustomed to furnishing its dead for the comforts of the journey. Hal moved the suitcases from one side of the room to the other, tonguing his toothpick in and out of his mouth. Then he paused and looked down at his mother.

"Now, just one thing, if you don't like the place, nobody ever said a woman couldn't change her mind."

She sighed and gave him a frail smile, too tired now to attempt words to reassure him. He carried the chair out of the room.

Ruth would have liked to continue that speech, but she knew Clara had no reassurance for her either, needing the little courage she had left for herself. Ruth would have liked to make promises and plans, too, but she had none of Hal's illusions that she could make anything happen.

"Is it still snowing?" Clara asked.

"Yes."

"Don't forget to put out something for the birds, will you?"

Ruth smiled. That and the taking of Clara's hand were the only expressions of affection left to Ruth, who had intended to keep small life offerings before Clara the winter long, but she was being asked to accept Clara, too, after these faithful years, as a bird of passage whose time had come. Had she really expected not to have to face anything but Clara's death? *I would have buried you under the lilac bush with the robins.*

Hal needed a drink, served him in the living room, where he could pretend for a while to be self-satisfied master of the situation, but he had done enough that day to leave the problem of Ruth's future alone. He was tired.

"What time in the morning?" Ruth asked.

"Just after nine." Hal looked at her steadily. "I don't ask you to thank me."

"I suppose I should be able to."

"You never were," he said with no bitterness in his voice, simply stating a fact.

Being his sort of man had always seemed to Ruth a thankless task, but she had not until that moment seen any point in it either. Perhaps all the years of bullying had been necessary preparation for these hard endings, which he was strong enough to manage without her gratitude.

"You've been good to her," Hal said quietly.

Ruth shook her head impatiently. Crude duty was all he would ever understand, a virtue she had rejected by the time she was ten years old.

"And you don't ask me to thank you either," Hal said, as if agreeing with her.

"You need another drink?"

"Can you wait that long?" he asked, giving her his deep, dimpled grin, punctuated by his toothpick.

"Maybe," she said, answering the smile, but she didn't want to wait rigid against his will. She wanted to give in to him in the one way she could.

Lying in the noisy dark of his deep sleep, Ruth listened again to the unusual quiet of the returning young. If they had all really been her children, if she had borne them and borne with Hal, he would have driven them all out of the house and Clara to her grave years ago. Thankless tasks all right, hard on a decent man unless he could believe in duty, which had also taught him to kill men and trees. She touched his handsome head, heavy on her breast. *Poor bastard.*

Chapter Five

"We had better do something about Christmas," Tom said to the back of Ruth's head as she sat watching the snow fall.

"Willard's going to Kamloops to his mother," Ruth said.

"And Joanie's going home, but that still leaves Mavis and Gladdy and me … and you."

Ruth had been sitting in the empty house since ten in the morning, her heart stiff with the loss of Clara, her body stiff with unaccustomed attention. She had traveled so far in that emptiness she had forgotten Mavis and Gladys and Tom, perhaps even, as Tom was suggesting, herself. She had no will to return, even to him.

"What is it you want then?"

"A tree, presents, a Christmas dinner."

"Why?"

"Look at me, Ruth," Tom urged. "I've lost my whole family, too, and you didn't let me just sit and stare. Christmas can be a lousy day, but trying to ignore it just makes it worse."

"I could ignore it," Ruth said. "I don't keep birthdays of the dead."

"All right, it's obscene, barbaric, commercial, and all things unholy, but it happens to be the only thing we've got."

"Hal used to talk about singing Christmas carols in the trenches, all good Christians together."

"Has he left?"

"Yes."

"Then we don't have to sing in the trenches," Tom said, offering a smile.

"It occurred to me last night that, if you all had been my children, you would have left me in peace years ago."

"Interesting, because it occurred to us last night that we'd been behaving like children long enough. We've decided to turn this place into a commune, everybody taking a turn at cooking and the dishes, except for Willard, of course."

"It's my house, Tom Petross," Ruth flared, "and I run it."

"Sure, fine; a commune with a dictator, that's all we meant."

"You begin to sound like Gladdy."

"Do I?"

The contrived innocence of his tone and expression forced Ruth to register the lively shifting patterns even in these remnants of her household. *Clara, Tom and Gladys are in love, and they want Christmas. Why?* tipped to *why not?* in one moment's unspoken information.

"All right," Ruth said, "we'll get the silly tree. Come on."

Snow softened the street, covering the evidence of neglect in the yards of deserted houses, turning loitering adolescents back into warful children, hilarious in snow forts facing each other on either side of the street. Tom ducked a snowball and fired back.

"Nobody is finally a pacifist," Ruth commented.

"Not in this elemental sense, no," Tom agreed, ducking and hurling another.

A snowball thudded against Ruth's back.

"If I had two hands …"

"Here," Tom said, handing her a snowball.

She lobbed it with high accuracy into the fort across the street.

"Got me!" someone shouted, falling melodramatically through the soft snow wall.

A hail of snowballs followed.

"We're outnumbered," Tom said. "We'd better run for it."

Patched with snow, out of breath and laughing, they arrived at the bus stop, where rather more sedate neighbors stared away from them with superior smiles. A neighborhood was a neighborhood after all, and one was expected to act one's age.

"We mustn't fool around too long, Tom," Ruth said, trying to catch her breath and her dignity. "I have to get dinner on."

"Gladdy's cooking tonight," Tom said.

"Maybe I didn't get this straight. Who's supposed to be the dictator of this commune?"

"You are, Ruth."

"And what's for dinner?"

"It's a surprise."

"But the mess in the kitchen won't be."

"I'm on KP."

"It begins to sound like a barracks."

"It's going to feel like home. Wait and see."

Mavis and Gladys were both in the kitchen by the time Ruth and Tom got home with the tree.

"Don't ask what it is," Gladys warned. "It's French with a Greek accent."

Ruth refrained from looking into the kitchen. She went off instead to find the stored tree stand and ornaments, the sharp missing of Clara no longer a silence in her head but instead a recording of all the sounds of the house to play back to Clara tomorrow. She was not, after all, dead. She was only a dozen blocks away in a pleasant room with a view of the water, resting instead of having to rise to the occasion.

Though Willard's chair was in the place where a tree should have been, Tom had not moved it. Instead he and Mavis had moved the couch so that the tree could stand at the corner of the big window. They were spreading a sheet there when Ruth came back in with the stand.

"The ornament boxes and lights are in the back hall," she explained, and then she glanced into the dining room. "Wine for dinner?"

"Yep," Tom said, "a contribution from Stew."

"Is he coming?"

"No," Mavis said, "but we had dinner with him last night."

"Has he ever changed his image!" Gladys said as she put a large bowl of salad on the table.

"And I like it," Mavis said.

"Who liked it was Joanie. I've never seen her turn on like that before," Gladys said. "I began to have pangs for poor old blue convertible."

"Don't start that until after dinner, Tom," Mavis said as he began to open the boxes he'd brought from the hall. "Let's make one mess at a time, or Ruth will veto the whole project."

"I'm going to veto it anyway," Ruth said amiably. "Tonight's fine. Tonight's a party, but I've been running this house too long, and I'm just not the co-operative sort."

"How do you know until you try?" Gladys protested.

Willard came in at that moment and raised his head in unaccustomed nervousness like an animal picking up a strange scent.

"It's all right, Willard," Gladys said, laughing. "It's only that I'm cooking dinner tonight."

"Are you sick?" Willard asked Ruth, a fear in his face Ruth had never seen before.

"No, of course I'm not sick. I'm never sick. You know that. It's a party, that's all."

"A party," Willard repeated thoughtfully.

"A Christmas party while we're all still here," Tom explained. "Joanie's going home tomorrow, and you're going to Kamloops, aren't you?"

"We aren't all still here now," Willard said, climbing over the boxes of ornaments to reach his chair.

Was it Clara he missed? Ruth couldn't be sure. For her the room was crowded with ghosts, not before her mingling with the present company, no, she didn't allow that, but at her back, the refused memories who lived on only in her dreams.

Joanie either didn't feel she had time to change into curlers or hadn't got the message that Hal had really gone, for she joined them the moment she got in and was some real last-minute help in the kitchen, remembering the coffee which Gladys had forgotten.

It had been so long since Clara had joined them for dinner that she did not seem as absent as she had during the day. She was only in another room, listening not for words but for the message of mood at the table, which tonight was resolutely cheerful. The presence that had not quite left them was Hal. Gladys used not one four-letter word the meal long, and Joanie played with her hair like a girl on a date. Willard sniffed his wine several times before he decided to drink it, but then it went down in gulps like a glass of cold beer.

"Do you like it?" Ruth asked.

"It goes down," he admitted.

"You're not going to go out tonight, are you, Willard?" Gladys asked. "Why don't you stay and decorate the tree with us?"

He shook his head. The laundry had to be done. Since he had to deal with a four-day holiday and a long bus trip, he had to guard his routine the more carefully while he had it.

Ruth was not allowed to take part in the cleaning up.

"You're just too organized. You make everyone but Tom nervous," Gladys explained.

Ruth was abandoned in the living room with nothing but a last cup of coffee to keep her company. It was the time of night she might go in to read to Clara. Would she be listening to her radio instead? Or, left in peace, perhaps she would learn to sleep.

In the kitchen, Joanie began a carol, her voice high, the words uncertain high-school Latin. Gladys joined in resolutely in English. Mavis picked up the harmony, and Tom hummed an octave underneath.

"The only thing I ever learned in Latin was 'Jingle Bells,' a class project to irritate the Latin teacher," Gladys admitted and began, "*Tineat, tineat …*"

"Oh, come on," Mavis moaned.

"All right, I'll stop if everyone promises not to sing 'White Christmas.'"

"I like 'White Christmas,'" Joanie protested.

Tom began a bad imitation of Bing Crosby, which came to an end with a grunt, undoubtedly caused by Gladys' authoritative fist. Mavis started a carol the others didn't know, her voice sure enough to carry it by herself. When she had finished, they sang together again, this time with unself-conscious pleasure, of peace, of joy, of salvation over the clatter of pots and pans, and they went on singing once they had come back into the living room until the decorating of the tree began, offering opportunities for argument.

"Why is it that men always assume they have to put up the lights?" Gladys demanded.

"Be my guest," Tom said, offering her the string he had been testing and was about to begin winding through the branches.

"It's not that I really want to do it," Gladys admitted. "But at home, Dad always put up lights, and then he didn't do one other thing. My sisters and I always did the rest, while he sat around drinking beer."

"Speaking of that," Mavis said, "I've got a bottle of brandy."

"My dad didn't even do that," Joanie said. "He thought Christmas was a pile of crap, but then he thought we were all a pile of crap too. He finally took off. That's why I have to go home. Mum's alone now. Neither of my brothers want to be bothered."

Tom didn't say anything. He had gone back to putting up the lights, whistling softly through his teeth. He was so resolute about Christmas because, among them, he was the only one who could not choose to go home.

"I'd go home if I could afford it," Gladys said. "I've got seven nieces and nephews, but Toronto's just out of the question."

Mavis came in with the brandy.

"Where's your family, Mavis?" Joanie asked.

"In Vancouver."

"And you're not going home?"

"I don't go home," Mavis said.

"This is home," Tom said, stepping back from his work to admire it, putting a hand on Mavis' shoulder. "Now, give me my brandy so that I can sit around and watch the rest of you work."

"Not fucking likely!" Gladys shouted, snatching at the glass Tom was reaching for. "Not until you've earned it."

Hal's ghost bellowed as loudly, but only in Ruth's hearing. She saluted him privately and took a sip of her brandy, which helped unclench the grief in her throat. The bright globes began to go up on the tree, turning slowly, giving off miniature reflections of the room.

"Where did this pretty glass angel come from?" Joanie asked. "I've never seen one like it."

"I don't remember," Ruth said.

"Put it high up, Tom," Joanie said, handing the ornament to him, "in the light."

"Angels we have heard on high …" Mavis began, and the others joined in, except for Ruth, whose voice could no longer lift to any line of melody.

There was no more way to stop the invention of angels than there was to stop the building of highrises or trips to the moon. Creatures foundered out of one element into another, always trying to leave behind the mortal climate of their birth.

"I can't understand wanting life ever after," Ruth said, nearly to herself, "except perhaps for other people."

"People don't like dying," Mavis said, "particularly for nothing."

"Oh, don't be morbid," Joanie protested. "Look at this pretty fish. I've never seen a Christmas fish before."

"Must be a lungfish," Mavis observed.

"My father always hung silver dollars on the tree," Tom said.

"How American!"

"Yeah," he agreed.

"Well, we had chocolate money," Joanie said. "I don't see anything wrong with that. I think different customs are interesting."

Mavis poured another round of brandy. Willard came in with his clean laundry and refused to join them for a drink. Joanie went off to pack for her departure in the morning. Tom went out into the kitchen and came back with the cart loaded with breakfast dishes.

"Tom!" Ruth called sharply, beginning to get up from her chair.

"The thing is," Gladys said quickly, "we thought we might find a place together, Tom and Mavis and I, maybe Joanie, too, but we need some practice at it if we're going to do it, to see beforehand if we could."

"You've got all the work of packing this place up," Mavis added, "and you'll want to spend some time with Clara; so it could be a help to you, too, don't you think?"

"It's a conspiracy," Ruth muttered.

"A peaceful revolution," Gladys said.

"A family solution to a family problem," Tom said, "and there haven't been enough of those around here. You've been carrying everybody and everything on your back, Ruth."

"You can tell us exactly what to do if you will," Gladys said.

I think I've had as many burdens taken from me as I can bear, she wanted to cry at them, watching her with such hopeful love, but she couldn't. They were right. She would need help because it was now time. Without Clara there was no point in waiting until the end, and these young needed to be set free.

"All right," Ruth said.

There by the lights of the Christmas tree, they laid out the plans they had already made, surprising Ruth with their knowledge of the work she did.

"It would be more practical for you to go on doing the ordering," Mavis said, "but we wish you'd teach us. Tom's used to restaurant quantities, and Gladdy'd get us into co-op buying of crates of wormy apples, and I've managed for twenty-four years never to set foot in a kitchen, except to get ice for a drink."

When the chores that usually occupied Ruth's restless night had been done, Tom and Gladys drifted off to bed. They had been so much together for the last week, Ruth was surprised that she had not realized until this afternoon that they had become lovers.

"Shall we have a nightcap?" Mavis asked.

"Why not? It might even put me to sleep."

"We're awfully sorry about Clara, Ruth," Mavis said quietly, as she handed Ruth her glass and sat down unaccustomedly near Ruth on the floor, a gesture far more like Gladys, for whom physical affection was natural. "We thought if we'd put our minds to helping once Arthur left, she might not have wanted … needed to go."

"You've always helped," Ruth said, "particularly with Clara."

"We could have done a lot more."

"It was time. I should have known it and done something about it myself."

"You couldn't have very well, could you?"

"It was probably better for Hal to do it."

Ruth was glad to be sitting with Mavis instead of Tom or Gladys, both of whom at this late hour, after the strains and bewilderments of the last few days, might need to ask questions. Even if Mavis needed to, she wouldn't.

"I think the three of us could live together, but I'm not so sure about Joanie," Mavis said. "I haven't got Gladdy's movement faith that we're all sisters, and I'm not sure about sisters anyway."

"I've sometimes thought it was hard for you to live in the same house with Tom and Gladdy."

Mavis smiled. "It has been, and it probably would go on being. I've been applying for teaching jobs all over the country; so I might not be around all that long anyway. I guess I don't much like the idea of moving into a room somewhere; it's too easy for me. Now that they've finally… got it together, it won't be as hard."

Mavis was not self-sufficient so much as self-protective. If Gladys had been sitting there, Ruth would easily have put out her hand, touched the young head, but Mavis was just out of natural reach. She would be more comfortable with options closed, and for Tom they probably would be, but for Gladys? Gladys could be genuinely grief-stricken over a mistake like Stew and Arthur; she might even learn to be more careful, but wherever Gladys was, no option could be entirely closed.

"I guess nearly anything works for a while," Mavis said, "if people want it to."

"If it isn't important," Ruth said, "and nothing should be important."

"You could be cynical, Ruth."

"I've never had that kind of hope."

"Will Clara see any of us?"

"I don't know. I'll see."

Was Mavis wondering as well whose hands were canny or gentle enough to settle Clara for the night, to get her up in the morning?

"I guess you must be tired," Mavis said, quickly looking at Ruth. "I'll get the lights and do the glasses. You go on to bed."

With the faint odor of Hal in her bed, a comfort she could not even explain to herself, Ruth did drift into sleep, and, though the glass angel hovered precariously, it did not fall. Then Tom was floating around the room on the strings of a puppet, and Gladys held up her arms to him, or perhaps it was Stew up there, or Arthur, and Ruth was reaching her own arms up, the face above her her husband's, descending on her, and he was heavy and naked again, held in her arms, as often restored to her in dreams as her children, all her children, were taken away. She was afraid. She had to warn him. "Hal, if you don't finally get out of the way of progress, it's going to fall on your head." And above them the tree began to fall, but very slowly, as if it might take days or weeks to reach them; yet Ruth knew, however long it took, there was nothing she could do, for it had all really happened years ago. Her father was singing, "Happy Birthday to you," the song he always sang to her first thing on Christmas morning. She had sometimes thought it was her birthday with all those presents. She wanted to wake Hal up. She wanted to tell him it was Christmas. She wanted to wake their child, singing. "We mustn't forget," she was pleading with him. "We mustn't forget her."

The room when she woke might have been a hospital room, so white and bright it was with snow.

Chapter Six

Ruth sat in the chair she and Hal had insisted on moving into Clara's new room, brutally bright on this shining winter day.

"It's hard to praise glaring beauty," Clara said.

"Shall I draw the blinds?"

Clara smiled, as if such a subversive act might restore them to familiar conspiracy, but she did not give assent. Ruth didn't know whether it was perverse courage or immobilizing fear that kept her from doing what she herself had suggested. Clara lay exposed in a frozen flash of light, and Ruth did not want to see how mortally frail she was, death as close as a change of expression on her face. Oh, Ruth had seen it before, not only in the old but in the mirror and in the faces of children. Familiarity did not lessen shock.

"Gladdy's taken to Tom's bed now," Ruth said, her liveliest offering.

"Poor Mavis."

"They're thinking of finding a place to share, the three of them, perhaps even Joanie."

Clara had nothing to say to that. It would probably be too much of an effort for her to go on imagining into the lives of all these young now that they no longer populated her days. Ruth should learn to let them go as well, but she hadn't the painful weariness to make it easy.

"I wonder what the world will be like without accidents ... mistakes like Hal," Clara said suddenly.

Without accidental birth, there would still be accidental death, children growing up without fathers, parents bereaved in middle age. But Clara was not really interested in generalities. She was speaking out of specific guilt, one that Gladys and Joanie would not have to experience, given the pill and easy abortion.

"He's not a bad man, Clara."

"No," she agreed, "not for someone who has no business here."

Do any of us really have, Clara? Could you tell me what my business is or ever has been? At least Hal thinks he knows, however rigid and silly it is, this being a man. The pity for him is only how little we let him get on with it. I sometimes think I was born an obstruction and not a very successful one at that. My mother married again. Hal went his own bullying way. The child died. And now you've left me, too. It's not much of a business, a lifetime of trying to keep things from happening when they happen anyway.

"I don't even remember him," Clara mused. "And there shouldn't have been any reason to. Will Gladys remember Arthur? Or Stew? Or Tom, for that matter?"

I've tried to forget, and so I dream orgies of the forgotten. I can remember if I have to. Am I to sit here now in this terrible light, wide awake, and let everything happen again before my open eyes? Everything that is lost to me still there? Why should I? Why should you? Nothing between glare and dark then, nothing.

"It can make such a difference," her father was saying, pleased with their own newly acquired electricity, about to teach his child one of a thousand lessons in generosity. "Won't cost us more than a few cents a day just to take this wire down to the Weedmans, and that's what we're going to do."

"Is it legal?" Ruth's mother asked.

"Never heard of a law against neighborliness," he said.

"They might get one of those electric heaters," she protested.

"Might get them one myself. Be easier on me than worrying about her firewood all the time now that he's no help to her."

Ruth was allowed to help her father, and stringing the wire along the posts he'd set was more exciting than mending a fence or building a new one because it carried that mystery of energy which not only turned on new lights in their house but made the inside of the new icebox cold as winter and turned the water in the little trays into ice. Her father had bought her a pair of electric scissors, and, though (as her mother pointed out) they didn't really cut as well as her old ordinary ones, they were still amazing, vibrating in her hand like something alive.

"This is going to be a big surprise to old Weedman. I bet he never thought he'd live to see the day ..." her father was telling her, the delight in his scheme a deep pleasure in his voice.

Only when they got to the Weedmans' shack, built too close to the river, flooded out twice even in Ruth's short memory, did Ruth feel any of her mother's apprehension about the project. Ruth was afraid of old Mr. Weedman, maybe not so much now that he lay in bed, one side paralyzed by a stroke, unable to talk. He didn't seem to her crazier now than he had just weeks ago when he was a strong, up-right man because he didn't talk even when he could, and now he was helpless. He hadn't ever been mean to her really. In fact, when she tried to think about it, she worried that she might have been mean to him. Old Weedman often helped her mother when her father was away. Last spring he had even put in their garden, but, when she tried to help as she always did with her father, he behaved as if she were a nuisance instead, something to be watched and shooed away like a chicken from new seed. Or if her mother sent her down there to the shack with a gratitude, a pie or a half worn-out sweater of her father's, Mr. Weedman glared at it and at her as if she might have been the person who put that knife scar right across his nose and cheek, but the worst time was this fall when she had been impatient for the watermelons to ripen. If her father had been home, he would have walked along the row with her, thumping the biggest ones, now and then making a small plug with his knife, until he'd found one for her. Old Weedman just shook his head to mean, no, they weren't ready, and turned his back on her. Though she was frightened of him, she felt he was denying not just her but her father. She thumped a melon or two loudly, hoping to confirm the deep, hollow tone of ripeness for herself, but she wasn't sure.

"Listen to this one, Mr. Weedman," she called to his back. "Or this one?"

He turned and looked down at her.

"There's probably one," she persisted.

He picked up the melon she had just tested, lifted it over his head, and let it drop to the ground. It split open, its flesh a pale, unsatisfactory pink, most of the seeds still white. He glared at her, then picked up a second melon and dropped it. Along the row of melons, he stooped, lifted, and smashed until the whole crop lay broken, not one ready to eat. Then he turned and left her in the melon patch to take in the lesson of challenging his authority.

"He's a wicked old man," her mother said, nearly as grief-stricken over the melons as Ruth was.

"I made him do it," Ruth had to say.

"You're just a child!" her mother contradicted. "He did it for spite."

Her father said, when he heard what had happened, "It's just you touched him in his pride, Ruthie."

Now they were stringing the magic wire up the side of the shack, and Mrs. Weedman was watching them, a handkerchief pressed to her mouth as it mostly was these days, held there like a bandage on a wound, but no scab could ever form to shut in the tears.

"You're a good man," she was saying to Ruth's father, over and over again.

Ruth could tell it embarrassed him, but he was used to that. Though Ruth often wished, when she was sent there, that it would be Mrs. Weedman who received whatever it was Ruth had to deliver, Mrs. Weedman's gratitude was nearly as uncomfortable as old Mr. Weedman's anger. "A lot of times it's like that," her father explained, "with two people, maybe a man and his wife, maybe even a couple of brothers: what one has too much of the other has too little, and, since there's no way to shuffle them together, you have to do the mixing up in your own head. Mrs. Weedman doesn't thank you too much because she's thanking for both. Mr. Weedman doesn't thank you too little. He's making up for her embarrassing the life out of you."

There were only two rooms in the shack, one with the stove where they ate and sat, one with the bed where they slept. Ruth hesitated by the stove, not wanting to follow her father into the bedroom, where the first light was to be installed.

"Morning, Pete," he was saying. "We've got a little surprise for you."

He went on talking cheerfully like that, stringing the wire up the inside wall and along the ceiling, and then he was asking Mrs. Weedman just where over the bed she wanted it.

"Now, we'll just be a few minutes turning the power back on," he explained.

He found Ruth in the kitchen, took her hand, and they raced back to their own house, the new wire marking the familiar way.

"Don't you want to come down to see it go on?" he asked Ruth's mother.

She was busy at the new sewing machine he had bought her, half nervous and half pleased about how it worked, and she snapped at him, "If I'm ever going to figure this darned thing out, I can't go chasing after every electric light you string up all over the neighborhood."

So only Ruth went back with him to witness the miracle, and this time she knew she'd have to go right into the dark bedroom.

"Now you watch his face when I turn it on," her father instructed her as they were about to go back into the shack.

In the dim natural light, she could just make out the old man, lying among rumpled bedclothes, strong of the smell of his stale body.

"Now!" her father said, and he pulled the little chain on the bulb that hung over the bed.

The room exploded into light, and there old Mr. Weedman lay, staring up at it, his eyes blank.

"He couldn't wait," Mrs. Weedman said, her voice carried on a shaking sigh. "He's so sorry. He just couldn't wait."

Her father on the walk back home was as silent as Mr. Weedman had ever been.

"What's the matter?" her mother asked.

"I think," Ruth said timidly, "I think Mr. Weedman's dead."

They went on paying for the little electricity Mrs. Weedman used even after Ruth's father was dead. But when Ruth's mother married again, her new husband said, "What the hell is this?" about the wire that led down to the Weedman shack.

"I never knew how to take it down," her mother confessed, "and I didn't want to call the authorities because I wasn't sure it was legal. He was always doing crazy things like that, trying to be kind, mind you, but he actually killed the old man. It was just too much for him."

❧

"I'm going to pull the shade," Ruth said, getting up from beside Clara's bed and going to the window, but even as she gentled the room into shadows, she felt that stepfather shaking and shaking her and shouting, "You're going to see the light about this if I have to shake the daylights out of you." Against her tantrum of protest, the wire had come down.

"A minister came to visit me yesterday afternoon," Clara said, "from the United Church. He said it was better to pray than to brood. I told him neither would hatch many eggs at my age."

"Clara," Ruth said, shaking her head in amazement.

"I do brood, of course, but I resented him. I told him I had only one thing left to do and that was to learn to cherish my mistakes."

"What did he say to that?"

"He thought I was talking about forgiveness. Tiresome man. I've been spoiled. I haven't had to deal with very many tiresome people. I don't think he'll come back."

"Mavis wondered when you might like to see any of them."

Clara sighed. "When they want to come."

Her face in this softer light looked very much more still at the mercy of life, and, where Hal might have ranted at her being worn out further by the very people he'd just freed her from, Ruth was glad.

"I won't tell them not to," Ruth confessed.

Clara closed her eyes, perhaps dozed, perhaps simply waited through a passage of pain. She had disciplined herself long since to keep her face from communicating the difference between rest and patience.

You've always made yourself comfortable in ways that surprise me. Who else would try to cherish mistakes? I understand that there's no for-giveness, but I can only bear it if there's no cause and effect either. If I hadn't unhooked those years ago and then kept unhooking them, I couldn't have survived the guilt. Cherish the mistakes? My father didn't kill old Weed-man; there was no mistake.

"If she weren't so stubborn, if she'd just learn not to go into the poi-son oak, she'd save us all grief," her mother said, addressing the back of her father's head, her voice raised to be heard over Ruth's crying.

He was unwrapping the gauze from around her thighs, having to use quick, sharp tugs where the bandaging was stuck to the draining blisters.

"She doesn't do it on purpose," he said quietly.

"I was only picking huckleberries," Ruth said, sullen against her mother's lack of sympathy.

"What neither of you will ever learn is that the road to hell is paved with good intentions. It doesn't matter why you do it; if you do it, you get poison oak."

"Dad doesn't even get poison oak," Ruth said.

"And you remember: no swimming until it's all healed, not even wading, or it will spread even worse."

"Try not to cry. Try not to scratch," her father said gently when he'd finished putting on clean bandages. "Do the best you can."

He gave her a small bottle of perfume, a glass bottle in the shape of a man whose black top hat unscrewed, to help conceal the awful smell of the sulphur salve.

Everything bad that happened was according to her mother a mistake, according to her father an accident. Her mother was always angry and full of ideas for further punishments to underline the lesson. Her father was sorry and wanted to lessen the pain.

The road was being lowered that summer along the cliff face right across from their favorite swimming hole. Two days a week no one was allowed on the river bar, and the old, higher road was closed for blasting. Ruth and her mother would sit on the screen porch, cutting up the early apples for making applesauce, bracing themselves for the next blast. Then in the evening when her father came home, they would walk down to the river to see what had happened, a new large boulder snagged against a tree trunk, a whole tree, its roots tangling in the air, half submerged in the river. Sometimes there were small torn manzanita bushes even on their side of the river.

"It's a mess now," her father said, "but it's going to make that stretch of road much safer."

"If people would just slow down, there wouldn't be any need," her mother said.

"Can't go backwards about that," her father said. "The world's going to go faster and faster."

Despite herself, Ruth's imagination went with her mother's. She saw the great freight trucks rounding the cliff edge, floating out into the air, and buckling in a slow-motion fall into the river. She had seen it happen once when she was out alone fishing, her small catch strung by its gills to hang on a stripped willow branch, lying beside her on the rocks. It was hard to believe even when she was nearly rocked off her feet by the impact and felt the rain of spray as the truck disappeared under the water in the deep hole below the riffle. Two other cars had stopped at the edge of the cliff. A man was shouting.

Another was climbing down the cliff face.

"You'll never get him out," the one at the top was calling. "I'll get the police."

Ruth did not stay to watch. She ran home to tell her mother. An hour later, when she went to find her fish, there instead was a snake, swollen with her catch, inching itself off into the willows. The river did not even swell over the place where the truck had gone in.

"They got him out," her father confirmed that night, "but not in time. Take a couple of days to round up the equipment to pull that truck out."

At the café, they said he'd come through maybe forty-five miles an hour, but someone else said his brakes had failed, and Ruth's father favored that story though he wasn't prepared to argue about it.

"Fate's a fool's answer," her mother said.

Her father's eyes rested in the far distance.

Ruth tried not to scratch, and she tried not to cry. She tried to stay away from the river even on safe days, but the heat in the valley was intense, up to 110 one day even in the shade of the fig trees. By three in the afternoon, there was almost always a relieving breeze along the river, which could cool her bubbling rash even under the bandages and carry the smell of it away from her. When she felt that comfort, she could see no real harm in letting the water cool her feet, but even the familiar shallows had been altered by the blasting. She turned her ankle in an unexpected pothole and fell in. The jolt of guilt was followed immediately by such deep relief from the itching that she lay in the water, sleepy with pleasure, floating downstream in the gentle current. Then, as she felt the strength of the water increase where it narrowed to the riffle, she guided herself toward shore, for she was forbidden to ride the riffle even when she didn't have poison oak. On shore she looked at her water-soaked bandages and knew they would take longer to dry than her shorts and shirt. She climbed to the top of a large rock, exposing herself to the sun and the wind, and watched an occasional car pass over the high road on the other side of the river, imagining that she was a log, marooned up here by the spring floods or blasted here by the road crew, as happy an accident as her birth which gave her the river and the great trees, no need ever to drive the long road to get here. Sometimes one of the truck drivers, familiar with the area, spotted her and honked, but, if she was a log, she didn't wave. She lay on the rock until her bandages were dry, the sun down behind redwood mountain, and then she ran home with a new fear about being late to greet her father.

He did not come home.

Her father lay broken, hurled to the ground by a god with a scar slashed across his face. But old Weedman was dead. God had the face of a falling tree.

"I did not kill my father," Ruth said, aloud but alone in the dark, and she knew even though she was only eight years old that she had to believe it.

∾

"I didn't really ever want to marry," Clara said without opening her eyes. "It wasn't pride so much. I didn't really want to. Did you?"

"I guess I did," Ruth said.

"I don't think I ever have done anything – anything really important – I didn't want to do."

Even now?

"Except perhaps leave you when Hal came back from the war."

"That didn't last long, did it?" Ruth asked, smiling.

"Nearly three years. Do you remember that awful woman, my landlady? 'Clara Wheeler, it's a mistake to come between your son and his wife.'"

"And you said, 'I don't come between. I come before and after. He says he doesn't want her. I do.'"

"Was I as outspoken as that?"

"Yes, you were, and she said, 'It's unnatural!', and then and there we had to find another place to live."

It should have been a horror story: a couple of women with a two-year-old child aren't priority tenants even without the perennial housing shortage of a city like Vancouver, and Ruth was young and proud and angry enough to refuse to take money from Hal in those days. Clara had a clerking job at the Bay. Ruth found a job as a waitress in the evening. They were only a month in a damp basement flat before they found rooms at the top of a house in West Point Grey with a little balcony overlooking the water and the mountains, a garden they could share, where they stayed comfortably until after Ruth's accident when she bought the house.

"I don't think I ever really believed in 'natural life,'" Clara said.

I did. I believed it after she was born. Did you ever know I didn't want her? A baby. But she didn't have my face. She looked like Hal. I wanted to call her Clara, but you said, no, she must have a name of her own, for a life of her own. I dreamed last night we had forgotten her.

"Prayer!" Clara said with a snort.

"My mother prayed," Ruth said. "She prayed for reward for the good and punishment for the wicked."

"Exactly," Clara said.

"She knew who they were, too."

"Is it a blessing the world's never been in anyone's hands?"

"Blessing?"

"We aren't cursed anyway," Clara said quietly.

Clara, Clara, this won't do. I need to take you home, wherever that turns out to be, so that we can stay among the living as long as there are any. Neither of us can live among the dead. We can't even call them by name.

Ruth was late to meet her child coming home from nursery school. She got to Fourth Avenue just as the light turned red and saw her daughter skipping toward the corner on the other side of the street. Ruth wanted to call out to her, to warn her, but she stopped obediently at the light and waited next to a tall man in a gray overcoat. When the light changed, the child took his hand. He looked down at her, startled, and then smiled. She did not acknowledge him, rode his hand across the street as if it were a bus strap, and released it when she was safely on the curb.

"Thank you," Ruth said.

The man nodded shyly and turned away.

"I'm sorry I was late," Ruth said.

"You mustn't be afraid for me," the child answered, skipping again.

How could you teach a child like that that the world was not really arranged for the protection of children? To be told over and over again by her mother that it was essentially a hostile place hadn't stopped Ruth from finding out for herself. So she never did say, "Don't trust strangers," and that hand-riding child turned into a hitchhiking adolescent, for whom Ruth and Clara did try not to be afraid. But inadvertently Ruth had taught her to be afraid for them. She had just had her tenth birthday when Ruth lost her arm, and always after that there was a trace of anxiety in the child's homecoming, as if she needed to count her mother's remaining fingers and toes before she was reassured that everything was all right. She was anxiously concerned, even irritable about Clara's first sufferings with arthritis, wanting her to try every cure from medicine to magic. She was a little mother to them both, and perhaps that had been the omen of her life running backwards: child as mother to the woman, a women's liberation slogan she would have approved, like Gladys, only there had been something wistful in her own child's face, as if she could have so easily been happy if only other people would be, too. She was too easily touched, too quickly compassionate, but Ruth never said to her either, "You've got to be tough."

All the fear Ruth tried never to have, all the teaching of platitudes, all the anger had come leaking out of her only in the last two years, too late and as useless as they had been when she had held them inside her whole self not so much as an act of will or faith as a way of loving who the child was.

❧

"They've decorated a tree," Ruth said. "They want Christmas."

"That would be Tom," Clara said. "I was too tired, Ruth. I just couldn't."

"I know."

Chapter Seven

After Ruth had bought books and bottles for Tom and Gladys and Mavis, she struck upon an even better idea for them for Christmas. If they were going to set up house, she could give them nearly everything they needed from her own. It would be an easy way of disposing of all the things she wouldn't any longer need. If they objected to the loss of a few dollars she might get from a sale, she'd turn their commune argument against them. The plan pleased Ruth, seemed to ease the weight of the shopping bag she carried over her shoulder as she walked back along her own Christmas-card street, mountain-ash berries capped with snow.

As Ruth turned up her walk, cheerful, nearly excited, as if Christmas might again be a celebration for the living, she saw that someone was waiting on the front porch: a young black man, short, slight in build, wearing an absurd knitted cap which grew from his head into a huge scarf he had wrapped around his neck and chest.

"Hello, lady," he said, coming down the steps to her and reaching a hand to take the shopping bag. "You her all right," he confirmed with a sharp look. "They told me in the beer parlor there's this lady with one arm who looks like Abraham Lincoln, and she helps anybody, even niggers, and I say, where is she at? And here she is."

"Isn't anyone else at home?" Ruth asked, smiling at him.

"I couldn't exactly say. I rang the bell, and I knocked hard, and then the door opened all by itself, but, since nobody did say come in, I stayed out here."

"Well, come in now," Ruth said. "We don't lock the door."

"You a little bit crazy, or is Vancouver really the Promised Land?

Lady, in Detroit, you wouldn't have no stove, no mattress, no furnace left here if you was just walking the dog around the block."

"In another couple of months, I won't even have a house; so I don't worry about it. What are you looking for, a place to stay?"

"That's right, and a way to work for it because I just ran fresh out of bread this morning."

"What's your name?"

"Boy."

"No mother of yours ever named you that, come on," Ruth said.

"She named me Boyd, which is either a feathered creature who can fly – and I don't fly – or the past tense of Boy – and I, thanks be to sweet Jesus, ain't past tense yet. This way, everybody knows my name. I don't even usually have to tell them, lady."

"Boy," Ruth said, shaking her head. "My name isn't lady. It's Ruth. Put that heavy thing down, just on the dining-room table if you like."

"It *is* heavy. Didn't you know Santa Claus had joined a union and won't carry nothing over thirty pounds?"

His bright patter had a nervous underedge, probably not just for this occasion, a tic turned into a talent.

"You can stay here for a month anyway," Ruth said. "But there's just been a successful coup in this house. I'm still the head of state but without much domestic authority. We're a kind of commune or family, depending on whose jargon you're using."

"You mean, everybody's got to vote?" Boy asked dubiously.

"No, nothing as clear-cut as that. Anyway, there's plenty you can do to earn your bed and board, no problem about that. I was just thinking I'd like to wrap most of the house up in Christmas paper and put it under the tree, and three hands would be better than one for that project."

"You *are* crazy, lady."

"Ruth."

"It's a sad name," he objected.

"Yours is ridiculous, but, if I'm willing to call you Boy, you can manage to call me Ruth."

"Yes, ma'am," he said and then added, "Ruth."

"What's your last name?"

"Wonder," he said, "and that's the truth."

"It is not," Ruth said.

"The safer I feel, the sillier I get."

She showed him Stew's room, which she hadn't tried to rent since Stew's departure.

"This here is for a son of the family," Boy said, "not for the likes of me. Don't you have no bed down by the coal bin?"

"We heat with natural gas," Ruth answered, refusing to be uncomfortable about her decision not to give him Arthur's room. If he wanted to parody himself, that was his business, but she wouldn't co-operate.

Downstairs there were voices in the front hall, the rise of Gladys' laughter, a hushing from Mavis.

"Come on and meet the others," Ruth said, and he followed her down the stairs and into the front hall. "This is, so he claims, Boy Wonder, here for a month, Gladys, Mavis, Tom."

Tom stepped forward to shake hands.

"Y'all look like regular Christians," Boy said, nodding at the parcels they carried. "But Santa Claus has already been and gone and ate up the baby."

"Where you from, Boy? Tom asked.

"I come from walking to and fro upon the earth, making out a report on Job's Daughters."

"We're not going to call you Boy. That's ridiculous!" Gladys protested.

"Listen, if you don't give me no shit about my consciousness, I won't give you no shit about yours, all right?"

Mavis chuckled. "You've got her number, but it won't dial that way."

"I'm a shit specialist," Gladys said, "and I'm not calling you Boy."

"My other nickname's Nigger. Take your pick," he answered agreeably.

Boy had not yet taken off his ridiculous hat, and he stood there small, riding on the balls of his feet, insisting that he start out this way.

"Boy will have to do, then," Mavis decided. "It's not really so difficult, given that hat."

"I knit this hat myself," Boy claimed, stroking the scarf across his chest. "And I can make corn bread, and I can shine shoes. I'm a one-boy campaign for preserving our native crafts."

"You've got the worst jokes I've heard in a long time," Gladys said.

"Lady, when you cook just for a joke, then you, too, will be truly free."

"Who is cooking tonight?" Ruth asked.

"You and I are," Tom said.

In the kitchen they organized themselves without conversation, and Ruth found herself listening for Willard.

"I have to remind myself he's gone," she said, without needing to use his name.

"How's she?"

"She fades in and out," Ruth said. "Anyone would without distractions."

"We've found a house," Tom said, "an old farmhouse down on the flats in horse country."

"How long would it take you to get to work?"

"Too long," Tom admitted, "but we all just liked it: fruit trees, room for a vegetable garden, berries. We can have it the first of February."

"I suppose Willard and I should move then, too. With Boy here to help, I should be able to close the place up in a month."

"Where are you going to go?"

"West End? I don't know."

"I don't suppose Willard cares."

"The future looks after itself," Ruth said, smiling.

"Why is Willard your problem?"

"I don't know," Ruth admitted. "I've never been able to answer that question about anyone … or anything, and somewhere back a while I stopped asking."

"People use you."

"Hal, you mean? I guess I use him, too. What is it Mavis says? 'We're social animals after all.'"

Boy and Gladys brought their political sparring in to dinner, Mavis being occasional referee.

"Sociological context is all-important, honey, if you and I are going to understand each other at all," Boy was explaining cheerfully. "Now, I'm a sort of James Baldwin reactionary, born too late for my style, a faggoty little nigger making up to white boys; so I got to come to a backward country like Canada where there's enough social lag for me to survive. I mean, you want to be *nice* to me, don't you? Tom here does, too. He wants to be my *friend*, and so this here is a tree I can swing in. They cut all that kind down by now in my native land, and that's the truth. I mean, I've only been in Canada a week, and the guilt here is just unreal, and you hardly got no niggers to make up to."

"How did you get into the country?" Tom asked.

"Underground railway," Boy said. "I walked."

"Any papers?"

"I got lots of papers: dishonorable discharge from the You-nited States Army, certificate of inferior birth, negative Wassermann, and I pee purple like everyone else losing weight."

"Where'd you go to college?" Tom asked.

"Berkeley," Boy said. "This here's a smart white boy, and he don't come from around here."

"No," Tom said. "I come from Iowa."

"That's a good laggy place from what I hear," and then Boy turned to Mavis. "You want to know, if I been to college, why I should still talk like a nigger, don't you?"

"You're the first black man I've ever met," Mavis admitted. "I don't know what to expect."

"The Promised Land!"

Ruth watched and listened, wondering if Boy could also keep quiet, but she was soon to discover that even by himself he sang and chattered. At breakfast, Gladdy shoved a large roll into his mouth and, leaving the house to do an errand with him, she wrapped his long scarf around his head like a gag. But his talking did not get in the way of his working. While he explained, "My mama, she say ..." the kitchen shone with his industry, and every wood surface in the house could be used as a mirror.

"I got a Lady Macbeth complex so big it could clean up this whole, old, sad world. Look at dat shine."

"He says anything that comes into his head," Mavis said, shaking hers. "Next to him Gladdy seems like a deaf-mute."

"I had a friend like him in high school," Tom said, "only he went into the Army and made a success of it. Too bad."

"A real friend?" Mavis asked.

"Well, I thought so. How can you say, any more?"

"Is he really ... gay, or is that a joke, too?"

"I don't think anything he says is a joke," Tom said.

"I wonder what Joanie will make of him," Ruth said, aware of Mavis' uneasy curiosity.

"And Willard," Mavis added.

"Willard won't make anything of him at all," Tom said.

"Where did he and Gladdy go?"

"To get the damned turkey," Ruth said.

Tom laughed. "Still not resigned to Christmas, are you?"

Ruth left them all to the ritual chores, made elaborate by Gladys' imagination, confused by Boy's inventions, and went to see Clara, but she had drifted too far off for Ruth to call her into the new interest of Boy or the Christmas preparations, and Ruth could not afford to join her again out there in the loss of the past. She stayed only an hour and then hurried home, ignoring the number of derelict houses on her street, glad of the tree in her own window bright with welcome.

The four were all sitting on the floor in front of the fire, bowls on their laps, shredding bread for stuffing.

"How is she?" Mavis asked, and to Ruth's shrug, "We'll all go tomorrow, shall we?"

"We'll see," Ruth said.

She did not want to think about Clara. She did not want to think about anything outside this room at this moment, Gladys and Tom leaning comfortably against each other, back to back, Boy and Mavis facing each other with resolute goodwill, a place for Ruth on the couch where she could enjoy the tree, the light of the fire on Boy's dark, pockmarked face, on Tom's fairness. Later she would say, "And now we're going to furnish the farmhouse." Later she would let them know that they could be let go, were free, but just for this time she held them in her dark eyes, in her quiet heart, for herself.

"What would old Scrooge think, looking in on this house to-night, Mavis?" Tom asked.

Mavis smiled, but her eyes were thoughtful. "I'm just glad I don't have to make his rounds tonight. There's not all that much love and forbearance around these days."

"That's cheerless of you, Mavis," Gladys said.

"You know I'm a reactionary. I'd even be a Christian if I could manage it and live in a Christian world where twice a year there could be at least a little kindly and generous hypocrisy."

"If you would consent to go to midnight mass with me," Boy said in a mock-formal tone, "I think we could still find some saints to try the patience of. And I could say a prayer for Martin Luther King, whose genu-ine love and charity was a matter of FBI record, and for my mama, who loved him, too."

"Are you serious?" Mavis asked.

"He can't be," Gladys said.

"I am. I am. Why don't we all go?"

"I wouldn't be caught *dead* ..." Gladys said.

"No." Tom shook his head.

"What about you, Ruth?" Boy asked.

"Churches make me sad," Ruth said, "but you and Mavis go if you feel like it."

"You don't have to be scared if you go with me," Boy said to Mavis. "If there's a bolt of lightning, it's bound to strike me, for I have lusted after Jesus Christ with a loving heart for lo these many years."

"You're outrageous," Gladys said. "You aren't going to go, are you, Mavis?"

"Yes, I think I am."

Ruth watched Gladys swallow a standard speech on the evils of the Church. She was comfortable enough gagging Boy or calling him names, but she had lost the ground under her feet too many times in the last couple of days to try arguing seriously with him. Mavis, on the other hand, didn't want to argue. She was fascinated by the contradictions he offered, fearful, perhaps in some part hopeful that the parody might be, as Boy put it, "the truth." He was off again, weaving scripture and ghetto rhythms and his own nonsense into a Christmas sermon.

"So when the lion lies down with the lamb, he's going to be wearing my little red shoes on his ears, and that I gotta see."

"Before you go," Ruth said, "there's a Christmas chore to be done. We have to furnish the farmhouse. I was going to get Boy to help me wrap everything up, but, since we still need it for a month, that didn't seem practical, so I've got some little red stickers instead. We're going to go round the house and mark everything you can use."

Against the protest she had expected, Ruth was firm. Tom gave in first, the most comfortable of them in her affection and therefore the quickest to see how much pleasure the idea gave her, how much relief from the grief of finally closing up the house. Once he had changed sides, Gladys and Mavis could not hold out long.

"If you're really sure, Ruth ..."

"I can't keep more than I can get into a two-bedroom apartment.

I'm never going to run a boardinghouse again. There's nothing really valuable, but it would be useful to you. The dining-room table, for instance."

"Oh, not the dining-room table!" Gladys protested.

"What would I do with it?" Ruth asked. "And it was given to me in the first place."

Having convinced them they could accept so large a gift, Ruth had less difficulty persuading them to claim their own beds, chests of drawers, Boy helping her with clownish descriptions of her priceless antiques. By the time he and Mavis went off to church, Gladys and Tom were settled at the dining-room table with Ruth to make a list of what they could use from the kitchen.

"What a Christmas!" Gladys said. "We'll never have to get married, Tom."

"Not even after our fifth child is born?" he asked.

"Ruth, aren't we wildly overdoing this?" Gladys asked. "You could get real money for these things."

"You can't put a price on being able to turn a burden into a pleasure," Ruth said.

"It seems a shame you didn't have kids of your own," Gladys said.

Ruth looked at her and realized that Gladys didn't even know, the conspiracy of silence Ruth and Clara had kept so successful that no one any longer knew not just about her death but about her life. The silence of grief had become a void, and that seemed to Ruth a monstrous betrayal. But how could they not know that she had lost her child when it had so much more obviously crippled her than the loss of her arm?

"I did have a daughter," she found herself saying. "She was killed in a car accident just a little over two years ago."

Gladys reached over and took Ruth's hand. "What was her name?"

"Claire," Ruth said and found that that long unspoken name made her smile instead of weep. "I wanted to call her Clara, but Clara said she had to have a name of her own."

"How old was she?" Gladys asked.

"Twenty-two – your age. Keeping on with the house, keeping it filled with young people was something I thought would help Clara … and me, and it has. And now that it's time to give it up, you help with that, too."

"Why don't you come with us?" Tom asked.

"I told you, Tom, if you'd been my own children, you would have cleared out years ago …"

"But we're not," Tom said. "Why are we less important than Willard?"

"Willard can't leave home, and he's been with me for fourteen years."

"It's not as if we're all going to opposite ends of the earth," Gladys said. "Give Ruth and Willard six months in a highrise and us out in the boondocks, and we may all be back together again in a house two blocks from here."

"Then be sure to take enough furniture," Ruth said. "And put the roaster on that kitchen list. Wherever I am, this is absolutely my last turkey."

"Do you have a picture of Claire?" Gladys asked.

"Lots of them, in a trunk up in the attic, which I'll have to un-earth sometime soon. She looked like her father, the same shape of head, the same lopsided grin."

"And that's why he needed to order us all around like that," Gladys said.

"There's no explaining Hal, Gladdy. Claire didn't get along with him any better than you do."

It seemed so ordinary, sitting there at the dining-room table talking about Claire without being afraid any longer that Gladys might blur and refocus into Claire. They couldn't, now that Ruth had so simply established them as separate people. The pity and rage, so long silenced, had transformed themselves into gentler emotions. But if Ruth, primed by Claire's name, no longer feared vomiting up the blood and bone of her loss, she would have to be careful, too, not to flood them with the relief of that discovery.

They were still at the table when Boy and Mavis came home.

"You could get drunk inhaling the air," Mavis said. "It's given me an awful thirst."

"Were there any saints?" Tom asked.

"My friend, the whole lovely church just strained with goodwill," Boy said. "I could have been born again if I'd let myself."

"Let's get everybody a brandy," Mavis suggested, cutting Boy short.

He was willing, and, when they came back into the dining room, they did not draw up chairs to the table, but stayed at the edge of the group as if whatever experience they had shared set them a little apart. Gladys was the first to start the move toward bed, and on her way she bent down quickly and kissed Ruth.

"Merry Christmas in the morning," she said, taking Tom's hand as they left the room.

Boy followed them.

"Are we going to have one more?" Mavis asked.

"We're beginning to make a bad habit of it," Ruth said. "Thanks."

"I wonder if Boy will come with us," Mavis mused.

"Would you like him to?"

"I feel as if I could learn something from him. I'm not quite sure what. Kindness?"

"You don't need lessons in that," Ruth said.

"Yes, I do, when it comes to myself."

"Well, that," Ruth agreed.

"I did feel like Scrooge tonight being taken to church to see the spirit of Christmas. People do want to be nice to Boy. He's right. In his place, I'd be cynical about it. I *am* cynical about it. But with all his joking, he's not. I don't know where he gets the guts to mock and like himself so well, calling himself some sort of moral throwback …"

"Another good puritan?"

"Not exactly …"

Mavis had no more to say, though obviously more to think. Left alone, Ruth did not feel the building tension she was accustomed to at that hour. Claire moved around in her mind like someone at home there, the absence of two years obliterated. Ruth sat, amazed with that sanity and peaceful.

Chapter Eight

When Willard came home, his face laced even more tightly than usual at the sight of Boy, whose antic speech about having been blackly soiled on the way down the chimney did nothing to reassure Willard. He ignored Tom's admiration of his new suit and responded to Ruth's questions about his mother in uninformative monosyllables.

"He's always like that," Mavis explained earnestly to Boy.

"This house has got to be big as a church, Mavis, where bigots and black boys read the same funny paper, same as the lion and the lamb. Don't worry about it."

When Joanie came home only a few hours later and took a visible step back from Boy at her first sight of him, Tom and Gladys joined Mavis in an attempt to protect Boy's feelings. They praised Boy to Joanie, trying to tone him down enough to reassure her. Boy reacted with a stepped-up campaign in his own character assassination. He invited Willard to join him at the steam baths that evening.

"When I'm going to get screwed, I like to keep it simple," he said cheerfully.

Fortunately Willard dealt with the invitation as he did with any other, wrapping his newspaper around him so firmly he looked like a large package from the fish store, but Joanie left the room without even offering an excuse.

"This is turning out to be a short season of peace and goodwill," Tom said, sighing.

"Not everybody likes glad tidings, honey," Boy said, patting Tom on the shoulder.

"It's your own silly fault," Gladys said fiercely.

"I know," Boy admitted, striking a pose of guilty dejection so comic even Gladys laughed, "but you got to realize there's just a little more of de old devil in niggers as de good book say."

"But you can't go round guilt-tripping everyone," Gladys protested. "It doesn't work with everyone."

"A soul without conscience is a soul lost," Boy said sadly.

"There isn't time for a prayer meeting now," Ruth called from the kitchen, in which she somewhat reasserted herself. "Mavis, go up and tell Joanie to come down to dinner and behave herself. Boy?"

"Yes, ma'am?"

"Come out here and be useful!"

"Yes, ma'am."

Once he was in the kitchen, Ruth confronted him with a large wooden spoon in her hand in contrast to the unthreatening tone of her voice.

"You don't tease Willard," she explained. "He's only got three quarters of his wits and he has a hard enough time keeping those about him without being confused. And he won't bother you even if you do bother him. Joanie's a silly little thing who'll get used to you if you give her a chance. I want you to make her feel comfortable at dinner."

"Yes, ma'am."

Boy was subdued during the meal, offering small courtesies without mockery, and Joanie was doing about the same thing with her piece of Mavis' mind that Boy was doing with Ruth's. If it was not an hour of domestic tranquility, digestion was basically served. As soon as the kitchen was cleaned up, Boy put on his hat.

"Where are you going?" Mavis asked.

"To get laid, but I'll be home for cocoa," he answered with a bow, and was gone.

Outside the blue convertible honked cheerfully.

"The universal solution," Mavis said wearily.

"They have enough in common to get along," Gladys said.

"What are we going to say to Joanie about the farmhouse?" Mavis asked.

She had to wait for an answer while Joanie came down the stairs and went out to the now impatient horn.

"I don't think we have to worry," Tom said. "I don't think she'll like it."

He was right. Even without telling her that they'd also invited Boy to live with them, Joanie found the place too far-out, too run-down, the country smells suspicious. She had already decided on a bachelor suite of her own in a new highrise near Stanley Park.

"Nothing to cope with but colored plumbing," Mavis said wryly to Tom.

Still, everyone was relieved. When Joanie decided to move at the weekend, they all offered to help. Ruth had given Joanie the furniture in her own room, which she could take with her, along with a basic setting for a table and a few of the smaller pots and pans.

"Thanks anyway," Joanie said, "but Stew's offered. He can borrow a truck from a friend."

"Why not ask him to dinner?" Ruth suggested.

Prepared for the change in his appearance, Ruth was still surprised when Stew smiled shyly in at the kitchen door. Clean-shaven, his hair conservatively barbered to his collar – and he had not only a collar but a tie – he looked freshly, even innocently made, his eyes less important in his face now that he also had a mouth, a jaw line. Ruth realized that she never lost her suspicion of a weak chin under a lot of hair. Stew had been hiding nothing but the authority of his class-blessed genes.

"Smells as good as ever around here," he said.

"You look *fine*, Stew. It's good to lay eyes on you."

"I should have come round before," Stew said. "I guess I felt there was more apologizing and thanking to do than I knew how."

"Not a bit of either. Clara was so glad to hear you were coming for dinner, I almost persuaded her to come back for the occasion."

"Joanie and I thought we might drop in and see her one day soon."

"She'd love it. It's too quiet a life for her there, though she says it suits her. I hear you're thinking about law school in the fall."

"If I can get in," Stew said. "I can't play my clarinet for the exam."

Stew had none of Joanie's difficulty with Boy, even took his flirtatious teasing without archness or alarm. Whatever else Gladdy did to the men whose beds she had shared, she gave them a liberal confidence about what it was to be attractive, and she was warm now with Stew as if neither of them had anything to forgive the other. Joanie bristled occasionally with self-importance, but they all felt too kindly toward her for solving her own problem not to jolly her back into a good temper. Boy worked right along with Tom and Stew to get her belongings stowed in the truck, and, aside from a couple of loudly sung songs of slavery, in which the others joined, he did nothing to offend the sensibilities of "little white pussy," his private name for Joanie. Once Stew and Joanie had gone, taking Tom with them to help at the other end, Boy relaxed into a simulation of an epileptic fit so convincing that both Gladys and Mavis tried to jab a pencil between his teeth until he laughed, rolled over and onto his knees, shaking his woolly head back and forth.

"Is she really that bad?" Mavis asked.

"She's deeelicious!"

"You scared me shitless," Gladys protested.

"Dat's de way ah live, child. It's cleansing. You'll see."

"Boy never heard of leading a life of quiet desperation," Mavis said.

"Ain't my bag," he admitted, getting up.

"I'm going over to Clara," Ruth announced from the doorway. "I need an hour or so in a rest home."

"Tell her I'll see her tomorrow," Mavis said, "and don't take any complaints about our having tired her out on Christmas. She's not turning into a vegetable, and that's that."

In fact, they had tired Clara, but she had been less distant about them since. She was even curious to meet Boy, though she was glad enough to postpone that experience for a few days at least.

"I wonder if it's the first time Willard's ever been propositioned for the steam baths," Clara said.

"I don't think he knew what Boy was talking about. Willard can ignore anything, and now that Joanie is moved out, the last three weeks will be simpler."

"Have you found a place?"

"I think so," Ruth said. "There's a two-bedroom apartment on the third floor of one of those big buildings on Beach. It's got a view of the bay and the mountains, and Willard might even enjoy that. Now all I have to do is persuade him to go and look at it. Sunday's probably the easiest day to break into his routine."

"Has he ever said he'll go with you?"

"No, but I'm sure he will. It's the only solution he doesn't have to think about."

Ruth had brought a pile of Christmas cards for them both to look through, most of them from people who had at one time or other stayed at the house.

"There's been a lot of traffic through that house in fourteen years," Clara said.

"Jim Wright. Now who was he?"

Ruth could have said "the boy with the beautiful voice," but she said instead "that actor friend of Claire's."

"Oh yes, I remember now," Clara nodded, "the one with the beautiful voice."

Something in Ruth wanted to shout *Claire! Claire! Claire! Claire!* against two years of silence, but, if Clara could keep from noticing that there was anything extraordinary about mentioning her name at all, perhaps Claire could come back into their life together as gently as she had into Ruth's.

The house was quiet and purposeful when Ruth got home. Boy and Mavis were taking down the tree. Tom had come back and was making pies in the kitchen with Gladys.

"You're on a long busman's holiday this week, Tom," Ruth observed.

"I'm practicing," Tom said. "I think I may have a new job the first of February, cooking at the country club. I could walk to work from there, and maybe, after I got to know a few people, I could find work for Boy."

"It's not a good place to work," Gladys said.

"She doesn't think the rich should eat," Tom said.

"I don't think you should cook for them, that's all."

"If you want me to cook for the Salvation Army, we'll have to move to town."

"I don't see why you have to *cook* at all," Gladys said. "If feeding people is socially significant work, it has to be the right people. You should be working for world relief."

"Let him get his citizenship first," Ruth said. "Before you have him bombing the wheat board, be sure he can vote."

Willard came in from the beer parlor in the fuzzy, nearly friendly mood that overtook him only on Friday nights.

"Pies," he said in an approving tone.

"How about a piece, Willard?" Gladys suggested. "These are nearly cool enough to cut."

When he hesitated, she urged him as if it were socially significant to see that Willard had a piece of pie. Allowing himself the indulgence, he enjoyed it, but in the middle of his pleasure, Ruth took advantage of it.

"I want you to come take a look at an apartment after church on Sunday," she said.

"I have my book," he said as if he were refusing a social invitation with a prior engagement.

"I know you do, but it won't take long, and I want you to know where we're moving at the end of the month."

"This month?"

"Yes."

"You said the first of March."

"That's when the buildings begin to come down. We can't wait around for that. I think you'll like the apartment. It's much nearer work."

"*This* is your house," Willard said.

"Not any more. The city's bought it, and it's going to be torn down."

Gladys and Tom watched Willard as intently as Ruth did to see if he really understood that. He chewed and made no further comment. When he had finished his pie, he nodded to them and went off to bed.

"Do they think about people like Willard, those bastards?" Gladys demanded. "They tear down whole hotels full of people like that, just barely sure of where they are in the first place, who don't have a clue where else to go."

"I think Willard knows he's all right," Tom said. "He trusts you, Ruth."

"Yes," Ruth agreed, feeling the dull burden of that trust.

"Christmas is back in its box another year," Boy announced, "and it won't pop out at you again without plenty of public warning."

"Boy, what are you going to do about papers?" Ruth asked. "Is there anything you can do?"

"White folks is always wantin' to be legal. No piece of paper ever goin' to make me legal 'less somebody wants it to, and somebody don't."

"How can you get work, though?"

"You got to know somebody who knows somebody who wants somethin' bad done, and there you are."

"*Gun* for hire!" Gladys said. "You've been watching too much TV."

"You don't understand. Guns is gross. I'm a cook like Tom here, only I cook books, and they don't put you on the payroll for that. They 'depreciate' you or write you off as an entertainment expense."

"I can believe that," Gladys said.

"That's illegal," Mavis said.

"*I'm* illegal," Boy explained, "and if you don't know how hallowed book-cooking is in this here old Western tradition, you ain't been reading your Dickens like I thought you was."

"I don't think it's right," Mavis said.

"Now Mavis is going to give you a little speech on living within the law," Gladdy said. "The crooks in Dickens are bad buys. They help the rich exploit the poor."

"That's right. That's right," Boy agreed. "That's what we're all about. That's what I learned in college: how to screw the poor. It was called Humanities 1-A the first year, but then we got into economics and accounting."

"Before this turns into a full-scale political battle," Ruth said, "I need to know what day you're all going to move."

"Maybe this little nigger crook's going to have to bunk in with Willard."

"No way," Tom said, laughing. "You're just the kind of confusion we need."

"We're moving the last Sunday," Mavis said.

"Then Willard and I will, too."

Willard did not go with Ruth to the apartment to inspect it. All he would say was "When the time comes" from behind his thriller. She went over by herself to put down a deposit and measure the rooms for placing furniture. Preoccupied with practical considerations, she did not notice the view until she had been in the apartment more than half an hour. "Do you see it?" she heard Tom ask. From behind the sealed glass, it seemed less real than when she walked the beach, but she could do that, too. She might even teach Willard a new habit of strolling along the shore with bread to feed the birds down in Stanley Park. There were two children on the beach now, playing on the crusted edge of snow in Christmas-new hats and jackets. They were conspicuous because they were the only children in this gigantic neighborhood of young singles and old singles, who paired and separated with the same uncertainty in their journeys from bench to bench. As Ruth walked back along her own street, she realized that most of the children had left it, too. She hoped, like her own young, that most of them were now out in the country where there were still no signs which said, "No Children."

"Could we," Tom asked, as she came into the house, "get a pup before we move? The thing is, I just talked to a fellow who gave his kids a pup for Christmas, and his wife can't handle it. He's got to get rid of it."

"Why not?"

"Actually," Tom admitted, "it's already here. Gladdy?"

The kitchen door opened, and a puppy of potentially disastrous size tumbled out into the hall, wagging its whole body for its joyful reunion with Tom.

"Your dog already," Ruth said.

"Well …" Tom said, kneeling to fondle it. "Always did like dogs."

"I don't suppose he's housebroken."

"Of course not," Gladys answered, standing in the hallway laughing. "I hope you and Boy know how to teach him because the rest of us go back to work tomorrow."

"We can keep him in the basement," Tom said, "with newspapers."

"We're making sure," Mavis said from the living room, "that by the time you move, you'll be glad to."

"Mavis and me are going to get us a little white pussy," Boy said.

The puppy made a dash in to Boy and began to attack his boots.

"This here dog, Tom, is a coon dog, did you know that?"

"Coon Dog," Tom said, and the puppy had a name.

"If you really are going to get a kitten, you'd better get it now, too," Ruth said, "so that they get used to each other. We might as well help the city tear the house down."

"How about that?" Boy said, turning to Mavis. "Just how about that?"

Children, that's what they were, sometimes earnestly playing house, sometimes quarreling among themselves, calling playground names at each other, "Pig," "Crook," "Nigger," and now they needed puppies and kittens to play with but to leave to Ruth for housebreaking, just as they began to leave the cooking to her again. And they were not children precisely because they were free to require this last indulgence. *I will not be glad to go, Mavis, no matter what shits on my shoulders, no matter what I have to bury in the garden.*

The kitten, a white one, arrived the next day, wrapped in Boy's vast scarf, and, though Ruth was momentarily murderous when it shat in a half-packed box of china, she had to laugh at Boy.

"Look at that. Scared shitless, just like Gladdy."

He cleaned up the mess and repacked the box, all the while keeping the kitten tucked into his shirt, a white burst of fluff just below his dark throat. And he saved a pair of Willard's shoes from Coon Dog. They found instead an old pair of Hal's boots.

"Now, if you didn't have no dog, what could you do with an old pair of boots?" Boy asked, chuckling.

He worked all day, cheerfully, playfully, and his energy never flagged in the evening when the others came home, sometimes too tired to appreciate his energy, combined with the dog's and cat's. So, after dinner, he'd put on his hat and say, "I'm going to get laid," and off he'd go, usually not for more than a couple of hours.

"I wish it were as simple as that for me," Mavis said. "If it is simple for him."

"Do you want to come with me to see Clara?" Ruth offered.

Mavis laughed and shook her head. "You two need your own gossip. I'm going tomorrow night with Boy. He wants to watch her color TV."

"His own particular ethnic right?"

"He could put it that way, couldn't he? We did have a real argument about his book-cooking the other night. He said he'd think about it, but he wasn't entirely convinced he should live in terms of peer-group values since, as far as he could see, none of us agreed anyway. Tom's toned Gladdy down a lot. Still, legality in her vocabulary is a dirty word."

"Don't mother them all, Mavis. They've had enough of that."

"Given the rate I'm being turned down for jobs, it may be the only opening," Mavis said.

The months of time suspended became days of hard, baffling work, quickly over. Without Boy, Ruth would have been defeated time and time again. Boy had quickly established four categories: You, Us, Salvation Army, and Fire, which proved adequate until she got to the boxes of Claire's belongings. Boy found her sitting on her floor in the attic, a photograph album in her lap, an open box of toys to one side, a trunk of clothes to the other. Discarding things for the living was one thing, for the dead quite another.

"What are you doing up here?" he demanded.

"Nothing."

He took the album from her and looked at the page she held open.

"A pretty man and a pretty child," he said.

"She *was* pretty," Ruth said, smiling.

"So you can take this with you," Boy decided. "The rest of this stuff goes to the Salvation Army. Can't see you and Willard playing dolls over there in your fancy apartment, and these," he said, holding up a skirt, "are even too small for me to play with."

Simple.

"Thank you," Ruth said.

"You don't need no truck to haul around the past. You just got to share it out among the family."

Boy adopted Tom's vocabulary. Was it their shared nationality and their being deprived of it that made them sentimental about its discredited institutions? The sense of family would not last long, or at any rate would not include Ruth in it after the move was made. Concern was a matter of domestic geography except for a very willful few.

The new domestic geography of the apartment could be made

comfortable only in terms of Willard's needs, his familiar chair by the television. Even Boy's noisy good humor, so useful in enlivening the dead spaces of the past, could not invade the dead space of this future.

"It's a terrible place, isn't it?" Ruth asked matter-of-factly as she looked around at their finished work.

"Takes a little living in, that's all," was all Boy could offer.

Glad not to be any higher off the ground than she was, Ruth could still begin to feel the weight of all those floors above her like a hibernating headache.

"No," she said to the suggestion of a final dinner. She did accept Mavis' offer to drive them over to the apartment, but Willard at the last minute vetoed that.

"We'll take the bus," he said, "the way we always do."

Just as if they were on their way to the movies. The snow was gone. There were lights on in only one or two other houses in the block. The signs of scavengers and vandals were everywhere: broken windows, half-ripped-away fences, a broken toilet in one front yard, laundry tubs in another. Ruth tried not to think of the uses to which her house would now be put. Instead, she held the image of them all standing there in the front hall where she could go home to find them after this particular movie was over. It worked until they arrived at the apartment house and Ruth got out the keys she and Willard would have to use for any coming or going. He was reluctant to take his, to be taught how to use them, but Ruth was firm with him, a new needful authority in her voice unlike the accustomed nagging. Again she saw a threatening looseness in his face.

"It's all right, Willard," she said. "You'll get used to it."

The movie had just begun, and it would go on and on for them both without ever setting them free or letting them go home.

"I don't like it here," Willard said, looking around the living room of the apartment.

"It needs a little living in," Ruth said. A very little living was all they could do. "Try your chair."

He sat down, still in his overcoat, and turned on the television. Ruth went to her bedroom, stretched out on the bed, and let the weight of the day and the place descend.

Chapter Nine

"I suppose he's always been morose," Ruth said, "only I had other people to pay attention to."

She was sitting with Clara, who was in her own chair now, developing a habit of being upright against the assault of young people who would not tolerate her withdrawal from their lives.

"If he doesn't like it, couldn't you get him a room somewhere? He'd probably be better off."

"I've suggested it. He pays no attention."

"Is he eating properly?"

"Oh, yes," Ruth sighed, "and carries on with his whole routine as if nothing had changed, and it hasn't, really."

"It's you who needs to get used to it," Clara said.

"I wonder if I will."

"Tom and the others wish you wouldn't."

"They have a marvelous sense of choice, don't they?"

"It's not a bad thing to have," Clara said.

"Neither is a million dollars or two arms …" Ruth winced at the sound of self-pity in her voice. "The fact is, I'm bored. It's not as if Willard were hanging around my neck all day. It's the first time in my life I've ever had any choice about what to do with myself, and I don't know what to do. I read. I walk in the park. I take up as much of your time as I dare. The only real complaint I have about Willard is that he doesn't take up enough of my time. Isn't it silly?"

"Have you met any of the other people in the building?"

"Of course, and we all say good morning. Maybe people who use

the elevator get better acquainted. But I don't really want acquain-
tances."

"You want something useful to do."

"Yes, but a job seems silly, even if I could get one."

"Mavis says you keep refusing invitations to the farmhouse."

"Well, I've seen it. They seem to think I should go out there
once a week. I don't really want a routine like Willard's."

"Yes," Clara said, smiling, "that's what they do to me, and I resented it, but now, you know, if Boy doesn't stop in a couple of times
a week to watch television, I miss him, and I get impatient for Mavis
to come back to read another chapter. I'm just as involved in Gladdy's
students as I ever was. As for Tom, well, Tom's Tom. Even Stew and
Joanie have been by."

"They always did visit you. With me, they learned to talk to my
back, and they don't really know what to do with me as a guest in
their living room, even if I did know what to do with them, which I
don't."

"What *are* you going to do with the money?"

"I don't know. It's a funny thing. I can't seem to think about that
until the house is gone, as if it weren't really theirs and the money
weren't really mine until they tear it down. It's like collecting life
insurance before somebody's dead."

"How soon is that going to be?"

"Not long, sometime this week. Oh, I'm not going to go watch
them pull it down, but I just need to know it's gone."

"Maybe you should invest in a business," Clara said.

"Clara ..."

"I don't mean a café for pensioners in the Gulf Islands, but Tom's
not going to be happy at that country club, and Boy meets too many
likely propositions at the steam baths not to get involved in something unpleasant before long unless there's something legitimate for
him to do. Even Mavis is discouraged about finding a job."

"So you think I ought to figure out a business to employ a fry
cook, an accountant, and a Ph.D. in Dickens, along with a shoe clerk

and a teacher of handicapped children? There wasn't much more than fifty thousand dollars after I paid off the rest of the mortgage, and bank loans for the likes of us ... forget it."

"Hal might be able to get one."

Ruth snorted.

"If I asked him."

"I wouldn't invest in a chocolate bar with Hal, and you know it."

"Not even for the children?"

"They're not children, Clara, and they don't need me. I just have to get over needing them, that's all."

"I don't know why you think that. Claire would have gone on needing you and you would have gone on needing her, and you wouldn't have denied it. We need each other, after all."

"We were a family," Ruth said quietly.

"What family have any of these got but us?"

"Gladdy's got an enormous family."

"In the East. What about Tom? What about Boy? Mavis hasn't seen her family for five years. They threw her out because they discovered she had a crush on one of her female teachers and wouldn't go to a psychiatrist about it. What kind of a family is that?"

"When did she tell you that?"

"The other night. Boy had gone off to his steam baths. She admires his openness about it and is trying to be more open about herself, though she doesn't really know what that self is. She's half in love with Tom and half in love with Gladdy and glad they love each other so that she doesn't have to sort it out at all. She said maybe she was neuter, and that would solve more problems than it posed."

"I doubt it."

"So do I, and I think we should be around to doubt, don't you?"

Ruth looked at Clara, no less physically frail than she'd been two months ago when she came here to die, but the appetite for death had gone out of her face. There was instead that gentle alertness and concern that had drawn Ruth to Clara all those years ago. Last month Ruth had been conspiring with the others to see that Clara did not turn into a vegetable. Now it was obvious that Clara was conspiring with them to keep Ruth from disappearing into her dead-ended life.

"If it weren't for you ..." Ruth said, with no intention of finishing her sentence.

"Go to see them next time they invite you."

"If I can."

Ruth tried to be more cheerful and gentle with Willard that night at dinner, and he rose to the occasion as well as he could, but having to respond in the simplest ways was a strain for him. His hands shook a little as he managed his knife and fork, and his face grew tighter and tighter until Ruth suggested that they watch television while they had their dessert. She wondered in how many apartments all over the West End people sat over their meals staring at the screen simply to avoid confronting the boredom and impossibility of the relationships they were caught in. At least it wasn't painful for her as it would have been if she had been with Hal. As she turned to pour Willard his coffee, she realized he had been looking at her instead of the screen. Ruth couldn't read his face. The mask of self-protectiveness had grown over the years like a cataract. Even if there was anything he wanted to communicate, he had no way of doing it. What feelings he had remained entirely his own.

"Chinatown tonight?"

He nodded and looked away, perhaps shamed in his way as Ruth was in hers of the inadequacy between them.

After he had gone out, Ruth sat looking at the album of pictures Boy had decided she should save. She was not as much interested in the landmarks – the birthdays, the graduations – as she was in finding Claire's face among the clusters of other young people on the front porch, in the back yard, on the beach, sometimes among her own school friends, often among the members of the household, never the center of the group except in Ruth's eyes. She did not want to think of the others like that, which was what Clara seemed to be asking of her. The most painful boredom was preferable to that kind of vulnerability.

The buzzer sounded. It was Gladys.

"Come along up," Ruth said into the hole in the wall, still self-conscious about it since she didn't have to use it often.

"Tom had to work tonight, and Mavis more or less ordered me out of the house," Gladys confessed. "She's so fucking cranky these days."

"Work going badly?"

"I don't think so. She's right on schedule with the thesis. It should be done in another few weeks. The job situation irks her, but, Jesus, if she'd opened her eyes a year ago, she would have known how it was going to be. We've got a friend with a Ph.D. in physics who's building log cabins, and he feels lucky."

"Don't you think she's going to get a job?"

Gladys shook her head. "Once she has her degree, she's not cheap labor any longer."

"Coffee?"

"Lovely. Your real coffee. You know, I don't think any of us were really old enough to leave home. Don't put that album away. I'd like to look at it. "

It was easier to have Gladdy here, curled up on the couch enjoying coffee, than to go to see them all at the farmhouse, perhaps because there they were trying so eagerly to show Ruth how well they got along on their own. It was not that Ruth didn't want to see them but that she still didn't know how except on her own terms.

"What did Claire do?" Gladdy asked.

"Design. Things with her hands. She hadn't really decided. She was a good potter. She made all the plates and mugs you have."

"And you gave them to us?" Gladdy asked.

"And she designed a couple of stage sets. She liked the theater, but she was a little afraid of it, too. She used to say she was looking for the real world."

"Oh, I know how that feels," Gladys said, sighing. "Sometimes there isn't a thing I do that doesn't feel unreal. I mean, what am I really doing living in a farmhouse with Tom and Mavis and Boy? I get so *mad* at them all, and then I think, what the fuck am I doing that's different?"

"The world's always seemed real to me," Ruth said, as if making an admission.

"Even now?" Gladys asked.

"Willard's bone-real, Gladdy."

"Oh, I know. My kids are, too, but I sometimes think, what's the point, you know? Sometimes 'bone-real' just doesn't seem good enough. And then I think, my God, I'm sounding like Joanie. It's just that, if we can't do something to change things, I mean fundamentally, what's living about? I don't admit it, but I can feel as cynical about politics as Tom. Still ..."

Gladys' eyes drifted back to the album.

"She looks so ... hopeful in this one."

"She mostly was," Ruth said, smiling.

"A car accident," Gladys said.

"She was hitchhiking," Ruth said.

"I have to go for an abortion next week," Gladys said, still looking at Claire.

"How did that happen?"

"Oh, I kept getting suspicious pap smears, so the doctor took me off the pill. Those doctors make me so fucking mad. They're all the same, sitting in their offices with a picture of the wife and kiddies, telling you if you screw around, you'll probably get cancer and deserve it. This one asked me how many men I went to bed with, and were any of them black. How do you like that? And Tom's driving me up the wall. Sometimes he sounds like the original 'voice for the unborn.'"

"He wants the baby?"

"He doesn't even imagine that. He's onto the wonder and mystery of it all, the chance out of millions that one particular life is conceived. By the time any kid was born, Tom would have such a heavy trip to lay on it, it would smother in its crib: the first lungfish born on dry land, Jesus H. Christ Petross! What man ever knows that a baby's chief contribution for a hell of a long time is shit and vomit?"

"He just doesn't want you to have an abortion."

"Oh well, he's too well trained not to agree that a woman has a right to control her own body, but when I told him to cut out all the poetry, Mavis said, 'It's his baby, too, of course.' Mavis! I said it's nobody's goddamned baby, and why do I have to live with a bunch of romantic reactionaries? We can't even take care of ourselves. What would we do with a kid? And if we got hung up on the creative miracle, I'd be dropping one every ten months, and the place would turn into a baby farm."

"Do you think you'll ever want children, Gladdy?"

For an answer Gladys burst into tears, but it took only a couple of minutes for that excess of feeling to spill over.

"That's silly," Gladys said, blowing her nose. "I'm not sad, Ruth. But I sure can wish sometimes that someone would invent something to replace sex. It's such a bind! Maybe I'll want kids. I don't know. I just know I don't want one now, and, if I ever did, I think maybe I'd rather it wasn't my own. Then it would be perfectly clear it was just a job, you know? Not some sort of trumped-up destiny."

"Just a job," Ruth repeated.

"Well, I don't mean it like that. I mean, keep it ordinary. Kids keep getting born to be their parents' reason for living, their parents' salvation, and that's wrong. Claire didn't save your life or your marriage or anything like that, did she?"

"No," Ruth said. "Children are more apt to cost you both."

"That's what I said to Tom. How do we know where we'll be or how we'll feel about each other in a year's time? We ought at least to know what we want to do with our own lives before we start messing with someone else's."

"And Tom can't see that?"

"Tom wants to marry me," Gladys said in a tone of such gloom that Ruth laughed. "Is it funny?"

"No, I don't suppose it is," Ruth said, "but people don't usually make it sound like the final tragedy of life."

"Even though it is for most people. I don't ever want to get married, even for kids. Tom says that's silly. Marriage doesn't have to be a prison, but that's all it's designed for. Otherwise there's no point in it, and it's such a stupid thing to fight about."

"I don't suppose it is."

"Will you tell me something? Why do you let Hal come back like that?"

"I don't let him; he just does."

"But he's so *awful*. You don't really have to put up with that."

"Gladdy, when you're young, it feels as if you have a lot of choices. Maybe you really do. I did marry Hal. What he thinks about that and what I think about that are different, and what I think can never be more than half of it."

"But he doesn't give you any space at all."

"He's given me lots of space, nearly the whole of it."

"Wow," Gladdy said softly.

"Clara says Tom doesn't like his job at the country club."

"No, he doesn't. There's nothing to like. And he won't solve that one until he gets over thinking there are private solutions to public facts."

"You're his private solution?"

"I guess," Gladys said. "He matters to me, too, you know."

Ruth's spirit was both lighter and more troubled when Gladys left, lighter because she had been taken out of herself for those hours, troubled because there was no way to protect Gladys or anyone determined to take life into her own hands. Claire smiled up at her from the page, hopeful, and Willard turned his key in the lock.

"Have to be off an hour early tomorrow," he said.

"All right."

The trouble with you, Willard, and the relief, is that you're so easy to please.

It was not until nearly noon the next day that Ruth discovered why Willard had to be off so early in the morning. The RCMP phoned her.

"There's a man in the house you sold to the city who claims it still belongs to you. He's barricaded himself in, and he's threatening to shoot anybody who sets foot on the property."

"Don't do anything," Ruth pleaded. "I'll be right down."

As Ruth turned into her old street, she was in a disaster area of razed buildings. Her own house and the one next to it were the only ones left standing, and they had already been torn at, tormented by children and scavengers, windows broken, planks wrenched from the porches. A small crowd, attracted by the red pulse of the lights of three police cars, was being urged back by a policeman with a megaphone. At the sight of him, Ruth felt bitter bile rise in her throat, and for a second she remembered Arthur quite clearly, not as he was being taken off but as he sat at the table, smiling at Gladys. Beyond the cluster of people, there were not only other policemen but also men with cameras, obviously from the newspapers and television studios. One man was speaking into a microphone. Ruth pushed her way through the spectators until she was near enough to the policeman to call to him.

"I'm Ruth Wheeler," she said. "I'm the owner of the house. You just phoned me."

"Talk to the man in the car there," he directed, "the one talking to that other one."

As Ruth looked where her attention was directed, she saw Tom turn away from the police car and start up the walk.

"Tom!"

If he heard her, he did not acknowledge it.

"Don't follow him, lady. He knows the guy."

Two policemen blocked her way.

"I'm the owner. Let me through. He might not listen to Tom," Ruth protested.

Tom was on the front porch, opening the door. The report of a gun startled everyone, and Ruth ran forward up the path, at the edge of which four early daffodils lay broken. Tom was lying across the threshold, a circle of blood widening on the shoulder of his sweater. Ruth knelt down.

"Willard!" she said sharply. "Come out here at once. You've hurt Tom. It's just Tom."

She looked up and saw Willard standing with the rifle in his hand.

"Willard, put that down and help me."

He came slowly, as if reluctant to obey her but unable to refuse. Then he stood in the doorway looking down at Ruth, watching her as he had been watching her the night before at the table.

"Why couldn't you tell me?" she asked him.

The gun report sounded behind them like a warning, but immediately blossomed where Willard's tightly laced face had been, and he collapsed backwards into the house. Ruth froze, like an animal, her body braced for the next shot. Instead two men were climbing over to reach Willard.

"Oh, leave him alone," she cried. "Leave us all alone."

Tom was in her arms, his head turned into her lap, a small trickle of blood at the edge of his mouth.

"Breathe, Tom," she whispered to him. "Breathe."

There were strong hands on her shoulders, trying to pull her away from Tom. She clung to him as if he were the last defense she had against drowning. "Breathe," she kept saying softly, over and over again.

"I'm a doctor," a voice was saying. "Let me see if I can help him."

Pried away, half carried down the porch stairs, Ruth wrenched free and stepped over the broken daffodils. Then she raised her shocked face to the man standing tall above her.

"You kill everything," she said, as two flash bulbs exploded.

"Is he dead? Is he dead?" a voice called.

"Stand back! Let the stretchers through."

She needed to bury the flowers there under the lilac with the bones of birds.

"Can she identify them?"

"Don't try to question her now. She's in shock."

"What have you done with Arthur?" Ruth shouted. "What have you done? They're *my* children, *all* of them, *mine*. You kill everything. Bastards! Bastards!"

"Are they both dead?" someone called out.

Ruth crouched on her own front lawn, holding the broken flowers, weeping, in a new burst of flash bulbs aimed over her head at the stretchers being carried down the walk.

Chapter Ten

"To cut down on the expense of superstars, everybody's going to be famous for fifteen minutes," Boy said, as he wadded up the front page of the newspaper and threw if into the wastebasket. "Miss Clara and me saw you on color TV last night, too, with them poor, pretty yellow flowers. So I told them shit-ass reporters down there in the lobby you'd had your turn, and anyway I can get you out through the laundry."

"How long do you think they'll stay?" Ruth asked.

"Don't know. Don't need to worry about it. Just pack up enough clothes, and you can stay at the farmhouse as long as you like."

"Willard's mother will be here tomorrow morning. I've got to do something about his things."

"Mavis is going to meet her. She and Mavis can come over here and take care of that."

"I'm frightened," Ruth admitted. "I felt a little crazy when I went down and tried to get out of the building."

"Nothing crazy about that," Boy said. "Ruth, just about this time yesterday, you was bein' shot at with guns as well as cameras. You can't be surprised if you're feeling just a little shy, you know."

"If only Tom had waited, if only he'd let me ..."

"Listen, it would just be you instead of him getting a bullet dug out of your lung."

"I can't understand why they let him, and then just ... just shooting Willard down like an animal. They intended to kill him."

"I already told Gladdy this morning, and I'm telling you now, it's a natural disaster, that's all, just like a flood or a fire, and you don't blame nobody. If you start hating what hurts and breaks us, you'll end up hating the waters of the earth. You'll end up hating the sky. Nobody intended nothing."

Ruth stared out the window. *I have hated the waters of the earth. I do hate the sky. But I'm frightened of the people down there. I'm frightened of them.*

"Miss Clara wants to lay eyes on you," Boy said. "Let's pack your bag."

Ruth sat down in Willard's chair, so tired suddenly that even the fear went out of her. Boy moved off and came back with a shot of whiskey.

"You drink, and I'll pack," he said.

The reel of events started to turn again in Ruth's head. Tom was going up the steps of the porch; he was opening the door. Then the sound of the gun, which had freed her ... the broken daffodils. Ruth shook her head sharply and took a sip of the whiskey. Tomorrow, next week, next month, if she could get there, it would begin to slow up, repeat itself less often, and then maybe she would think about it. Now her throat still ached with her own screaming, and she saw that screaming face, mouth pulled downward in a grotesque stone mask of grief, as it appeared on the front page of the newspaper all over the city.

"Don't you have no bras, lady?" Boy called from her bedroom.

"Ever tried to put on a bra with one arm?"

Boy chuckled.

Ruth took the last bit of whiskey against the pain in her throat and got up to help him.

"Now we elope," Boy said, shutting the case firmly.

He had discovered the utility stairs and the basement exit, and he made such an exaggerated and silly drama of their escape that it turned into a game without believable meaning. Ruth remembered hurling snowballs with Tom those snowy months ago, but the film slipped, and again he was climbing the steps.

"We'll see Tom later?" she asked.

"When I get Gladdy at work and we change shifts."

"Does he really need one of you with him all the time?"

"We need to," Boy said. "Nobody much wants him out of sight, that's all."

"He's a damned fool!" Ruth said.

"He's a heeero, which in my private dictionary means he's still alive. The man's breathing, just like he said you told him to. That ain't foolish."

Boy let her out of Mavis' car at Queen's Court and didn't pull away until he'd seen that she was safely inside.

"I couldn't have got here without him," Ruth said when she had finally reached Clara.

"I had to see you," Clara said. "It wasn't enough, talking on the phone, not after television and that terrible picture."

"We're never spared anything, are we?" Ruth said, the waves of nausea and exhaustion coming over her again. "I need to lie down."

There, in Clara's presence, Ruth slept. When she woke, Clara's face was the deep reassurance it had always been.

"When you go back to the apartment – if you go back to the apartment, I'm going with you," Clara said.

Ruth did not try to stop or hide the tears of relief that spilled down her face.

"I should never have come here," Clara said. "Boy said I'm not to say 'if only' one more time, and that's right, but I can only stop saying it if I'm at home with you."

"I don't think I'll ever go back to that apartment again," Ruth said, "but I'll find us a place to live."

"Ruth, I'm so sorry. I need to comfort you, and I can't unless I can comfort myself. I'm a very angry woman."

"Yes, so am I … and afraid."

"Did he … did he suffer?"

"No," Ruth said.

"I can bear Tom's pain as long as he's going to be all right, but I couldn't forgive if Willard …"

"I can't think about it at all yet," Ruth confessed. "I keep living through it. I expected to be shot, too. I expected them to kill us all."

"It must have been terrible."

"It's so *real*," Ruth said.

"Did Willard say anything?"

"Not a word. What would he have said?"

"It's a troubled world," Clara said softly, at that place where there is no difference between a joke and a cry of pain.

"He was the one person I thought I could protect ... spare."

"You did, Ruth, for years..."

"If only ..." Ruth began and shook her head.

Boy was right about that, and it was not something he had taught them. Ruth and Clara would have had to be cretinous not to have learned long ago that "if only" is the cardinal sin in the survivor's handbook.

"I do need to be with you, Ruth."

"And we have to get out of here," Ruth said. "I do know that ... now."

But she was as afraid of inventing the future as she was of reinventing the past. To try to make anything happen was to risk even graver consequences than to be victim and witness. Willard was dead.

❧

Tom dozed in his hospital bed while Mavis read Dickens. Ruth and Boy and Gladys came into the room quietly.

"I'll stay now," Boy said, handing Mavis the car keys. "You all go home and get some dinner."

As Ruth stood looking down at Tom, he opened his eyes and smiled. Ruth felt her own face soften, give way to smile in return, and she was for that moment free of her own death's head in the newspaper, free of the image of his face in her lap, bleeding. *You're a lungfish, all right. You can breathe.* She bent down and kissed his forehead, then stepped aside for Gladys.

"I'll be back after dinner," she said.

Mavis signaled them away as Boy settled in her chair.

"I didn't think we could leave him with Tom," Mavis admitted out in the corridor, "but he really doesn't chatter. He said he'd always wanted to be a batman or a male nurse for somebody gorgeous like Tom."

"He must be worn out," Gladys said. "Mavis and I finally did go home to sleep for a couple of hours. He was there all night."

"And rescued me from the reporters this morning," Ruth said.

On the street and in the car Ruth held herself rigid against the fear of the day before. Anyone walking along might have a gun. Anyone driving along might swerve into their path, the intention to kill as real and as ordinary as stopping for a red light. Only when they turned off Marine Drive and drove the quiet road by the golf course down onto the river flat did Ruth begin to breathe more easily, and the farmhouse, where she had felt so alien, welcomed her now in evening twilight and the green fragrance of spring, Coon Dog barking at them, jumping up, circling round. Ruth went out into the kitchen among her own pots and pans, among the pottery Claire had made. Once she had been hurt by the realization that things broke much less easily than people. Now she was glad of their durable familiarity. There was no teacart, but Gladys and Mavis moved about more confidently than they had in a kitchen entirely Ruth's, aware of what she needed since there were also no clamps for one-handed lifting. Needing their help was a comfort.

"I'm glad I'm here," Ruth said as they sat down at the old table.

"I'll get the tea cart and the clamps tomorrow," Mavis said.

"And we can move everything else over here next week," Gladys said, "before Tom comes home."

Ruth smiled again, her face still uneasy in the effort, as flickering as Arthur's had been.

"We've got a lot to figure out," Ruth said, "when we can. Clara wants to come home."

There were a great many questions, practical and emotional, but none of them wanted to confront or be confronted. They were exhausted. For Ruth, Willard's mother and Willard's body were the barrier between her and any other problem.

"I'm going to meet Mrs. Steele in the morning," Mavis said, as she and Ruth were doing up the dishes, "and I'll take her over to the apartment for Willard's clothes."

"I'll have to see her," Ruth said.

"Have you met her before?"

"No."

"Maybe we could have lunch or something like that," Mavis suggested.

"Thank heaven she wanted to take his body back to Kamloops," Ruth said.

"Do you suppose … ? Gladdy's afraid all her talk put the idea into his head."

"He might have thought it up in church. He might have read it in one of those penny dreadfuls of his. You can blame the city hall, the police, Gladdy, Tom, me. I suppose Mrs. Steele has thought for a long time he shouldn't have been born. Even Clara can think that about Hal."

"Is it all a way not to blame Willard himself?" Mavis asked. "He could have killed Tom."

Ruth was shocked at the hard anger in Mavis' voice.

"Well, what else could the police have done?" Mavis asked, then added quickly, "I'm sorry, Ruth. It must be awful for you, and there's no point in talking about it, but Gladdy's so wrongheaded and Tom's so unrealistic that something like this could get either one of them killed."

"It's hard to be so frightened, I know," Ruth said.

"Sometimes I wish I just didn't *care*," Mavis said.

For Ruth, the caring she had tried to wish away herself, the terrible vulnerability of it, was now not armor so much as deep distraction. As the obsession of events began again in her head, she could force her concern for any one of them between her and the horror. She did not know how, with fifty thousand dollars, she could invent a world for them all to live in again. She had no conviction that it would work, but she knew, even if she had to ask Hal for help, they all had to get out.

Boy was still asleep when the others left in the morning, Gladys to be dropped at work, Ruth at the hospital, before Mavis went to meet Mrs. Steele.

"He won't be as groggy today," Gladys said. "I'll catch the bus down after work, and you can meet me there at dinnertime."

She kissed them both before she got out of the car.

"She's scheduled for her abortion day after tomorrow," Mavis said quietly.

"Is she going to go through with it?"

"I don't know. She hasn't said anything about it."

"I'm going to tell Tom this morning that I'll be ready to talk business with him anytime he is."

"Business?"

"Ever since I sold the house, he's been after me to go into business with him, and now that Willard's gone …"

They were driving down Broadway, just a few blocks from the house, and the fear of the traffic was building in Ruth again.

"What kind of business?" Mavis asked.

"He was thinking of a café in the Gulf Islands."

"I can't see Gladdy and me as waitresses," Mavis said wryly, "though Gladdy thinks we'll be lucky to have any sort of job at all in another six months."

"When does your grant run out?"

"In May, and surely I'll have a job by then," Mavis said, "but Gladdy thinks they'll be cutting back staff by then, and she'll be the first to go. It's a shame. She's the best they've got."

Mavis stopped in front of the main entrance of the hospital.

"I'll be out here at eleven-thirty," Ruth said.

Tom's color was reassuring, and, though Ruth was aware and concerned about his weakness, she had to be careful not to reach out to his returning strength.

"We mustn't talk a lot," she said against his excitement at her proposal. "There's plenty of time."

Back on the steps, waiting for Mavis and Mrs. Steele, Ruth found herself wondering if she had made Willard face the problem of the house on his own, if she had followed her desire rather than her duty, might he still be alive, settled into some other routine of minimal comfort? The responsibility for what he had done was such a heavy, meaningless burden for them all. Ruth read it in Mrs. Steele's face the moment they met, so clearly the mother of the man, a face as revealing in this backward movie of life as Hal's. But Mrs. Steele looked as Willard would have looked if he'd had all his wits about him, intelligent enough to suffer what was really happening.

"Is he really going to be all right?" was her first question. Reassured that Tom was healing, she asked, "Should I go to see him? I want him to know how sorry I am. I want him to know if there's anything I can do ... I have a little set aside. I never knew when Willard might need ... he's my only one. You were always so good to him. I've always wanted to thank you. I couldn't ... I just couldn't handle him once he was grown, but I didn't think he'd ever ..."

From the brace of Mavis' shoulders, Ruth could tell that this monologue had gone on ever since Mrs. Steele's arrival. It took Ruth a few minutes to adjust to the flow of articulate feeling coming from a face so reminiscent of Willard's.

"He had such a hard time expressing himself. Oh, I knew he was upset when he was at home, but he couldn't say anything about it, more than what a troubled world it was. I never thought he'd do anyone harm ... not that. But he wasn't normal ... ever. You do what you can. It's awful. And you were so kind to him, taking him with you like that ..."

"I'm sure he was trying to help me," Ruth said.

"If I'd let him stay home … he didn't really want to go back after Christmas. I knew that, but I made him go. I had to force him sometimes. I had to try to make him have a life of his own, some kind of life."

Though the car was claustrophobic with her distress, it was obvious that they couldn't go into a public place for lunch. Mavis took them to the White Spot drive-in, and they sat chinning themselves on the high narrow trays, the food they had ordered nearly untouched.

"It's so hard to know what's right," Mrs. Steele was saying. "You do what you can, don't you? And you try to believe that you do. I tried to be responsible. I wanted him to have what life he could, and he seemed all right. You were so kind to him. How *could* he have done such a thing?"

"It was an accident, Mrs. Steele. He was trying to do something he thought was right. Nobody's to blame," Ruth said firmly, and she met Mavis' eyes as she said it.

"He should never have been born," Mrs. Steele said, weeping.

"That's nonsense," Mavis said with gruff kindness, "unless it's true of us all."

Against her vow of yesterday that she'd never go back into that apartment again, Ruth insisted on accompanying Mavis and Mrs. Steele. She did not have to explain that the police had already been through Willard's things, looking for esoteric or political motives for a simple stubborn gesture against change and loss.

"What a lovely place!" Mrs. Steele exclaimed. "What a beautiful view! Now, why couldn't he be happy with this?"

"It was lonely for us both," Ruth said.

Mavis was folding up the teacart and putting the clamps in a paper bag.

"I don't know what to do with any of this. Could Tom use any of these clothes?"

Ruth shook her head. "We can put them in boxes and call the

Salvation Army if you like. That's what I did with my daughter's clothes … finally."

Mrs. Steele was crying in a grief with so much shame in it that she obviously did not know herself whether she was burdened or relieved. Mavis stood in the doorway watching her as if it were a performance in a film rather than something taking place in the same room. Her detachment irritated and troubled Ruth. Was she imagining her own death and her mother's ambivalent sorrow?

"Help me," Ruth said quietly, startling Mavis into activity.

Finally they were able to deposit Mrs. Steele at the railway station to supervise the loading of Willard's coffin onto the train.

"I need a drink," Mavis said.

Perhaps the only choice she had was anger, and it did relieve Ruth of the necessity of comforting her, but Ruth wanted to get Mavis back into a human circle where she had to care whether she wanted to or not.

"Let's wait until we get home."

Gladys was in the main lobby of the hospital and met them as they came in the door.

"Don't go up now. He's tired," she said.

"Is anything wrong?" Mavis asked.

"No, really, he's all right. Stew was in to see him, too, and he's just tired."

"We all are," Ruth said.

Anticipating that, Boy had a welcoming fire burning and dinner ready to put on the table. Only Ruth and Mavis wanted a drink. Boy, who had already eaten, wanted to be off, and Gladys wanted to get out of her teaching clothes.

"I suppose," Mavis said, after a couple of silent sips of whiskey, "he was trying to talk her into having the baby."

Ruth put down her drink and absently stroked Coon Dog, who lay at her feet, his head across her shoes.

"I guess he misses Tom," Mavis said. "What are you thinking?"

"Trying not to," Ruth admitted.

Gladys came in and joined them by the fire. Though her face was pale and rather puffy, the languor of her body in the soft robe gave Ruth easing pleasure. The kitten jumped up, stretched, and climbed to Gladys' shoulder, where it began to chew a strand of her hair.

"Wouldn't it be nice if we could all just sleep for a week and wake up to everything solved?" Gladys asked with a sigh.

"It would take longer than a week," Mavis said, "or we should all have slept through the last three days."

"I'm hungry," Ruth said, surprised. "I guess we didn't really have lunch."

"I'd rather drink my dinner."

"Well, you're not going to," Gladys said, asserting herself suddenly by taking possession of the bottle. "Alcoholics are boring."

"How do you know?"

"My sister, the one with the five kids, is a drunk."

"The one doesn't necessarily follow the other," Mavis said, following Gladys out into the kitchen.

I don't know what you ought to do, Gladdy. There's no wisdom in me. Today I wondered if the unwanted ones wore out more quickly like a badly made pair of shoes, the damage done even before life surprises you into joy or regret, and, if that were so, you shouldn't have this one, the womb already become a cell for the condemned, who'd have to come into the world only by means of a pardon, being forgiven instead of given life. But that's all nonsense. I didn't shorten my child's life. I am not guilty of all the grief I feel, and there's no wisdom in that either. There's only fear and anger.

"Come eat," Mavis said.

Gladys only flirted with the subject through dinner, wanting to know who ever coined the term "nuclear family," wondering if Willard was a victim of genetics or brain damage or childhood illness, thinking maybe she'd like to work in a gas station if she lost her job, speculating about the toilet training of the world's leaders.

"How can we be serious about anything if we don't understand anything?" she demanded.

"Simple," Mavis said, "people are seriously silly."

"I'm trying not to be, Mavis," Gladdy shouted, "but I don't think having an abortion is like Willard's shooting Tom!"

"Did he say that?" Mavis asked, shocked.

"No, I said it," Gladys admitted. "Everything's so fucking unreal and super-meaningful."

"Talk about it," Ruth said.

"I don't want to be scared or bullied into having a kid," Gladys said earnestly. "And I don't want to kill anything either. I guess it's just too fucking awful that the first really revolutionary act of my life would be to kill Tom's child. It does seem about as sensible as Willard's trying to kill Tom, and I probably talked him into that. I can feel so guilty and confused about that, I think the baby's got to be born now because I killed Willard. And that's just fucking stupid. It's all crazy."

"What *did* Tom say?"

"He said we could just go ahead and have it and love it, and was that really so hard to imagine? I don't think for Tom a baby's all that different from a puppy, you know? A bit more responsibility for a while, but then it grows up and leaves home."

"What is so hard about loving a baby?" Mavis asked.

"Then why don't you have it?" Gladys demanded.

"Easy," Ruth said, back in the familiar role of referee.

"Look," Mavis said, stung to anger, "we've had this argument about twenty-five thousand times in the last three weeks, and it doesn't have anything to do with Tom's being hurt or Willard's being dead, but I'll tell you this, if Tom were the one to be buried, you'd have the baby, and I don't see why Tom alive is less important than Tom dead."

"Would I?" Gladys asked.

"Yes, you would! I'm going to bed."

Gladys sat, staring at her hands. Then she looked up at Ruth, who smiled at her.

"I'm glad you're home," Gladdy said, "because the only way I can see to do it is if we all have this baby. If there's no other solution, it's got to stop being a problem, right?"

"That sort of a problem anyway," Ruth said. "Now, let's all get some sleep."

"Yes," Gladys said. "I'll just say good night to Mavis."

Chapter Eleven

The farmhouse was neither large nor convenient enough for Clara to join them there. Once Tom had come home from the hospital, his convalescence was all that prevented them from looking for a place where they could all be together again. The chief debate, as they studied the ads, was where to look.

"Why are you so fixed on an island?" Gladys demanded of Tom.

"Why are you so set against an island?"

"Answer both questions," Ruth said.

For Tom the isolation and definition of an island were its advantages. Urban sprawl might not be permanently daunted by the twenty-mile barrier of water, but it could be postponed. The very fragility of an island, with its clear limits of fresh water, of good growing soil, made people live more thoughtfully in their environment, perhaps more thoughtfully with each other as well. Oh, Tom knew about small-town pettiness and gossip, he'd grown up with it, but he also knew about small-town interdependence, which required kindness and resourcefulness. And the Gulf Islands were not like small towns of homogenous culture. Very different sorts of people chose to live there.

"With one thing in common," Gladys said. "They're all dropouts."

Tom argued that there was just as much opportunity to be responsible in a small community as in a large one, perhaps more, since the scale was still human.

"That's the only thing that worries me," Boy confessed. "I don't expect there's much choice in steam baths over there."

"You might find a friend instead," Mavis suggested.

"I got friends, Mavis, and I got a bias against mixing lust with other pleasures. It gets complicated."

Mavis did not pursue that argument. She sat at the edge of most of the discussions, too intent to be detached but making it clear that she held herself and her own life in reserve. She still hoped that a teaching job would insure that she was, at most, only a summer member of the community.

Boy supposed that, for the sake of his friends, he could combine their need for mainland supplies with his need for sexual simplicity. When Clara was consulted, she had no objection to the distance from hospitals.

"At my age, you don't worry about dying, you worry about being kept alive."

So Gladys was the only one who continued to resist the idea. Tom had enough sense not to use her pregnancy as a weapon in the argument. Finally Gladys used it herself against herself.

"I guess I won't be marching in demonstrations for a while," she said, "until whoever this is can walk anyway, and we aren't talking about the rest of our lives, are we?"

Tom didn't answer.

"Even if we are," Ruth said, "we don't have much real say even about day after tomorrow."

No one took issue with that view now, not even Gladys. They had all been too much wrenched out of themselves for any naïve confidence. Still, on the day after tomorrow, they were all together on the deck of the Gulf Island ferry as planned, looking out at the silhouette of Galiano Island. "About sixteen miles long and a mile wide," Tom was saying, "except at the fat southern tip. Macmillan Bloedel owns about seventy percent of the island in tree farms."

"Don't object," Mavis said to Gladys, who was about to. "It means you have a capitalist enemy right on your doorstep. You don't even have to go to the mainland when you're looking for a fight."

"Don't seem quite fair to fight with trees," Boy said. "You know,

I half expect the waters to part so that we can just walk the rest of the way."

He expressed an excitement, a sense of extraordinary purpose they were all experiencing, even Ruth, for whom the beautiful day, the escort of sea gulls, and the ferry horn which sounded three short and one long blasts for landing were simple omens of hope. It was a moment in which she felt truly innocent of all that had happened, blessed with the present.

"We have to go down to the car," Mavis said.

Coon Dog barked joyfully at them and made it more difficult to crowd five people into Mavis' Volkswagen.

"What we need is a bus," Mavis grumbled, but a laughing shove and hug from Gladys made her grin.

"I seen them ads for bugs floating on the water," Boy said. "But you just drive right out onto dry land, hear?"

The ferry jarred up against the pilings, and then slowly maneuvered into place. The sign GALIANO ISLAND – STURDIES BAY arched over the dock, and a tattered British Columbia flag snapped in the late April breeze. The ramp was lowered, and they were driving up onto land from the narrow dock to a narrow country road.

"The real estate office is the first turn on your left," Tom directed.

They had come to look at the café, which still had not found a buyer, probably because anyone willing to work long hours needed more reward than the thin trade the winter island could offer. Even in summer, people arrived on the island to visit friends or hike for the day, bringing their food with them.

The kitchen was well equipped, and there were the beginnings of an outdoor patio. The indoor eating space was drab and dark.

"But we could make something of it," Tom said, "a driftwood counter and stools here ..."

"And get rid of those curtains," Mavis said. "Maybe even open up that whole wall to light ..."

"If it were bigger ..." Gladys said.

"Yes, ma'am." Boy grinned. "Buy it and tear it down."

Once they had explored the place, asked all the questions they could think of from the details of financing to the frequency of power failures, they had spent only an hour.

"What are we going to do for the whole day?" Boy asked.

"See the island," Tom said.

Ruth wasn't sure why this tiny island reminded her of the red-wood landscape of her childhood. In miniature it seemed done to scale, Douglas firs tall enough to dwarf the hills, here called mountains. The little valley that crossed the island was about the size of the valley she had grown up in, though it had been more dramatically defined by the river as well as the hills. Here there was the sea at the end of every road whether they arrived at the shore or on a hilltop, and on that gentle spring day it did not seem to imprison so much as embrace this island and all the others they could see, a colony of lands in friendly sight of each other, stretching down into American waters.

"What kind of a tree is that?" Gladys asked.

"A madrone," Ruth answered, remembering the walking sticks her father had cut to carve designs into the hard, green wood through its peeling red bark.

"An arbutus to Canadians," Mavis corrected. "How did I fall among such a crew of outlanders?"

"I don't think I was ever properly introduced to a tree before in my life," Boy said. "How do you do, arbutus?"

When they came upon the graveyard, Boy's fear of the place made him noisier and more boisterous than ever.

"Look at dat!" he crowed. "The local Chinese grocer!"

"This grave says 'Japanese,'" Gladys said, studying the one next.

"Probably the only piece of land we didn't expropriate during the war," Mavis observed.

"Wonder how many Indians and niggers is buried here," Boy said, "under white men's names. Least these little yellow jackets keep their sting."

Tom had gone further and found a path through the fringe of trees to the rocks that overlooked the west entrance to Active Pass, the chief shipping lane through the islands. He was watching one of the large Vancouver Island ferries and absently rubbing his damaged shoulder when Ruth came to join him.

"I like it here," he said quietly. "Do you?"

"Yes," Ruth said, "I feel at home."

Three eagles played in the high air above them.

"They live here," Tom said, "up on Mount Galiano. Old lady would like that, wouldn't she?"

And the graveyard, or perhaps I'm the only one it matters to, a place finally to bury my dead.

"I think that's Indian land across the way there on Mayne Island, a deserted reservation," Tom said.

Boy came skidding down to join them. "Gladdy said I ain't got no business being so loud in a graveyard, but we could be the last human noise there is on this sweet earth before aerosol cans and the jet stream take away the veil from the sun and radiate us into angels. Then, when the Martians come, there won't even be no common-cold germs to kill them. Spose they'll know which of us killed each other and which of us died of the sun?"

"The small-change philosopher," Tom said, putting a large, gentle hand on Boy's head.

"Who with Ruth's nickels and dimes now has to teach the so-ciological fry cook how to run the last café on earth. Man, we're important people."

"But where are we going to live?" Gladys asked as she and Mavis joined them.

"Took God seven days to make the world, Gladdy. Give us at least two to make our own," Boy said. "We've got some adding and subtracting ahead of us 'fore we know where we are."

It was several weeks before they were ready to pose that question seriously. Tom had dutifully looked into a number of other possibili-ties, sometimes alone, sometimes joined by the others, who, after the day on the island, were as ready to find fault with anything else as he was, who overlooked with him the obvious problems of the café. The formal decision to buy the café was made in Queen's Court with Clara, who had put maps of the Gulf Islands and Galiano up on her wall so that she could explore the geography of a real place to end her life, which she did not intend to do now until after she'd seen another child born.

That night, as Ruth prowled the farmhouse with her familiar insomnia, she came upon Tom reading in the living room. She had been aware of this new habit of his on several other nights and had avoided an encounter, but now that the decision was made, perhaps he needed to talk about it.

"Are you worried about it?" she asked, standing behind the chair opposite him.

He shut his book and put it aside, which Ruth took as an invitation to sit down.

"I guess so," Tom said, "I've talked a lot of people into a lot of things."

"We're not really playing follow-the-leader."

"That would be easier," Tom said. "Ruth, if Gladdy doesn't like it, if she decides after a while it's not her sort of thing, I want you to know that wouldn't change it for me."

"That's nothing to promise, Tom."

"No, just something to know."

"But, what about the baby?"

"I don't know. She might leave it with me."

"Have you two had a fight?"

"Not exactly. But Gladdy just doesn't like conventions, and, though she's great on planning the future of the whole bloody world, she thinks her own ought to take care of itself. Or at least I shouldn't take care of it. If Mavis does get a job, I'm not sure Gladdy wouldn't go with her."

"With Mavis?"

"They sort of … got it together, you know, while I was in the hospital."

"Mavis?"

"They've always mattered a lot to each other, and I guess women know how to need each other in certain ways. Mavis is a special person for me, too. I don't know where Boy and I get the idea that friendship and sex don't mix, gay or straight. The only difference between Boy and me is that I want some kind of commitment. It's not that I want to be possessive, really. If Mavis is part of it for Gladdy, I can cope with that, but I don't think Mavis wants to be just part of our lives, or maybe she's afraid of it. I can't talk to her now. If she does come along, I'm going to look like a man with a harem when really Mavis and I are part of Gladdy's. All right, but what if we aren't enough, even so?"

"Are they together now?"

"That's right," Tom said. "Sort of every third night." He laughed.

"Are you sure about the island?"

"It's a bad cartoon, isn't it? But I can't help it, Ruth, I want to try."

The house they found might have been built for them. It was forty years old, a farmhouse originally, but one of the owners had been an artist with a large family, and the outbuildings had been attached to the house and turned into additional living quarters and a studio. It stood on rock overlooking Active Pass, surrounded by ten acres of arbutus and fruit trees. Half up for sale, the owner would prefer a lease for minimal rent in exchange for good caretaking and repair.

"We could grow our own vegetables," Tom said.

"And chickens," Mavis said.

"Do you know anything about chickens?" Boy demanded.

"Not a thing."

"Well, I do," he said glumly, "and it don't take no Ph.D. In English to deal with the stupidest creatures on God's earth, next to the goat, which can't teach its kid the difference between its tit and its ankle."

"I thought you were a city boy."

"I am, but I once spent a month on a detention farm, a ghetto holiday, it's called."

"Can we really afford it?" Gladys asked, her face amazed with pleasure. "A place like this?"

"Put your accounting hat on, Boy," Ruth said, "right now."

If they could buy the café outright without a mortgage, Ruth's disability pension and Clara's allowance from Hal would pay the rent and the utilities with enough left over for modest emergencies.

"The café's got to feed us," Boy said.

"It will," Tom promised. "At least that."

"Come with us, Mavis," Gladys said. "You just have to now."

Mavis let Gladdy hold her look for a moment and then she turned to Tom.

"Please," Tom said.

"Time to stop playing hard to get, Mavis," Boy said.

"What would I do?"

"Everything," Gladys said, "just like the rest of us."

Ruth watched Gladys, whose need for freedom would always have to be a world of enough alternatives not to seem as confining as it was. She was their spoiled child, their gaiety, their center of desire, and Mavis' only hesitation now was the approval of the others.

"Clara needs you, too," Ruth said.

"It's crazy," Mavis said, "but I do want to."

The owners of the café were only too glad to accept a cash offer, and, though Ruth had no illusions about it as a business, if it provided occupation for them and fed them, that was all she asked of it. Arranging the lease for the house took longer. The absent owner, a widow who could not live there alone but could not quite bring herself to sell the place, wanted to be sure she was not renting to hippies.

"If I could say you were a family ..." the real estate agent suggested dubiously.

"We are," Tom said, "four generations of us soon."

"And I'm a faithful old family slave who refused emancipation," Boy explained.

"You'll sign the lease yourself?" the real estate agent asked Ruth.

"That's right."

"It makes me so fucking mad!" Gladys said, fortunately after they had left the office, "that you have to be fifty before anyone will trust you."

"But I think we're going to get it," Tom said. "I think we really are."

"Imagine what a place like that would cost in the city," Mavis mused. "I think we ought to celebrate the recession."

In their pleasure, Gladys forgot her irritation and joined in the mock parade Boy was leading back to the car, Coon Dog barking frantically to be let out for the game.

When they got back to the farmhouse on the mainland, Hal was waiting for them, sitting on the front steps playing with the kitten.

"See you still don't have the sense to lock your doors," he observed to Tom, who was the first out of the car.

"How are you, Hal?" Tom asked coolly, keeping a firm hand on Coon Dog's collar so that he wouldn't jump.

"Oh, I keep from getting shot at," Hal said, looking past Tom to Boy.

"Boy," Tom said, "this is Hal Wheeler, Ruth's husband."

"Massa's come home," Boy said with a deep bow.

"I thought we might go along over and see Mother," Hal said to Ruth.

"Fine."

They had not backed out of the drive before Hal began, "Now what the hell *is* all this anyway?"

"Have you seen Clara?"

"Yes, I've seen her. First she chewed me out for not coming back for the shoot-out at the house. I told her I didn't need to find out what was going on. As usual, I could read all I wanted to in the newspapers or watch it on TV. What else can you expect of a houseful of half-wits and deserters and tarts? But you won't listen to me, never would, and you don't care a damn what's happening to me with my wife's face smeared all over the papers, bawling at the police for clearing out a slum. 'That your old lady, Hal?' Jesus!"

"There wasn't any reason for you to come back."

"I was way the hell and gone in the North," Hal said more quietly. "I didn't see the damn paper until a week after. It shook me up. I can tell you that. If you've got a woman who grieves like a stone, what are you going to do about that, eh?"

"Nothing," Ruth said.

"Nothing," Hal repeated, glancing over at her. "You look all right."

"I am all right."

"*Then* she tells me she's getting out of Queen's Court and going to live on some island with you and that crew of, of …"

"Hippies?" Ruth supplied wryly.

"Hippies and niggers!"

Ruth sighed.

"And she says I'm supposed to pay for it!"

"I would have asked you if I'd needed to," Ruth admitted. "In fact, all I need is the money you pay for Clara at Queen's Court."

"So all of you can live on it?"

"In a way," Ruth said, "but let me really tell you about it."

He did listen then, grudgingly, with an occasional explosive remark.

"When I said 'the country,' I didn't mean an island. You can't even build a road to an island, not over twenty miles of water!"

"It's a nice boat trip."

"In good weather. What if Mother's sick? What if she needs to get to the hospital?"

"There's an ambulance boat, there's a seaplane, and it doesn't worry Clara. She doesn't want to be kept alive."

"That's obvious!"

"Hal, I need to get away from this city, and I need Clara with me.

We both need young people around. If the café does any kind of business, after a year or so we wouldn't need your money …"

"It's not the money. But I work hard for it, Ruth, and why I should turn it over for a bunch of no-good, dope-smoking …"

"They're as much my children as Claire was."

"That little nigger, too?" Hal asked bitterly.

"Boy, too."

Ruth had not spoken so openly to Hal in years. She had fought free and then stopped fighting and simply endured his occasional invasions. Now, puzzled with herself, she was asking him not only for his help but for his understanding.

"They won't stay, you know. They'll get bored, and they'll take off. That sort always does. I see plenty of them on the road gangs, one paycheck and that's it. And what will you do then, stuck with a café even you admit won't return decent money on your investment?"

"There's always help," Ruth said.

"How can you go on thinking that? How many times do you have to get broken to learn?" he shouted in frustration and concern.

"'Til I'm dead," Ruth answered.

They were parked by this time in front of Queen's Court.

"I guess I'll have to be dead before I learn there's no point in arguing with the both of you. If you've got to be women, I wish you'd change your minds just once in the right direction."

"I think I have," Ruth said, smiling.

She found that even Hal's presence didn't dampen her excitement as she hurried to Clara to tell her about the house, and Clara listened with such delight that even Hal could continue to protest only in silence.

"Do you think I might get, well not binoculars, because they're too heavy to hold, but opera glasses maybe … for watching the birds?"

"What you need is a wheelchair built like a tractor for those country roads," Hal said.

"I do need a wheelchair," Clara admitted. "It's come to that."

"We might be moving in ten days, if the lease goes through," Ruth said.

"I'll be ready anytime," Clara said. "Doesn't it sound marvelous, Hal?"

"You know what it sounds like to me," Hal said.

Leaving Clara, Hal grumbled all the way to the car. Then he stood like a cartoon of aggressive belligerence and confronted Ruth.

"I'm not taking you back to that broken-down country slum tonight. We're going to a decent hotel."

"I don't have anything with me," Ruth protested.

"I'll buy you a dress, and then we'll go somewhere for dinner and behave like human beings for a change."

The toothpick tilted up. The dimple deepened.

'Til death do us part, Hal, maybe the only thing you can say about me is, "One thing about my old lady; she never turns down a good screw," and maybe the only thing I can say about you is, "In bed he doesn't screw. It's the one place he knows how to make love."

When Hal dropped her off at the farmhouse the next morning, Ruth felt comically guilty, as if Gladys might confront her with the immorality it was to keep on going to bed with a man she couldn't talk to, husband or not, but Gladys had gone to work. Only Mavis was at home, far too lost in her own moral brooding to require any explanations from Ruth.

"Where's Boy?" Ruth asked.

"He's gone off on some sort of secret mission of his own," Mavis said. "If we don't get him out of this city soon, he's going to be dumped across the border or shot in the head, probably by some off-duty policeman at the steam baths."

"He could be with Clara watching TV."

"Why doesn't someone offer me a job and fish me out of this craziness?" Mavis demanded.

"Would you take it?" Ruth asked.

"I don't know," Mavis admitted, "but I'd like the choice."

The following morning in the mail, Mavis was offered a job

teaching remedial English in the Maritimes. After a night with Gladys, Mavis wrote to refuse the job.

"She said, if I took it, she'd go with me," Mavis said to Ruth.

"Tom thought as much."

"Did he? I don't know, Ruth. I don't know how this can work either. It's like all those desert-island jokes, isn't it?"

"A bad cartoon, Tom called it."

"Did he?"

"You'll have to learn to talk with Tom again," Ruth said.

"I used to think *he* was unrealistic. Is he a saint or just a … a weak fish?"

"You know his answer to that."

"The weak fish that saved the world! But if I don't love him, if I don't love Gladdy, I don't see how I'll ever be able … This isn't the way I thought it would be. Gladdy was beside herself, and it seemed the only human thing to do. That's not true either, is it? I've always wanted her. I just didn't think she'd ever want me, not with Stew and then Arthur … and then Tom, and I thought what a mess it would be. I was right about that anyway." Mavis paused and looked at Ruth. "Boy says my only problem is that I haven't had an education for catastrophe, but my instincts are okay."

Chapter Twelve

"Here we are!" Boy shouted from the cab of the U-Haul truck. "Spat out of the belly of the whale at the last."

"That ferryboat scares you," Tom observed, as he eased the truck over the speed-control ridges of the dock.

"Shitless, man, shitless," Boy admitted.

Ruth between them pondered Boy's loyalty to the enterprise, given that fear. Perhaps what was fearful in each of them was a measure and an offering, like the child Gladys carried, driven with nervous care by Mavis in the car behind them. Then, as they drove past the café, its grounds untended, some of its windows broken, the simple sign CAFÉ badly weathered, her concern shifted to the thing they had bought, more derelict than she had remembered.

"What we are we going to call it?" Tom asked.

"Jonah's," Boy said at once. "And then every time I make it back here with the hot dogs, I will be assured that I'm about the Lord's business."

"Well, it's better than Ma's," Mavis admitted when Tom tried out Boy's suggestion, "or Pop's."

"Who the fuck was Jonah anyway?"

"A reluctant radical who ran away the first time he was supposed to preach death and destruction. Then, when he finally did and God didn't kill everybody, he sulked in the sun under a gourd," Mavis explained.

"And the Lord, he say, listen, man, I can't kill a bunch of poor sods who can't tell their left hand from their right hand, now can I, not when they's already running around in sackcloth and ashes."

"What about Sodom?" Gladys demanded.

"That's a different story, child. He couldn't get nobody to repent buggerin' angels."

"It's all so much bullshit," Gladys said impatiently.

Nearly the first thing they did, however, once they had settled the house, was to paint the new signs for the café on huge gray pieces of driftwood, in the spirit more than in the shape of the whale, to greet Clara when she arrived, brought from Queen's Court by Mavis and Ruth. Her delight in the name, in the place, renewed their energy. While Clara sat for hours in her new wheelchair in the corner window watching the birds, sometimes through the field glasses Tom had set up on a stand for her, the others worked around her.

"I'm grateful it's too late to put in much of a garden this year," Ruth said at the end of the first week. "There's so much else to do."

There were daily crises: bashed thumbs, flat tires, broken pipes, unbudgeted-for expenses, forgotten essentials which could only be purchased on the mainland. Then Coon Dog strayed, and, because the postmaster had warned them that farmers shot dogs to protect their sheep, Mavis spent nearly twelve hours looking for him before he turned up on his own. Tied up, he howled, so Clara kept him indoors with her until one of the others found time to take him out for a run.

"So much for the happy myth of big dogs in the country," Gladys said.

"Walking's good for you," Mavis said.

"Good for the baby, you mean."

Gladys was testy any time either Tom or Mavis tried to spare her work or suggest what she should eat or how she should behave because she was pregnant.

"I'm not sick, you know. Peasant women just drop their kids between the rows of beans."

Gladys had, in fact, never looked lovelier or stronger. It was Tom who needed to be watched, still convalescent and forgetful of himself. He didn't take the sun as both Mavis and Gladys did, and often in the evening there were pale shadows of tiredness on his face. He was determined the café would open on the first of June. It was Boy who watched him and manipulated him into taking breaks by sitting him down with a new financial problem or complicated question about ordering. He persuaded Tom that it was his responsibility to make first contracts with the wholesalers and to pick out the bus they needed, which would require a day in town away from the hard physical labor of remodeling the café.

"Actually running this place is going to feel like a holiday," Gladys said as she and Ruth stood together painting.

"Maybe," Ruth said, "but we're going to take a day off *before* it opens, all of us. There's no point in living in a place like this and working ourselves to death."

"But it's fun, too, isn't it?"

Ruth smiled at her paint-spattered young companion. "Yes, yes, it's fun."

"Boy's *not* going to name the baby," Gladys said fiercely, going back to work.

"Who is?"

"I don't know, but we're going to have a look at the baby first. It's not so long now, not much more than three months. Once the café's ready, Tom wants to fix up the nursery."

Gladys and Tom had taken the two rooms, which had once been storage sheds and were now attached to the house. Ruth worried that they wouldn't be warm enough in the winter, but Tom and Gladys had insisted, and there were two extra bedrooms in the house, which they could use if and when they needed them. For this time, there was a tactful physical distance between Tom and Mavis, who had chosen one of the three back bedrooms upstairs. Space and their common preoccupation with work seemed to have eased what tension there had been among them.

"A whole day off?" Tom repeated dubiously when Ruth confronted him with her proposal.

"Tom, do be serious enough about this project to live to see it,"

Mavis said. "You need a break more than anyone else does. We *could* open tomorrow if we had to, and we've got five more days."

"Miss Clara," Boy said, "you and that wheelchair are coming with us in the new bus. We're taking you down the boat ramp at Montague and launching you onto the beach. How about that?"

"Sounds to me like turning play into work," Clara said doubtfully. "I'm perfectly happy here, perfectly."

"If you go, old lady," Tom said, "I will."

On a weekday in May, even though the beach was part of the only public campsite on the island, they had it to themselves. Once Clara was settled and braced on the flat rocks next to the boat ramp, the others set off to explore, except for Ruth, who settled herself comfortably against a log, and Gladys, who stood near Clara's wheelchair, skipping rocks into the flat sea.

"Do go off with the others," Clara urged. "I'm fine right here by myself. It's such a lovely place."

It was, and Ruth wanted to share it with Clara in quietness, a rare luxury in these busy days. They could not really rest their eyes on the serene distance of mountains on Vancouver Island with Gladys like a restless child in the foreground. She had stayed behind for a purpose, however; that was clear. So Ruth and Clara waited. After Gladys had skipped at least a dozen rocks, she turned toward them.

"Why didn't you marry Hal's father?"

Ruth would have liked to protest the question, given the mood she wanted for the day, but to do it she would have had to deny Gladys' need to ask it.

"I thought at the time because he didn't want to," Clara said, "but I've come to believe I didn't want to either."

"Did you live with him?"

"No. We didn't … in those days, not as easily as now anyway."

"Tom won't say it, but I know he thinks that our not being married is going to be bad for the café. There seem to be plenty of women on the island with kids and no husbands, but that seems to be okay; people can feel sorry for them."

"Do you maybe want to marry Tom?" Ruth asked.

"If only anything were a clear choice! I don't want to marry Tom because otherwise the churchgoers won't eat our hamburgers. That's fucking ridiculous!"

"What I think," Clara said, pulling a sweater a little closer around her, "is that people really do what they want, and one excuse for it is as good as another, unless you regret it, of course."

"If the hamburgers are good enough …" Ruth said, smiling.

"But what if they're not? We'd never know, would we? It might be my fucking language or my fucking bastard."

"Or my bastard, or Boy's blackness, or Ruth's one arm, or Tom's draft dodging," Clara said. "If business is good, Gladdy , it will be because the café is run well and thoughtfully for the people who need it. If somebody wants to do the café harm, indigestion is all that's necessary, and with the number of people my age on this island, there will be plenty of that, no matter how you cook."

"You aren't any *help*," Gladys protested, "either of you. I *want* an excuse."

"Then you have loads of them," Ruth said. "Now, go find the others. They'll be missing you and we won't."

Ruth and Clara said not one word to each other after that. They watched Gladys amble away down the beach, then break into an easy run. Then they turned to the large view of the sea, the mountains, and the sky. Ruth did not have to say, *I wasn't much good with them alone. They need both of us. And I need you. As long as you're here, nothing will fall apart. That's silly, I know. I mean, I won't fall apart.* The song of contentment she felt was a melody so familiar between them they had only to be still to listen to it.

Gladys was the first to return, bringing shells and pine cones for Clara's identification, but the others were close behind her.

"You three!" Mavis said. "It's just like a Fellini movie."

"What do it all mean?" Boy asked. "Who can tell my fortune: the sibyl in the wheelchair, pregnant Venus, or one-armed Fate?"

"The thing about Fellini movies is," Gladys said, "that they don't mean anything."

Tom and Mavis went back to the bus to get the lunch, deep in earnest talk while Boy and Gladys threw sticks for Coon Dog to be certain he'd be exhausted by the time they began to eat.

"Is Coon Dog the only one going swimming?" Gladys asked.

"Have you put a toe in that water?" Boy asked.

"Sure. It's not that cold."

"You want to give your child a cramp in his own sea before he's even born?"

"I'll go with you," Mavis called, "if you'll go right now before we eat."

Gladys would not have bothered with a suit, but Mavis, who had seen to it that the suits were in the bus, reminded her it was a public beach.

"I know, I know, and that's no way to sell hamburgers. All right, I'll race you."

Only Boy refused to watch, his fear of water overcoming his protective obligations.

"You can swim, can't you?" he asked Tom, and the moment he gave a reassuring nod, Boy rolled over onto his face and stayed there.

Mavis in a bathing suit mildly surprised Ruth. Her shoulders did not seem so square and self-protective. It was a handsome body, only ill served by the convention of clothes which insisted on dividing people in half, and there playing in the water with Gladys, she had graceful strength. Ruth turned and smiled at Tom.

"She's going to marry me," he said, glancing from Ruth to Clara.

"Yes," Clara said, "she is."

The license arrived in time for them to be married in Vancouver the day before Jonah's opened, with Boy and Mavis as witnesses. Ruth wanted to spend the day with Clara, but the young people got away only because she could finish the chores that remained. Alone at the café, Ruth worked hard against the filmstrips in her head, Tom not on his way to be married but back there going up the old porch steps, the blood bloom on his shirt, the flowering wound of Willard's face. Ruth had not lacked an education for catastrophe, but it did her no good. The horrors that took up only a few minutes of actual life had to play and replay themselves until they finally took up the space of dreams. The young people picked her up at the café on their way back from the evening ferry, and it was hard for Clara afterwards to remember that Ruth had not been with them for the wedding.

Over a hundred islanders responded to their invitations on opening day. If there hadn't been a power failure for an hour just at noon, the amateur inefficiency of Jonah's staff might have been disastrously exposed. A power failure meant not only no hot drinks or food, but no water, since the café depended on its own well and pump. Also it was unwise to open refrigerator or freezer since there was never any way of telling how long the power might be off. People shouted out warnings about the danger of spoiling supplies, happily accepting pieces of pie and cake, cooling coffee and un-iced soft drinks. In that slow, visiting hour, Tom and Gladys, Mavis and Boy moved among their customers like diplomats, not one "fuck" or dubious prayer to be heard. If customers were later amused or jarred by verbal eccentricities of Jonah's staff, today they were making a good impression. Ruth stayed in the background, where she intended to be, for, except on special occasions like this one, her one hand would be more useful at the house, where she thought of Clara enviously in her wheelchair by the window watching the weather and the birds.

Reading the weather preoccupied them all. Though the weather chart would have denied it, storms seemed to boil and stream up from the southwest off the Olympic range in Washington, or the sun snagged there illuminating those far mountains while a low, flat gray sky hung over the islands. Then a perfect summer day for the whole gulf might not reach Vancouver, a weather trap in a cul-de-sac of mountains. Islanders were always restless for rain. Very few wells on the island could supply enough water for gardens, but, if it rained too much, it was time to fret after the sun so the tomatoes would ripen.

"I wish people liked the same variety of weather as the vegetables," Tom said. "Then we could pray together."

"God ain't always persuaded by lobbies," Boy said.

That particular rainy day, he was right. Day trippers swarmed off the ferry and sought the shelter of Jonah's for coffee courage before they elected one of the trails Mavis had marked on a large island map, and they came back early to dry off, wait for the ferry, and spend money. But, as the rain continued, day after day, people regressed to winter habits, gloomily predicting there would be no summer, recalling another year when mud season lasted until it froze. For two weeks the ferries brought only campers from California and the prairies who had forgotten they'd come to the rain forest to escape the heat and cursed the great leaking shelter of trees, the closed-in sky. Accounts at the end of the first month were not encouraging.

"Well," Mavis said, "we aren't going to be counting on day trippers all winter. Now's the time to begin training islanders. We don't have to wait for September for pensioners' dinners."

"You noticed Jonah's ain't all that popular with the old folks?" Boy asked.

"That's what I mean," Mavis said. "We have to start encouraging them."

"They think we're hippies," Gladys said.

"Then perhaps it's time I started inviting a few people for tea," Clara announced.

"Tea?"

"Tea. There's nothing like a good, stiff afternoon tea to reassure people."

Clara's social strategy worked, though it tired her enough to worry Ruth. The first pensioners' dinner was a real success without heart attacks or later rumors of food poisoning. When the July sun finally came out, there was no grudging gossip about the clutter of tourists at Jonah's, open by seven in the morning to catch the early ferry breakfast trade, never closed before nine in the evening, seven days a week. With four of them and Ruth as occasional stand-in, they could do it. August accounts were even more encouraging than July's, but they did not content themselves with easy business. Boy shopped more and more shrewdly both on the mainland and on the island. If an island price was a bit higher, he commented on it but accepted it, because a farmer who sold his lambs to Jonah's was more apt to stop for coffee there, take his wife out to dinner. Fishermen began to bring in salmon and cod, and Tom, at first reluctant to be away from the café for any reason, was persuaded to join a fishing party, the catch so good that it was a profitable day as well as a rest and a change for Tom. Boy set up space in the budget for buying a boat after he made it clear he'd get into nothing smaller than a ferry. They could set crab traps, collect clams and oysters, once they had a boat. As the blackberries ripened along the valley road, they had picking parties for pies through the winter. They had their own apple and cherry and plum trees, and Coon Dog finally had a function to suit his name, keeping raccoons and deer from early harvesting. Even without Clara's insisting, they would have had to share with the birds. There was plenty. The freezers bulged with free crops from the sea and the island.

They talked of raising their own pigs and chickens, of setting up a smokehouse, of next year's vegetable garden. The tired strain had gone from Tom's face. Mavis had stopped looking every day for the mail, and Boy rarely spent a night in town. Gladys was smugly convinced she would have twins, at least.

Ruth took long, exploring walks, following old lumber roads into the forest, climbing up to Bluff Park, which overlooked Active Pass, crowded with fishing boats, which often had to be herded out of the shipping lanes by the Coast Guard, or climbing higher still to the top of Mount Galiano, the whole of the island beneath her, the mountains of Vancouver Island to the west, of the mainland to the east, the Olympic range making a southern border. Often now she could be several hours alone, her childhood with her in the soles of her feet on earth again. She had nearly stopped smoking for the pleasure of the fragrance of the woods, field grasses in the hot sun, berries. If she did take Coon Dog with her, the deer acknowledged her with soft stares before they lowered their heads again to browse. Even in August, while Jonah's was crowded with tourists, Ruth rarely met anyone. If she did, there was always a friendly exchange, an offer of a piece of chocolate or a drink of water, the metallic taste of it from the canteen another gift from the past, from her father, a man not much older than Tom. There was no grieving irony in that for Ruth, a looking forward instead to Tom with his own child, giving the gift of place in his turn. She took her discoveries of wild flowers and leaves of unknown trees back to Clara.

They all carried fragments of their days back to Clara, and as she taught them needle and cone shape to name the trees, they taught her the names of island children, of old-timers and newcomers. Gladys described and imitated so well that Clara could, when Boy or Mavis took her for an occasional ride, identify people along the road. Every time she was right, saying "George" or "Sarah" or "Skyler," Boy would try to match her with "hemlock" or "spruce" or "willow."

"This place was just one big blur of green to me at first," he said, "and that's as bad as not being able to tell one nigger from another, isn't it?"

"You've been a city boy," Clara said.

"Yes, ma'am. I could tell you a Shell Oil tree, a Macdonald's tree, a White Spot tree, and that was about it, and I thought that birds-of-a-feather stuff was lousy propaganda."

"Nature's as bad a bible as any other," Clara admitted.

"'Less you read it like you do, for pleasure."

"What are you thinking, so silent there in the back seat, Ruth?"

"I'm thinking it's a good thing you're embarrassed instead of spoiled by compliments."

"You accusing me of sweet-talking Miss Clara?"

"You sweet-talk everyone, Boy, and we all love it," Ruth said, laughing.

"Tell that to Gladdy. She said she had the prize for bad-mouthing until I came along."

"Are you quarreling with Gladdy?"

"She say I'm a nigger chauvinist every time I call that baby 'him,' and I say, 'She-it, man, what am I supposed to call him, it?' And she say, 'She-it, woman, why not?' It ain't what you can call racial strife, which I handle better. This battle of the sexes is just too scary with so many kinds of sexes, along with prenatal wondering."

"Do you want her to have a boy?"

"*Twin* boys," Boy decided, "even up the balance."

Gladys' temper did flare more often these days, and Boy was usually the target. It sometimes seemed as if he put himself in the way of it, a kind of decoy away from Tom or Mavis, but he could tease her into laughter as well, where Mavis could only nag and Tom worry at her.

"I now know what a sex object is," Gladys said tiredly one evening, sent home to keep her swollen feet and ankles up.

"The last two weeks seem as long as the whole nine months," Clara said. "Even I can remember that."

"But, you know, I wouldn't want them out in a test tube where I could watch them grow. Maybe a window in my belly would be all right. Do you think I'm going to turn into one of those women who dig motherhood?"

"Maybe half the time," Ruth said.

"I wish Mavis were having one, too. Two for me seems greedy."

"Boy wants twin boys."

"Boy's a pain in the ass, and, when I tell him so, he says it's his social duty. Maybe it is."

They heard a car door slam. Coon Dog was already lying across the back door, his ears starched with hope, his tail pounding. Mavis came in first, letting the dog shove past her to greet Tom.

"That creature is getting as big as a bear," she said.

"Me?" Gladys asked.

"Not you, lovely. How are the ankles?"

"Which ankles?"

Tom came in, bringing the dog, Boy behind him carrying the cashbox.

"We made so much money today," Boy announced, "that we get to start a college fund for she-it."

"Do you see what I mean?" Gladys demanded of Ruth and Clara.

"There's an old rule of survival, Boy," Ruth said. "Don't tease a pregnant woman in the last month."

"Who's teasing? I believe I am the only one around here with the proper respect for motherhood and apple pie and so on."

"And on and on," Gladys said.

"How are you feeling?" Tom asked.

"*I am feeling fine!*"

"And now for the nine-o'clock news," Boy said. "The mass murder on Galiano this evening of an ill-assorted group of dropouts is just another instance of what premature lactation in a pregnant woman ..."

"Premature what?" Gladdy asked.

"It's a Latin term for the milk of human kindness," Boy explained.

"Let's count the money," Tom said. "You can kill him as soon as he's done this month's books."

The money-counting ritual absorbed them all, and, when it was over, Ruth wheeled Clara into her bedroom.

"They're tired, all of them," she said. "Maybe it's not such a bad thing that business falls off after Labor Day."

"Do you suppose Gladdy will ever learn to be impatient with herself?"

"I expect so. It's so hard to avoid learning, but I'm not sure it's healthy, are you?"

Mavis' light rap on the door stopped Ruth from answering. Together they got Clara ready for bed, a nightly ritual they all enjoyed.

"I think," Mavis said, "I'm going to be driving the school bus.

How's that for my first job after my Ph.D.?"

"Do you really want to do it?" Ruth asked.

"After Labor Day, Boy and Tom can run the café. Gladdy's going to be busy with the babies. It would bring in a few dollars. I like the kids …"

"Are you a bit sorry you're not going off to that job in the Maritimes?"

"It was pretty dead-end. If a good job ever does turn up, well …"

Mavis had finished giving Clara a sponge bath and was gently rubbing her back.

"You should really have been a nurse," Clara said. "You have such good hands."

"Probably, but my father's a doctor," Mavis said, "and my mother was a nurse. According to them, I didn't have the right qualifications. You have to be stupid, obedient, and a good lay. Power's such an ugly thing. I wonder why I want to go back into the system at all as anything, but sometimes I do."

"Not to be pushed around," Ruth said.

"To be somebody," Mavis said. "To be safe."

Once Clara was settled, Ruth and Mavis went back into the living room. Only Gladys was there, playing with the cat.

"You in the mood to give another back rub tonight?" Gladys asked.

"Sure," Mavis said. "Come on up."

Power had never been a choice for Ruth, that dream of vindication, authority, freedom to be who you were and have what you wanted. It had been real enough to Mavis, still was; though, when it was offered to her, the job and Gladys to go with it, she had turned it down. For Tom's sake? For the children's? Or because, really confronted with power, she did find it ugly, for the winner as well as the loser. Still, Boy couldn't go on forever acting out the tension Mavis and Tom courteously refused to deal with.

Ruth stepped out onto the terrace and sat down in one of the summer chairs. A ferry sounded at the entrance of the pass. She heard its engine long before it came in sight, its bright lights momentarily dimming the summer stars. Only after it passed did she notice Tom, sitting below her at the edge of the cliff.

Chapter Thirteen

Because Gladys insisted, Mavis went with her and Tom in the water taxi to Salt Spring Island, where the hospital was. It was late Saturday afternoon when they left. Ruth went down to the café to take over the dinner cooking, and Boy waited on tables. They didn't get home until after ten o'clock. There had been no phone call.

"I wish we'd told them to phone anyway, every little while," Clara said fretfully.

Boy, nervous and unusually quiet, finally decided to take the dog for a walk. Ruth heard him come in several hours later, long after she had settled Clara in bed. She went down to tell him there had been no call yet.

"We should have let her have them at home the way she wanted to," Boy said. "It's unnatural, them over there, us over here."

"Safer there."

"What's safer?" Boy asked with a hard, short laugh.

"They'll be home soon enough," Ruth said, wanting to reassure and deflect him.

"It's a bad sky out there," Boy said. "Sky's going to cry on us any minute now."

"Boy, Boy," Ruth said, "what is it? Babies get born every minute. You don't have to be frightened."

"You're talking about white odds, lady. I got five little brothers and sisters born and buried pretty much the same day. Last one my mama, she cut off his ear; so God wouldn't want him. God ain't that fussy, turns out."

Ruth's hand was on Boy's head, cupping his ear, knowing that kind of maternal insanity for the children being born this night, the grim bargains for life one is willing to make, sacrificed ears, scarred faces, ugly names. *Overlook these children and let them live. We've been bound by enough fear and grief. These two are already paid for.*

"It's a good thing you're not keeping Tom company tonight."

"Nobody keeps that man company, you know that?"

"He's healing," Ruth said.

"Why doesn't Mavis phone and tell us how many heads there are anyway?" Boy demanded.

No phone call came that night. Boy and Ruth went sleepless to the café in the morning, apprehension having settled to dread because someone should have phoned to say something, anything: a false labor, a long labor. They could not all have died of it or even been struck dumb.

The morning ferry from Salt Spring, due in at eight-ten, was half an hour late. Mavis, with three parallel fingernail scratches across her cheek, walked into Jonah's with the first of the foot passengers.

"Why didn't you phone? What is it?" Ruth demanded, following Mavis into the kitchen away from the curiosity of early coffee seekers.

"I couldn't ... not on the telephone."

"She hurt you," Boy said, touching Mavis' cheek.

"No, Tom did; it's all right. There were twins, a boy and a girl. The boy didn't make it, but the other one's ... fine. Ruth, you're going to have to help them."

"Does Gladdy know?"

"Yes, but it's Tom. He went berserk, not in front of Gladdy, thank God."

A customer banged a knife against a glass, and Boy turned with an angry oath.

"Easy," Ruth said.

"I'll deal with him," Boy said. "I'll fry his brains for breakfast."

"I think you'd better go over, Ruth," Mavis said.

"Do they know why?"

"A simple thing – the cord. Tom hates her."

"The baby?"

"Gladdy. He called her a whore and a head and a dyke and a murderer. I hit him. I had to. I had to do a lot of things."

"Where is he now?"

"At the hospital. Somebody's going to have to help him, but not me."

"We'll close up right now," Ruth said.

But it was nearly an hour before they could clear the café of people. Mavis made no attempt to help. She sat on a stool in the kitchen and stared at the near trees.

"If that tomfool wanted a whipping boy, why didn't he ask me along?" Boy muttered at the dishes he was loading into the washer. "What nigger ass is for."

"You wouldn't have done," Mavis said quietly.

"Wouldn't I? Wouldn't I?"

"He hates her," Mavis repeated.

"He's hurt," Ruth said quietly.

"Why did he have to blame anyone? He's got a baby. Isn't one enough for his fantasy to father a new species?"

"He wanted a killer whale because they sing so pretty, because nothing on earth is trying to kill them, not even their own kind," Boy muttered on.

"Did you see her?" Ruth asked.

"The baby? No. Tom did. He saw them both, but he only looked at the dead one, the boy."

"Did you see Gladdy?"

"Yes, they were nice about that; it's a little hospital. She's pretty doped up. I don't think they even gave her a chance to go into shock."

"I'm going with you, Ruth," Boy said. "Otherwise you're going to get needed in too many directions at once."

He phoned for the water taxi before they locked up and drove home to Clara.

"Will you tell her?" Mavis asked Ruth.

"Yes," Ruth said, "and then, listen to me, Mavis, you're to tell her exactly what happened, everything, because you've got a lot of understanding and forgiving to do before we get back."

"I won't be here when you get back."

Ruth reached out and turned Mavis' damaged face to her. "Have you forgotten who persuaded Gladdy to have this baby? Have you forgotten you love her?"

"I wish I could! Tom tried to rape me about four hours ago and I wish I could forget that, too."

"Don't say that," Boy said softly. "Don't say that."

"He hates me. He hates Gladdy. He hates us."

"It's only stupid, stupid sorrow," Boy protested.

Mavis began to cry.

It was Boy who had to explain to Clara. Ruth took Mavis to her room, undressed her to discover her fine, always shoulder-sheltered breasts bruised, her thighs bruised. Ruth got a basin of warm water, a washcloth, and a towel. She bathed Mavis with a hand taught its gentleness by Mavis, her face, her neck, her bruised breasts, her hurt thighs, while Mavis lay passively crying.

"Sleep now. I'll have someone look in on Clara, and we'll phone this evening."

"Don't let him hurt anyone else," Mavis said. "Don't let him hurt her or Boy."

Ruth went down to find Boy and Clara sitting together, holding hands.

"I'll call to get someone in," Clara said at once. "You must get to them as quickly as you can."

"Is Mavis all right?" Boy asked.

"I think so," Ruth said. "I think she'll sleep. You may have to help her, Clara."

"Yes, all right," Clara agreed. "But go now. I'm sure the water taxi's waiting."

"We'll phone as soon as we can."

"A little girl, Ruth," Clara said.

Boy drummed the steering wheel as he drove back to Sturdies Bay. Ruth watched the road, carrying her toward so much hope and grief commingled that she didn't know how much she could help herself, never mind the others.

"I am mad at *him*," Boy said, drumming a rhythm into his words. "I sure am mad at *him*!"

"He's going to be mad enough at himself not to need any help with that."

"If he ain't still crazy."

As they got out of the bus in the parking lot, they saw the water taxi come alongside the dock. Both of them ran, aware now that some hours had passed since Mavis left Tom. It was eleven o'clock, at least half an hour still until they could reach him.

It was a beautiful day, with the sense of high summer though it was the middle of September, even the air on the water fragrant with berries and sweet grasses.

"There were whales in the pass this morning," the boatman told them.

"Is it true they have no enemies?" Ruth asked Boy.

"Not the killer whales," Boy said. "Maybe after we'd learned to breathe, we could have taken a turn back into the sea, too, and never had to learn to walk upright at all."

The film Ruth hadn't seen in weeks suddenly began to turn in her head again, Tom walking up the front steps, the report of the gun, the blood bloom on his shirt, the flowering of Willard's face. *Breathe*, she thought to him. *Breathe.*

They were approaching Ganges now, only a five-minute taxi ride from there to the hospital, and there was one waiting.

"You got a speech all prepared?" Boy asked Ruth on the way up the hill.

"No."

"I've written me a whole sermon and even got the first and

second lessons picked out, thinking it's best to speak to the man before I bust his head."

Ruth shook her head. Boy in this manly necessity wasn't funny enough to laugh at or serious enough to discourage. He'd have to stand on a chair to hit Tom. And Tom, in whatever extremity, would never lay a hand on Boy except in affection. If anyone had ever suggested that Tom might one day lose his considerable but carefully controlled temper, let out all that anger and frustration and grief he'd tried so hard to heal in himself instead, Ruth would automatically have feared for Gladys, whom he needed to be so much surer of than he was or perhaps ever would be. It was really Gladys he had attacked this morning, the bitch, the witch, Woman, who would not finally ever give, give in, give up, who threatened the center of him, who killed his child. Ruth was not afraid he would hurt anyone else now, but she was afraid of his suffocating in the stench of his own anger. *Breathe, Tom, breathe.*

They hurried into the hospital and saw Tom, standing in the corridor, his back to them.

"Tom," Ruth said, and he turned, startled.

"Jesus," Boy said softly. "The devil got here before me."

Tom had a black eye, four or five stitches over his eyebrow, and a badly swollen lower lip.

"Where's Mavis?"

"At home," Ruth said.

"Is she all right?"

"Yes," Ruth said. "Upset, but all right."

"I told Gladdy we'd been in ... an accident."

"What she hit you with, man?"

"I don't know, but she should have done it sooner and harder."

"Are *you* all right?" Ruth said, taking his arm and leading him over to a bench.

"I think so," Tom said. "They just let me up a little while ago, to see Gladdy."

"You're green, man."

If there had never been any question that Tom was trying to kill Mavis, nobody could doubt that her own instinct had been murderous.

"You two stay here," Ruth said. "I'll be back in a minute."

She found a nurse, who took her to a doctor.

"A nasty cut, slight concussion, that's all. He's lucky. It would be a good idea if you took him home to rest. He wouldn't say anything about it. Neither would the young woman who brought him in."

Ruth went back to find Boy sitting quietly holding Tom's hand just as he had been holding Clara's earlier that morning. *Boy Wonder, you must have been given all the grace of your mother's five dead children.*

"Have you got a room?" she asked Tom.

"Yes."

"The doctor says you've got to get some rest. You go with him, Boy, and come back in an hour or so for me."

"The other one …" Tom said. "The other one's all right."

Boy, without a word, took Tom's arm and directed him down the hall.

Finally Ruth could turn her attention to Gladys and the child.

"Oh, Ruth, Ruth!" Gladys said, reaching up her arms.

Ruth, in that fierce, needful embrace, only needed one arm. Gladys still held her, locked, to ask about Mavis, to be sure nothing dreadful had happened to her.

"I said, 'Tom, don't lie to me, just don't lie to me; that's the only thing I can't stand.'"

"She's a bit shaken up, but she's fine. She thought she ought to come home to us, better than phoning, and Tom was all right and here with you …"

"You wouldn't lie to me …" Gladys said, holding Ruth off now, looking hard into her face.

"Not about anything important, Gladdy, you know that."

"It's hard," Gladdy then said softly, "crying for so much. Tom says we have a baby. We have to be glad for her. He's such a good person. A kid needs at least one good parent."

"Have you seen her again?"

"Yes, and she's just fine. Oh, but it scares me. Think how close they were. Think how separate she is now ..."

"Like all of us," Ruth said firmly. "Who does she look like?"

"You," Gladys said at once.

A pain tore in Ruth's chest. "She can't look like me."

"Well, I know, but she does. She has marvelous, fierce eyes."

"All babies do."

"Tom said I could name her. I want to call her Ruth."

She must have a name of her own, a face of her own. Clara? Clara, you refused, and it was no protection for Claire. Nothing is.

"May I?"

"Boy says Ruth's a sad name."

"It's a loving name," Gladys said. "Oh, fuck, Ruth, don't you cry!"

Before Ruth left the hospital, she was allowed to see the baby. She did not see then the fierce eyes, which had given the baby her name. She was asleep, her small, ancient face remote, storing up reserves after the violent shock of birth, the first invasion of air from which had to follow a thousand tests of the tiny intricate mechanism expelled, deprived, required, little Ruth, born so literally in the shadow of death.

Boy was with Gladys when Ruth got back.

"Well, what do you think of her?" Gladys asked.

"I think she's going to look like Tom."

"But have more sense because she's a woman," Boy said.

"Tom really is all right, isn't he?" she asked them. "That's a bad cut over his eye."

"He's all right," Boy assured her. "He's already giving me hell for shutting up Jonah's, giving the café a bad reputation, etc., etc. I told him he didn't have another mouth to feed for at least a couple of months and to take it easy. I think he read somewhere about a tribe where the men have all the labor pains and do all the moaning and groaning while the women just get on with it. One of these days

I'm going to take away his library card and see if we can get his head straight."

Ruth telephoned Clara to say and to hear over again for each one, yes, they're all right, yes, we're all right, yes, everyone is all right.

"I think we'll be home on the night ferry. Don't let Mavis do anything silly before we get there."

"She's got to drive the school bus in the morning," Clara said.

"So she does."

"She's all right."

It was a long trip back by the island ferry, which put in at Pender and Mayne before it finally arrived at Galiano at just past six, but it gave Ruth and Boy time to put together their separate segments of the afternoon.

"I've got a note for Mavis from Tom," Boy said. "I told him she was thinking of clearing out."

"Did you tell him to write it?"

"Yeh, you know, he wasn't in a very practical frame of mind, thought maybe he ought to go to jail or a shrink or both, even has this theory about acting out the war he wouldn't fight, having his own Vietnam right here in Canada, getting himself shot at, ravaging native women, all that negative manhood finally strangling his own baby boy. He told me maybe the only solution to it all is to lock up or shoot every white man there is. I told him eating that sort of shit was a luxury he couldn't indulge in since he already had one woman mad as hell at him and another that was going to be if he didn't get his head straight and get it straight fast. I said to him, 'Man, you just made yourself an ugly mistake, a *mess*. You don't eat it; you clean it up, and that don't mean giving Mavis or me or anybody a treatise on the failure of Western man; it means telling her you're sorry and making her believe it.'"

The need to sleep came to Ruth suddenly, and she did not resist it, floated on the surface of it, so that when the dreams came of wounds, of falling, of loss, she could run them backwards until everyone she had loved or needed was restored to her, father, husband, daughter, until she held two new children as she had held her own in two strong, protective arms.

Boy woke her when it was time to get off the ferry at Sturdies Bay. As they walked up the dock to the bus, people greeted them with questions about the closed café, about Gladys. Ruth and Boy paused to explain because, though they had lived on the island only a few months, it had become their community with a right to know the details. Ruth was not shy to speak about the death of the boy child; she found it more difficult to tell the living child's name. Boy said, "Ruth," with none of the reluctance he had once had at the name. Between them, they managed.

When they arrived home, Mavis had dinner ready and was sitting drinking a glass of sherry with Clara. The scratches across Mavis' face faded in comparison with Tom's stitched eyebrow. Her self-consciousness about them was slightly embarrassed, her reserve restored. Boy did not immediately give the note he carried for Tom. Ruth did not know when Mavis received it. The attention through dinner was on Gladys and the baby, and after dinner each retreated into that part of the experience which was his or her own.

Ruth walked out into the gentle evening and took up Tom's favorite position at the edge of the cliff where she could watch the last of the fishing boats working their way home against the tidal currents in the pass – out there among the superior killer whales which Tom had caught in the net of his imagination and offered to Boy or Gladys or anyone who would listen.

Gladdy had called him "good" this afternoon, a word Ruth had also used, not always with irony, to separate herself from her husband, and she heard again old Mrs. Weedman biting those words into her tear-soaked handkerchief, "You're such a good man," at her father's embarrassed back. For her mother, goodness was no excuse. It could kill, like anything else. A margin of safety was all her mother ever aspired to, to cajole, avoid, outwit, to admit nothing. She would not have been surprised at any of the damage done in the name or strain of virtue. "It doesn't matter *why* you do it, *if* you do it …" "Oh, for pity's sake!" she'd cry, always in irritation, so that even now pity was for Ruth the final, bullying shrew, the humiliation.

I can pity the strong, like Tom (the poor cowboy all covered with gore). I can pity the dead child. Oh, I can pity the living earth. But for life's sake, I can't pity Mavis or the living child. I can't.

"It's about time to put Clara to bed," Mavis said, standing behind Ruth.

"Yes," Ruth said, turning back to the house.

"Ruth, I want to apologize for all that melodrama this morning."

"For pity's sake," Ruth burst out. "We're all all right."

Chapter Fourteen

Clara watched through the field glasses an eagle attack a gull. "The eagle is a hideous, magnificent bird. I wish Puss weren't white; she's so easy to see. Mind you, it makes her bad at catching birds as well. Mating and killing don't look all that different up in the high air, but the birds aren't confused about it. Why are we?"

"Stop reading that bad bible of yours and see Tom and Mavis out there cleaning up the yard," Ruth said.

"They're making friends again, aren't they?"

"Yes."

"I don't think it occurred to her to feel sorry she'd hit him until she saw him this morning."

"It's an ugly cut. What did she hit him with, do you suppose?"

"Her beloved brandy bottle. She said at least she'd proved a point: you can't be raped by a good friend as long as you're in the company of a brandy bottle. She could have killed him."

"I think she intended to."

"Boy's all right down at the café by himself, is he?"

"Until dinnertime. Tom will go down then."

Tom and Mavis were walking back toward the house now, holding hands, a habit of affection Boy had taught them all, which made them look not so much like lovers as like the presently reconciled children they were.

Later Mavis explained, "We're going to tell her we had an insane row and leave it at that."

"Accurate," Ruth said.

"Accurate enough."

"And you and Tom?"

"Well, we have enough sense to be afraid of each other now. Would you call that 'a new respect'? And we've decided to talk to each other, or try to. He probably feels more cosmically guilty than he should, more at home there than at home, and he thinks I'm more cosmically angry than I should be. I don't really understand why I could have killed him without a qualm, and still I'm sorry to see him hurt. I guess, if, by accident, you don't kill something, your instinct is to take care of it."

"I sometimes wonder," Clara said, subject of Mavis' gentle hands at her nightly sponge bath, "if you'd all do better without such a persistent audience."

"I doubt that any of us would have survived the test," Mavis said, "but I think lately we've been playing to the nonexistent gallery and should quit. Maybe with little Ruth around, we'll all begin to grow up. What do you think?"

"I think little Ruth will," Ruth said.

"Ruthie," Clara decided. "That's easier."

"Here we are," Boy's voice began, "the soldier of fortune and his importunate batman, home from a very romantic dinner for two by candlelight."

"Candlelight?"

"The power went out again," Tom said. "I'm glad it didn't here. It's too bad generators are so expensive. Even so, I think we could pay for it pretty quickly by feeding everyone in the neighborhood every time the power failed."

"Public service at a profit," Boy said.

They went out into the kitchen for beer.

"I will be glad when that baby comes home," Clara said.

An unusual number of people, perhaps thirty, met the water taxi on Friday, the booze boat it was called that day because on Fridays people could order liquor and the boatman would pick it up at the Salt Spring liquor store. Some of them actually did collect bottles, but most were candidly waiting to welcome the newest island resident, little Ruth Petross, who came off the boat in her father's arms, followed by her newly lithe and slender mother. There were bunches of flowers from the finest of the island gardens; there were hand-knitted baby blankets, sweaters, booties. One of Jonah's most regular customers, a single man who worked on the road crew, had made a mobile of pinecones and driftwood, owls and pussycats putting out to sea.

A happy, slightly embarrassed Gladys was being so loaded down with gifts that Boy and Mavis and Ruth had to help receive them. The welcome had taken them all by surprise, not because the island had ever seemed unfriendly but because they had been working too hard and had been too much absorbed in their own company to make any real friends in the few months they had been here, or so Ruth would have thought; yet here they stood among a large number of friends, most of whom had obviously planned this reception some weeks ago. On an island whose main population was pensioners, the birth of a child was obviously a rare and special occasion, and this child, a sur-vivor, was at once inside a circle of human protection. She tolerated the attention, frowning over the high wall of her father's shoulder with intent disapproval. A baby has to be taught to smile. Finally the crowd moved in a slow procession up the dock. Boy reached the bus first, deposited his share of the presents, and ran back to Jonah's. The others got into the bus to take the baby home to Clara, into whose arms she settled at once.

"Now doesn't she look like Ruth?" Gladys said, smiling down at her fierce-eyed baby.

"She is Ruth," Clara said, "Ruthie."

"A real islander," Mavis said, bringing in a second load of presents.

"I've got to go to work," Tom said. "I'm sure that whole crowd went back to the café, and Boy's cooking is enough to lose us all Ruthie's new friends."

When he had gone, Gladys turned to Mavis and held her hard and long.

"You're never to leave me," she said then, "no matter what."

The happy, impossible requirements of love had returned to the house. Mavis was in no mood to protest. Ruth and Clara smiled on them. Only the baby went on fiercely frowning at her mother, a hard, mistrustful scrutiny, an absolute judge.

"Sometimes you terrify me," Gladys said to her, taking her from Clara's arms. "You're so little, and you're so yourself, and you're so wet. Come help me change her, Mavis. Come see how lovely she is under all these clothes."

"She's going to have a top-heavy family, that little one," Clara said, "two mothers, two fathers, a doting granny, and great-granny."

"Today it felt as if she belonged to the whole island."

"It's a good place," Clara said, "for all of us."

Tom and Gladys had obviously come to some understanding together that Ruthie was not simply theirs but a member of the community. Either of them relinquished her easily to be changed, bathed, walked when she was colicky. The only possessive one in the household was Coon Dog. They had worried that he might be jealous, and sometimes he was, but of other people, not of the baby. He guarded her constantly, growled if a stranger wanted to admire her when they were out for a walk.

"That poor, mixed-up dog," Boy said. "He thinks he's her mother. *I'm* her mother, Coon Dog, can't you get that straight?"

"Is that why you never stay off the island any more?" Gladys asked him.

"Well, I'm into a new phase, called the politics of survival. Mavis always was warning me I'd meet up with an off-duty policeman in them steam baths, and I did meet a real dicky-dick one night who wanted to mix business with pleasure. 'I ain't got no business, man,' I said. He was kind enough to reply, 'Then you ain't got no business here.' And I got to thinking just maybe he had a point. I like this little island, and I like this little baby, and you all, too. Why not stay alive and well? Lust ain't a big thing after all."

"Isn't it?" Gladdy asked.

"Look at it this way, if we can live here and not give a good goddamn about all those historic events goin' on down there in our motherfucking country, I can get along without the steam baths, too. I don't need it, any of it."

"Hasn't Boy told you?" Tom asked in a tone of mock innocence. "He's a volunteer fireman now."

"This here stupid white boy thinks I'm sublimating like mad with that great big fire hose, while he goes to them meetings just to be a heeero."

"We *don't* give a good goddamn any more, do we?" Gladys said over the teasing of the two men.

"Well, the war's over," Boy said. "Who wants to go home?"

Gladys looked over at Tom, suddenly seriously studying his own hands. "You want to go home sometimes, don't you?"

"No," Tom said. "This is home now, and there's plenty to do here."

"For you," Gladys said. "But what about me? What about Mavis?"

Tom looked over at Mavis.

"I've started an after-school prison camp for my four worst passengers," Mavis said. "If I can save the world from them, I guess that's enough to do … for now."

"Oh, Mavis, you never had any politics to give up!" Gladys said impatiently.

"Neither did you," Mavis replied.

"Don't you realize, Gladdy, we're not dropouts, we're refugees?" Boy asked. "Tom and I say we don't want to go home, and we don't, but there's no real amnesty down there for either one of us, and there's no way to live like a human being even if there were. He'd have to play white man and I'd have to play nigger. Even over there on the mainland, now, what's there for you to do? What's there for Mavis? You were the best teacher that school had, and what was that to them? Mavis has this fine, impressive Ph.D. Who wants it or her? You do have some choices, sure. You could go on welfare like a good radical. You could picket the school board, even get your head busted for TV or get shot at. But we've all tried that. What good is it?"

"I know," Gladdy said, "but sometimes I look at Ruthie and think, what happens if Galiano isn't big enough for her and meanwhile we've let the rest of the world go to hell?"

"It's not going to be a hard winter just out there in the world," Ruth said from the edge of the conversation. "It's going to be a hard winter here on the island."

"Way prices are going up and jobs disappearing," Boy said.

"But aren't we just sitting here saying, 'We're all right, Jack?'" Gladys asked.

"We're trying to *be* all right," Tom said.

"And we may be running a soup kitchen before this winter is over," Boy said, "for more fun than profit."

"Well, I'd *like* that," Gladys said.

"Pray for a severe depression," Mavis said. It's the only thing that will make Gladdy happy."

"Silly as that sounds," Clara said, "a lot of people were happier with less."

"Now, don't get me wrong," Boy said. "I don't like being poor, and I never have and I never will. Money's no misery in *my* pocket. Niggers never did get out of the depression, and you've got to admit, Miss Clara, about the only real fun of it was getting out of it."

"I don't want us to be *poor*," Gladys protested. "I want us to be *good*."

There was no cynicism in the shouts of laughter, but some people – and Gladys was certainly among them – were better off not worrying at goodness the way she did, wanting it not for herself so much as for everyone else on her terms, grand and impossible. Ruth knew what Gladys really needed was more to do. Since Ruthie was everyone's child, motherhood was not a full-time job. The café didn't need Gladys in the slow winter months, and work on the place would be finished with the last fall cleanup. Mavis found occupation for herself; it was her nature to. Gladdy would racket around with suggestions for other people until someone provided her with uses for her energy.

"There's so much just to see," Clara said when Ruth raised the question with her.

"I know, but she's not like you. She's like me."

But Clara was absolutely absorbed in the fall migration. "It's a question of robins again. They have such weak instincts. You'd think that would be incentive to develop intelligence but it only makes them indecisive."

Clara did, in her heart, prefer birds. Ruth went to Mavis.

"Is *that* the trouble?" Mavis asked.

"Everybody's happier with enough to do."

"You know, there are several women on this island with really little kids and nobody at all to help them. Why don't we start a nursery school?"

"It wouldn't pay at all, would it?" Gladys asked when it was suggested to her.

"You said you wanted to be good," Mavis reminded her.

"Maybe when Ruthie's older and needs somebody to play with ..."

"The kids need you now. One of those women is so zonked out on drugs most of the time she doesn't know whether the kids have eaten or not. Another's living on about fifty dollars a month, trying to raise enough to feed her kids."

"Well, why didn't you say so?" Gladys demanded.

Three days a week Gladys rode the school bus with Mavis to collect and protect her five small charges against the aggressions of the older children, who, under Mavis' direction, now did more singing than fighting, in the seats up front anyway, but they couldn't be trusted beyond that. When the little ones got over their fear of the noise, they began to enjoy the songs. With Gladys in the back, willing participation increased, and before a couple of weeks had passed, the children had graduated to singing rounds, which were more competitive and easier than harmony.

Once she and Mavis brought the little ones home, they were busy bathing, washing and mending clothes, feeding. There were sore throats, earaches, infected cuts.

"It's more like a clinic than a play school," Gladys complained.

But gradually there was more time to take the children for walks down to the beach or up into the woods. On rainy afternoons Mavis told them stories, and Gladys set up projects, finding good supplies from the trash at Jonah's, cans and boxes, tinfoil. Tom hammered together a low table so that they could all sit around it on the floor, eating the leftovers from the café in Tom's invented soups.

As the weather worsened, Tom and Boy often came home by seven in the evening because there were no customers after the six-ten ferry, and, though the women were glad to have them, the men fretted over how little the café was bringing in.

"Tell you what we ought to try," Boy said one night, "hot dinners at home, just down here at the south end, maybe three times a week. Lot of these old folks just won't come out after dark."

That project, on the surface of it, was an instant success. They had twenty-five subscribers at once. The difficulty was that only some could really afford to pay even the carefully low cost, and Boy began to discover some of the problems confronting eighty- and ninety-year-olds.

"I'm sorry I'm late," he'd say. "But there she is just back from the hospital and chopping her own wood. I said to her, 'You crazy, lady?' and she said to me, 'No, cold.'"

The days Gladys and Mavis didn't run their nursery school, they began to make day calls on Jonah's shut-in customers, warned in advance that this one was stone-deaf, that one proud as sin, this one suspicious, that one poison neat. "That old man just stink!" Boy would say, and Gladys would discover he was also an old goat.

"Oh, Gladdy, everybody's an old goat where you're concerned. I'll go," Mavis said, but, when she came back, she confirmed, "He's an old goat."

"Got to admire him," Boy said. "No teeth. Can't hardly see."

"*You* admire him," Gladys said. "I'm glad it's mostly an island of widows."

"What I don't understand," Mavis said, "is why so many of these people choose to live alone and why their families let them. I do admire them, but it's so hard a life, and, you know, a lot of them don't have to. There's Pioneer Village over on Salt Spring for pensioners, and some of them have the money to live in town."

"'Oil heat?' she said to me. 'Terrible for the complexion!'" Boy laughed. "That old lady is near as pretty as Miss Clara and vain about it, let me tell you."

"Three generations on this island," Gladys said. "The stories! Someone ought to be writing them down. You know, I'm getting to know everybody in the graveyard, too."

"We just got a letter from her son in Winnipeg," Tom said, "with a check for five hundred dollars. He says to help subsidize what must be the lousiest business venture in western Canada."

"Hey!"

"I wish I didn't have to agree with him," Tom said ruefully.

"Well, it doesn't matter about the time. We've got plenty of that, so we don't have to price it, but it sure is hard to pass on costs, and now we don't have to quite so much."

They were, in fact, making just enough to pay their bills, which was more than Ruth had expected. If business held through the winter, they could use last summer's profits to begin to buy a boat or a generator.

"We've got nothing but good worries, Tom," Ruth said to him, resting a hand on his shoulder.

He smiled at her with an expression both older and more vulnerable than she had seen before.

Preparations for Christmas this year began well in advance, this time without sorrowing irony, without need to give the lie to the dying year. The groaning of the foghorns there in the blanked-out sea, the first brush of snow reminded them.

"We can cut our own tree this year," Tom said.

The filmstrip for Ruth was a snowy street, she and Tom returning snowball fire against hilarious children, then running together, laughing. "All right, it's obscene, barbaric, commercial, and all things unholy, but it happens to be the only thing we've got."

"Are we going to church this year, Boy?" Mavis asked.

"We'll all have to go, won't we?" Gladys asked.

Ruth heard Willard's voice saying, "We aren't all still here now," but Clara sat contentedly in the window, and the baby played with her feet on a lamb skin by the fire.

"Makes a big difference, living inside a Christmas card," Boy said.

Mavis and Gladys were collecting arbutus berries with the children, finding green, yellow, and orange as well as deep-red ones, for making necklaces. Tom fashioned Santa Claus, snowman, and Christmas-wreath cookie cutters out of used cans and brought home extra pounds of dough from the café. He candied orange and grapefruit peel in slices and chips for the children to use for decorations on the cookies. On his dinner rounds Boy delivered holly wreaths which Clara had made and also took orders for Christmas shopping in town. The day of the Christmas sale at the community hall, Jonah's was closed so that Boy could take as many as were able to go in the bus, so that Tom could supervise the serving of refreshments. Clara did not go to that, but she went to the children's carol service, chiefly prepared by Mavis on the school bus, and also down to the dock to meet the Christmas ship from Seattle, which toured the islands with gifts for all the children.

"I thought the bus driver would get a holiday," Mavis said, nearly as busy delivering children to celebrations as she had been getting them back and forth to school.

Boy took his last trip to the mainland three days before Christmas, a huge list on his clipboard, his cap riding comically high.

"One of us should go with you," Ruth said.

"I'm not taking nobody over there," said Boy firmly. "You want to see Father Christmas in his riot helmet, the latest roadblock, and the Salvation Army, just turn on your TV. I'll be home for cocoa."

But he was not on the night boat.

"I knew he had too much to do," Ruth said.

"Or maybe he wanted to treat himself to the steam baths. It's Christmas, after all," Gladys said.

"He would have telephoned," Mavis said. "I don't like it."

"The traffic, the roadblocks, he probably just missed the boat," Clara said. "He'll phone in a while."

"The roadblocks," Mavis said. "Why don't we ever think about the fact that Boy doesn't have a legal license?"

"I'll call Tom," Gladys said.

Tom was too busy at the café to worry. Boy would phone in a while. He'd be all right. The others did not have Tom's distractions. Their own last preparations couldn't begin until Boy got back with the supplies.

Boy. Boy Wonder. Little, illegal, loving Boy, so indifferent to his own vulnerability that he could make you forget it yourself. Once the Christmas roadblocks had gone up, they should never have let him off the island. Ruth was now bitterly suspicious of one of the few police services she had been grateful for, keeping drunks off the holiday roads.

At nine forty-five the phone rang, and Ruth reached for it.

"Ruth? It's Stew."

"Well, Stew!" She said and felt the others relax again into waiting, unfocused worry.

"We've been meaning to call, meaning to come over to see all of you, but with the school and all …"

"It's a busy time for everyone."

"Yes, but, Ruth, I've just had a call from Boy. It's about your bus."

"Is he all right? What's happened?"

"He dodged a roadblock, said he didn't have a license and couldn't have got through, but he's sure the police saw him and probably got the license number of the bus. He's left it out on the grant lands and wants me or one of you to pick it up."

"Why didn't he call us?" Ruth asked.

"He said, once the police started checking … he said it was only a matter of time for him anyway. He didn't want to cause trouble over there for you. He wanted me to give you all his love and wish you a merry Christmas and be sure the bus and all the supplies got to you safely."

"But what's he going to do?"

"Disappear."

"Disappear?"

"Ruth, I really would like to help out. I mean that, but it's sort of awkward for me. If the police are wanting to check the bus and I don't own it, and they maybe already have a line on Boy … with law school and all …"

"That's all right, Stew. Somebody will go if you know just where it is."

"I wouldn't wait past tomorrow," Stew said.

"No, somebody will go over in the morning."

"Joanie and I sure want to get over there one of these days. We really do, and anyway we wish you a very merry Christmas."

"Yes," Ruth said. "Merry Christmas."

"That bastard! That fucking bastard!" Gladys shouted when she heard what Stew had said. "He deserves to be a lawyer!"

"Where will he go?" Clara asked. "Where will Boy go?"

"Well, anyway, now he has a choice," Mavis said quietly. "He's always known how to hide in a city. Now he knows a little bit about the bush."

"They won't catch him," Gladys said confidently. "Not Boy."

Tom, late in getting home because he'd been doing Boy's deliveries, whitened at the news, swore, said he would go in in the morning and find not only the bus but Boy and bring him home. "We can hide him in our own woods if he has to be hidden."

"You're not going in," Mavis said firmly. "If the bus gets stopped, they could just as easily hijack you across the border."

"I'm a landed immigrant. I'm here perfectly legally," Tom answered haughtily.

"So fucking what?" Gladys demanded. "Don't you remember about being on TV about just that little issue?"

"Mavis will go," Ruth decided, "on the morning boat."

"Why didn't Stew talk sense to him?" Tom demanded. "Why didn't he help him?"

"He wished us all a merry Christmas," Mavis said dryly. "How much goodwill do you expect?"

"We can't get along without him," Tom said.

"I'll look for him, Tom," Mavis said.

"You won't find him," Gladys said. "Not if he doesn't want to be found. Nobody will."

Chapter Fifteen

Mavis had no trouble retrieving the bus, supplies stowed carefully down to the last item, nor was there a roadblock to delay or detain her on her way out of town. She was home on the afternoon ferry.

"No, he hadn't checked into the steam baths, and, after that, I realized I didn't know where else to look."

"He'll come back," Gladys said, "when he's sure it's all right, in a month or two, or get in touch with us. He's not like Arthur or even Tom. He's been running all his life. He knows how."

Not like the rest of us, who didn't know we had to or didn't know we could, drifted instead, snagged, were jarred loose, drifted, snagged again, not knowing the road blasting and the razing of buildings meant to kill, never mind the evidence of dead fish and uprooted trees along the shore. Snapped daffodils, fallen birds' nests, accidents of progress, like old Weedman, like Willard. We did not know until we were grown, not even Hal that we had to, if we could, run or fight, the choice on this occupied earth.

"I'd knitted him a new cap," Clara said.

"I'd got him a nearly complete collection of James Baldwin," Mavis said.

"If you start hating what hurts and breaks us, you'll end up hating the waters of the earth. You'll end up hating the sky." *I just wanted to get us away to a safe place, an island. If we'd kept you on it, if we'd listened to your fear of the water … if, if, if! Make a safe place and a child can die in the womb. There is no place our violent mistakes can't reach. We plant time bombs in our own flesh.*

"Stop the noise in your head, Ruth," Clara said.

"Is it in my head?"

Mavis looked up, then moved to look out the window.

"It's the police helicopter," she said.

A moment later Tom arrived, passenger in a police car.

"If you offer those bastards a cup of coffee this time …" Gladys threatened in ludicrous anger.

Ruth could not have offered them anything. Fear flowed hot in her bowels and stank in her throat.

Mavis went out of the house and came back in with Tom and two policemen.

"They have a search warrant," she said quietly.

"Well, they know what they can do with it!" Gladys shouted.

"Don't!" Tom ordered sharply, but it was Mavis who went to restrain her because Tom had seen Ruth. "It's all right, Ruth. There's nothing for them to find, and I think they know that."

The two policemen went immediately up the stairs. Clara, meanwhile, watched the police helicopter land on the lawn by the orchard.

"What is *their* business," she asked Tom, "aside from frightening the birds?"

"They're going to search the grounds. It's not just that he's an illegal immigrant; he's wanted for fraud."

"Book-cooking," Mavis said quietly.

Gladys wrenched away from her. "Why don't you join the bloody pig force, both of you? You're so co-operative and you've got perfect qualifications: rape," and she smiled brilliantly at Tom, "and assault with intent to kill." The same smile shone on Mavis. "Why don't you?"

"Stop it!" Ruth ordered. "Now stop it!"

Ruthie's waking cry from the nursery had even more authority. Gladys went to get her, and Ruth moved mechanically out into the kitchen to heat her bottle. *They teach us to hate each other.*

"Mrs. Wheeler?"

One of the policemen stood in the kitchen door.

"Yes."

"This house is rented in your name?"

"Yes."

"Did you know Boyd Wonder was an illegal immigrant?"

Ruth carefully lifted Ruthie's bottle out of the boiling water.

"Did you know there's been a warrant out for his arrest for over a year?"

Did you know his five brothers and sisters were buried on the day they were born? Did you know God has an ear from one of them?

"Mrs. Wheeler, I've asked you two questions."

"The first of my tenants you inquired about was illegally deported. The last of my tenants was shot to death. I am afraid of you, and I want you out of my house." Her eyes blazed at him, fire in stone.

Tom stood tall behind the policeman in the doorway. "You've searched the house. I've answered all those questions. None of us knew."

The policeman turned to Tom. "Is she ... a little ... ?"

Over the policeman's head, Tom met Ruth's eyes, and she read in them what startled and gave sharp comfort: he was not afraid; he was laughing. Behind him Ruthie raged.

"We need to feed the baby," Tom said, "and I have to get back to work."

The policeman followed him docilely out of the door and went to speak with those who had arrived by helicopter. Ruth handed the bottle to Gladys and then hurried out of the room to have not only her house but her bowels emptied of her terror, but, even as it burned out of her, she saw the laughter in Tom's eyes. *Nigger in the woodpile/ Nigger up a tree/Nigger in the closet/You can't catch me!* The helicopter racketed into action, vibrating at the window, then rose up off the lawn and hovered a moment before it drifted out over the sea.

In Gladys' arms Ruthie tugged at her bottle, and in her softening eyes Ruth saw again her father's laughter. Clara sat, watching the helicopter through her field glasses.

"Obscene," she said in a tone as factual and impartial as if she were identifying a new bird.

"Who *told* you, Gladdy?" Mavis asked.

"Boy. He said he wasn't going to be around to play decoy forever, and I should know one or two of the basic facts of life."

"Do you understand them?" Mavis demanded.

Ruthie turned her head from the bottle and began to cry.

"Just feed her," Ruth said.

Mavis turned and walked out of the room.

"I shouldn't have said that," Gladys said. "I know that."

"Feed the baby."

"You and the police, Gladdy," Clara said, her frail head shaking itself.

❧

The helicopter the next day hovered a Christmas greeting, but did not land.

"Merry Christmas to you, too!" Ruth shouted, and the next day, "Happy Boxing Day!" but then she grew accustomed to it, a routine as accountable as the hourly ferries through the pass. Coon Dog did not. He barked murderously every time.

"It gets to seem like a daily message from Boy," Mavis said.

She had taken up most of Boy's chores, dinner deliveries, weekly trips to town for supplies, while she and Gladdy divided his hours at the café with Tom. She was the first, therefore, to be aware that other islanders did not grow as quickly resigned to police surveillance as they did.

"There are rumors," she admitted to Ruth and Clara at their nightly ritual, "and questions. It's not the helicopter so much as the patrol car. Funny, in the summer most people seem to want police on the island, but now they resent it. They don't say anything to me about resenting Boy, but I think some of them do. A couple of people have canceled their dinner orders."

Tom couldn't be sure the slight fall-off in trade at the café wasn't just the January slump, and he was probably being hypersensitive about increased references to hippies.

" 'Mind you,' they say, 'we like most of our own hippies, but some of them … the sort that bring the law onto the island …' That stupid helicopter delivered two parking tickets to some kids up at Coon Bay the other day."

One morning Gladys came in tight-lipped and white with only three of the five children she and Mavis usually took care of.

"What is it?" Ruth asked.

"Oh," Mavis said, "it's nothing. Their mother's just high out of her mind on something or other."

"She says I'm a witch," Gladys said, "and that's why my baby died."

"And Boy's a nigger," one of the children offered.

"Do you know what 'nigger' means?" Mavis asked.

"Bad."

"It means black."

"He's cocoa," another child said, fondness for the drink and the man in his voice.

The heavy snow came late, finally grounding the helicopter. The next morning all five children were waiting for the bus, and that afternoon the two who had canceled dinners signed on again along with half a dozen new customers. Mavis traveled with a shovel to dig herself in to her customers, to make paths to their woodpiles and out-houses. Twice in the week she had to call the doctor, once for a heart attack, once for a winter cold tipped into pneumonia.

"Oh, Clara," she said, "I'm glad you're not snowed in out there or in Queen's Court either."

"Vanity, mortal vanity is what it is," Clara said. "We're a nuisance wherever we are."

Then Ruth, Mavis, and Clara all seemed to pause and listen, for they were so used to Boy's picking up any biblical possibility and making a comic sermon out of it that they did not know what to do with their small assertions without him.

It was well into February before the rain began again, the slush more traitorous than the deep snow had been. Now Mavis came home with reports of broken arms, cracked hips, car accidents, but for Ruth the first ominous wonder was a yellow crocus under the eaves of the house.

"Spring," she said to it, and she looked out across the thin, old snow on the lawn as if it hid not simply the sodden grass but the human wreckage of all her life. Then the noise in her head was in the sky, and Coon Dog began to bark. The pilot of the helicopter gave her a grave salute as he hovered for a moment over the orchard.

"Ruth?" Gladys called. "The real estate agent's here to see you."

Ruth turned back into the house.

"She'd decided to sell. She wanted to give you notice, but I told her nobody would be looking for property for another couple of months anyway, and it wasn't a good idea to leave the place untended. I said how well you were taking care of it. I told her what good tenants you were."

"We have a lease until June," Ruth said.

"I told her that, too."

"Why is she suddenly in a hurry?"

"Oh, she's a silly old woman. She's heard rumors. She doesn't want the responsibility ..."

"We need another year," Ruth said, "just one more year ..."

"I tried," the real estate agent said. "She really doesn't want you in the house. She thinks she could break the lease, under the circumstances. I don't think she will, but she won't renew it."

"Perhaps she could sell it to the police," Ruth said wryly over the noise of the helicopter still hanging above them. "It seems to be their favorite spot on the island."

"I want you to know, Mrs. Wheeler, that nobody else wants you off the island, any of you."

"Thank you."

"And whatever it is about Boy, he was very good to all of us."

"It won't be easy to find another place ... like this."

"No, but something will turn up."

Ruth shut the door on the kindly bearer of bad news and turned to Clara and Gladys.

"This movie sometimes runs forwards and sometimes runs backwards," she said.

"What was it Boy called us?" Clara asked quietly. "Displaced persons? Refugees?"

"I'm so *sick* of it!" Gladys said. "So sick of it all!"

Ruth and Clara watched her slam out of the house, startling Ruthie awake. Ruth went to her and scooped her up out of her crib. She was heavy now for Clara's arthritic knees, so Ruth held her on her own lean, trousered lap. She and Clara were the only ones constantly aware that Ruthie was a radio receiver for all the emotions in the household, and when she was with them, they willed a calm, amused shelter for her, which served to calm them, too. Coon Dog butted his large head into Ruth's lap as well.

"It's all right," she said to him.

Mavis and Tom came home together, already having heard the news.

"It isn't the end of the world," Tom said firmly. "We don't really need a place as big as this, and it was going to be a problem eventually, fencing off the cliff, fixing the roof."

"There's a farm up island," Mavis added. "Someone said the owners might be looking for tenant caretakers – inland but good soil, much better than this."

They were both watching Gladys, who sat on the floor, her tangle of hair screening her face, playing with Puss.

"Gladdy?" Mavis called to her.

"I'm going to Toronto next week," Gladdy said, still not looking out from behind her hair.

"Alone?"

"With Ruthie. Mother's sent me a ticket. They all want to see the baby."

"For how long?"

"I don't know. It depends …"

"Of course, your mother wants to see the baby," Clara said.

No one else offered a comment. Given pause, they did not know what to do without Boy there to take it. What sort of noise would he have made? He was the only one who had found it easy to rebuke Gladys, but her wanting to see her family was natural enough. She couldn't very well time it for a period of calm in this household. There seemed to be so few. Still, her trip was read by everyone in the room as a desertion.

"Tom," Ruth said later, "I'm sure Mavis and I could manage if you went along with them for a week or two anyway, and there's money for the fare."

"I'm not invited," Tom said.

"Surely ..."

"Ruth, I told you last summer: Gladdy's plans don't affect mine."

"She's not leaving us, is she?"

"I don't know. I don't think she does. She does want to see her family, and she wants to get away."

"Tom?"

"I can't hold her. I don't even want to any more. She's got to figure it out for herself."

"And Ruthie?"

"Haven't you heard about kids' lib? We don't own them either. Oh, she's right, Ruth, in so many ways she's right, but I can't do anything more about it than I do."

It was Mavis who took Gladys and Ruthie in to the airport on her way to pick up supplies, leaving Ruth and Clara with an oddly empty day on their hands.

"Well, I left for good and all," Clara said firmly, "and I didn't get away with it. Why should Gladdy?"

"She's less stubborn and more willful."

Clara sighed. "I hardly have a chance to rest my eyes between the seasons now. I'm not really tired of seabirds, but it might be nice to be inland for a change."

Without the baby, without Gladys' nursery children under foot three times a week, Ruth hadn't enough to occupy her in the house. Most afternoons, therefore, she pulled on boots, slung her windbreaker over her shoulder, and went out into the fickle March weather, predawn snow still on the ground at the north edge of the woods, small, nearly secret violets in the spring grass, the salmonberry in bloom, the deciduous trees pulsing with sap. Wind gusted on the bluff cliffs, on the shore, sending occasional small but fierce hailstorms rattling through the trees and onto the stones, bouncing on the turf. Sometimes Ruth took shelter under huge cedars, but more often she took the weather like a tree herself. Always as a child her fantasy had been of something washed ashore or onto a high rock, but she had not drifted here, like a log storm-broken from a boom, marooned and placid. She had chosen this place with the stubborn intention of taking root, and so had Tom. If they had to move from their cliff inland, they could. Boy had been blasted away, and now Gladdy had gone in a moral high wind, which might finally wrench Mavis loose, too, but she and Tom and Clara would stay.

It is not a safe place. There is no such thing. But I've chosen it, my last compensation.

Because they would almost certainly have to move by June, there was no point in the garden they had planned or in the long-term repairs they had considered. Without work to do on the place, Tom wouldn't be spelled during the daylight hours, and he was restless when he got home at night. The old habit of nightly reading to Clara, often neglected in the past months for counting the day's take, for tending Ruthie, for preparing for some special event or other, was rediscovered, but Tom found it hard to keep his mind even on the books he had chosen. Mavis offered to play chess, and sometimes Ruth, in her sleepless wanderings, would find them still absorbed in a game at two or three in the morning, though Tom had to be up by six-thirty to open the café, Mavis soon after to drive the school bus. There by the dying fire, in concentrated conflict, they waited.

"Sometimes I feel like a character out of D.H. Lawrence, and

I've never approved of him," Mavis said.

"Why?" Clara asked.

"Oh, it's all so homey and elemental and intense. He wins a game. I win a game. But really the war between the sexes is all over, for us anyway."

"I don't suppose there's been any word from Gladdy?"

"None."

"We could phone, couldn't we?"

"Tom won't. Oh … I won't either."

The daffodils bloomed. The alders quivered into tassels. The deer came back to browse. The household worked and waited, counting small profits at the end of March. Mavis was doing the books.

"How long is it now?" Clara asked Ruth.

Since Claire, since Arthur, since Willard, since Hal, since Boy, since Gladdy and Ruthie? Where do you begin?

"Since we've had a letter from Hal?"

"Nearly a month," Ruth answered. "It's going to take him a long time to give in to coming to the island."

"I could ask him."

If I cannot have my heart's desire, bring any one of them home, from the mainland or the dead, any one I've ever waited for, as a sign, even my own husband, even your son.

"If you like," Ruth said.

Clara must have been writing the letter at about the time the accident occurred, the road grader tipping out of control, Hal falling. *Look, out! Look out, Hal! Progress will finally fall on you, too.* He'd been flown in to Vancouver before they telephoned Ruth. A badly fractured hip and leg, the necessity of at least two operations before Hal could walk again. But a heart attack had caused the accident. The operations now might kill him.

Ruth sat with Clara for half an hour before she caught the evening ferry.

"Are you going to make the decision or is he?" Clara asked.

"He is if he can."

"If he can't?"

How often Ruth had wished through the years that she could take the lives of those she cared about into her own hands, make the safe and sane decisions for them that would keep them alive. Now, faced with that possibility, helplessness in contrast was a blessing.

Mavis brought in coffee.

"If Hal doesn't want to risk it, Ruth, if he'd rather … we can take care of him here. He doesn't like any of us much, but we haven't tried very hard either. You say I'm a good nurse."

"I'll tell him," Ruth said. "Thank you."

Ruth stood on the aft deck of the ferry watching the island grow smaller and smaller. She had not left it since Ruthie was born.

Chapter Sixteen

If Hal had ever been hurt or sick before, Ruth did not know it. Though she had tried to think about the decision that confronted him, the conversations she had held in her head were with the energetic barrel-chested bantam of a husband she had always contended with, toothpick cocked at her, dimple signaling. As she was led down the long orthopedic ward by a nurse, she had to control irrational amusement rather than dread, for all the men here looked done up for a cartoon or a farce, great leg casts suspended in the air, bandaged heads, and they assisted her mood, calling out cheerful crudities as if this were a beer parlor instead of a hospital ward. So much at home most of them must have been here a long time, but they were nothing but movie extras waiting for the comic lead to be brought in.

At the end of the ward was a curtained-off space, and there in an adult-sized crib lay a small old man, cheeks sunken in, breathing heavily. Ruth turned back to tell the nurse, but in the second before she spoke the mistake, the shape of his head recalled her eyes to him.

"We're keeping him as comfortable as we can," the nurse said.

"Did he lose his teeth as well?" Ruth asked.

"Oh, no, we just take the bridge out."

"Bridge?" Ruth looked away from the nurse in sudden, guilty embarrassment. She did not even know Hal had a bridge.

I've got to pretend. I've got to behave as if this hurt man is my husband. I can't let her know I'm not sure.

"I'll bring you a chair."

Alone, Ruth finally really looked at the man in the crib, and still she could not believe it was Hal lying there, a much older brother perhaps, even his long-forgotten father, but Hal? She had never seen him sick, not even with a hangover. If it hadn't been for the handsome curve of his skull, she would have rushed out of that curtained cubicle and said, "It's a mistake. It's the wrong man." But she was now inside the farce, had a part in it, a humiliation to suffer, just for someone's amusement. The nurse handed her in a chair. She sat down on it and stared, but she could not make Hal's face of the face before her, and what if he woke and saw her there, a perfectly strange woman with a face of stone? She would terrify him.

He groaned and turned his head slightly.

"Hal?" she said softly, doubtfully.

He opened his eyes, and, though they were bloodshot with bewildered pain or drugs, she knew at once that they were Hal's eyes in this otherwise strange face.

"Ruth," he said, and immediately closed his eyes again.

Then the unrecognizable lips began to tremble and tears leaked out from under the lids of his eyes. Crying? Hal crying? She was afraid to touch him, but she had to. She reached out her hand and cupped his head, forcing herself to look, too, to learn this face until she could recognize it. It was as if the tears had changed the landscape of his flesh, made deep gullies in his cheeks, washed out the dimple. She began to brush them away gently with the palm of her hand and felt the crying go deeper into his chest.

"It's all right now," she said. "It's all right, Hal."

Gradually the tears stopped, then the catching breath in the chest.

"It hurts," he said softly, the voice of a bewildered child.

"The nurse can probably give you something soon."

He opened his eyes again, and the familiarity of them forced Ruth to stop tears of her own for a man she had never known except in his pride and his anger. She had not even known him in his grief. Now reading the pain and the fear, for his sake she would have turned away if she could, but she had to share this with him. He couldn't do this alone.

"Are they … ? "he began. "Have they decided?"

"We have to decide."

"What the hell …" he protested weakly, turning his face away.

"You don't have to have the operations. They can …"

"I wouldn't be able to walk; that's what they said."

"Well, Clara can't either …"

"She's an old woman. What good would I be?"

The tears began again.

"You've been good enough."

He gave a bitter grunt.

"On the island …"

"Don't tell me about that island."

"I could take care of you. I want to take care of you."

He was crying out of control again.

"Hal?"

"I don't want to be one of your cripples. If you didn't want me when I was good for something …" But he couldn't go on.

You had to be too damned good, you poor, proud bastard.

She was holding his hand now, pity and impatience rising freshly from old guilts, old angers.

"Tell them … to get it over with," he said. "I'm still good for my life insurance."

The nurse came in to give him a shot and then gestured to Ruth to leave him. The doctor was waiting just outside the ward.

"Have you decided?"

"What real chance has he … either way?" Ruth asked.

"Hard to say."

"He said … to get it over with, but I'm not sure he means it."

"And you, Mrs. Wheeler?"

"You kill that man's pride, and you kill the man. It's stupid! Stupid! Stupid!"

The doctor stood and waited.

"Get it over with. He said, get it over with."

"We can do the first one tomorrow. Then, in a month, if every-thing goes well …"

"And he'll be able to walk."

"Yes," the doctor said, "he should be able to."

Ruth walked back down the long ward, this time identified with that closed-off cubicle before which all these clownish characters fell silent. Her own mirth was also forgotten. She sat down again and took Hal's hand.

"Tomorrow," she said.

He looked out at her from behind the bars of his crib, a wavering hope in his eyes. She smiled at him.

"Don't you know you're indestructible, Hal?" she said, grudging him this lie, the sort he had always wanted and she had always re-fused, ungenerous to his silly, mortal ego even now. "Don't you know if anything could have killed you, I would have years ago?"

"You've been a bitch of a wife, it's true," he said, "except in bed." A shadow of a dimple appeared for a second, and he rested.

Ruth sat through the night with him, listening to the changing sounds of the ward out there beyond the curtains, the moans, the cryings out, the curses, a long, long reality before the farce of the day could begin again and each bluster through his bad joke again. A nurse brought her a light meal, brusque with concern as Mavis might have been. Toward morning, Hal was restless.

"If I don't make it, Ruth …" he said once.

What? She wanted to ask him. *What do you want me to do?* But again she wrenched the refusal of that possibility out of her grudging heart.

Once she thought he whispered, "I'm afraid," but it was too low for her to be sure.

Was there nothing she could say now when this might be her last opportunity? Nothing true. What he had never wanted from her he certainly didn't want now. Then couldn't she, just this once, lie to him with all her heart? Accept the farce and really let him be the hero of it? His pain and his fear pleaded with her: lie to me, lie to me with all your heart, make me real, make me immortal.

Dawn came and with it the clatter of breakfast trays. The orderlies would be there soon to prepare him.

"Did you bring your dress?" he asked suddenly.

"Dress?"

"The one I bought you."

"Of course," she said. "You're taking me out to dinner tonight, aren't you?"

"Well, maybe not tonight, but listen, Ruth, when I get out of here, we're going to do a little living, right?"

"Right," she echoed, rock-face for his hope.

"I mean, our own life. You've been items in the newspaper too many times, you know, star of screen and radio and all that. When I get out of here, I want a wife, understand?"

"I understand."

"A little real living …"

The orderlies were there. She leaned down and kissed him.

I do understand, Hal. I'm just such a bad liar. I'd give you the strength of my own heart if I could. It's what you want, all of you, even Tom: our lives. In that impossible bargain, the tables somehow get turned and we take yours instead, over and over again, my father, old Weedman, Willard, even Tom's son. Galiano is an island of widows. I don't want your life, Hal. Keep it. Keep it.

She had to take her hand away from his, but she waited for him then, walked beside him as he was wheeled along the corridor and stood fiercely smiling at him until the elevator doors shut.

Two and a half hours later, Hal was dead. The doctor was angry about it. The hip was going to be a handsome job, and then Hal's heart betrayed them, and he couldn't even help carry the sense of failure.

Spared, Ruth thought stupidly, spared, too, ever knowing that she'd lied to him not only about his life but about her dress as well.

"He filed his funeral arrangements with us, Mrs. Wheeler," she was told at the desk. "Memorial Society. So, if you have no objection …"

He was to be cremated, his ashes disposed of without ceremony. When had he decided such a thing, who had always behaved as if death were irrelevant to him? After Claire was killed perhaps, in one of those urgencies of goodness to take care of things, to settle things for himself.

"Just sign here."

Why not? He'd refused to cross the water while he lived. She needn't defy him now by carting his dead body or his ashes to a place he couldn't even build a road to.

She was brought his things. She took his wallet and his watch and left the rest for the hospital to dispose of, including his teeth. She'd have to contact his company to find out where his other belongings were, probably in a motel room somewhere in the interior. Or did he have a woman there? Ruth had often wondered about that. The company would know. They'd have to deal with whatever personal claims there were on him, aside from herself and Clara.

In his wallet, there was over three hundred dollars in cash. Hal never accepted the concept of the credit card. Money, to be real, had to be in hand. Filed behind it was a fresh white envelope with her name on it in his surprisingly small, neat hand.

Inside was a list of Hal's assets, not only the hundred-thou-sand-dollar life-insurance policy but a third share in a beer parlor in Kamloops, five acres of land which would front by next spring on a new road, five thousand dollars in bonds with the safe-deposit box number, and a technical explanation of her widow's pension. The only personal statement was at the end. "I didn't think Mother would outlive me. Take care of her." It was not even signed.

When had he written it? Probably right after the doctor told him what his chances were/weren't. Ruth looked at the writing itself, try-ing to find in its constricted neatness something of the angry pride he must have felt, the good son, the good husband, providing even now. She had no idea he'd invested money in a business, in land.

Always such a ready spender, needing to be, and always generous with his mother, with her, too, when she let him, Ruth had imagined he spent generously on other people, too. Had he away from them lived instead simply and to himself? He must have, at least most of the time.

She could not keep her mind on him or on what she should do next. The formalities seemed over with. It was only one o'clock. Perhaps she should go get some lunch. And come back for … for?

But I can't go home like this to Clara, not with nothing but his watch and wallet. I'll get her some flowers, that's what I'll do, and a bottle of really good sherry. I've got lots of cash. I might even get her a new sweater.

Ruth ate lunch and then wandered out into the windy April day, the city white in the sun, the mountains an eye-hurting brightness. She should go down to the beach, walk that shoreline again, a Broadway bus to Dunbar, and she could walk from there, back down through her old neighborhood, see the house …

Ruth sat down on the bench at the bus stop. She was confused. She knew that. She was tired. But it was a lovely day, and she had four hours to kill.

Maybe she'd like a new novel, something light.

The bus stopped, and Ruth got on it, smiling at people as she walked down the aisle to a seat.

City people don't smile back. I'm glad we live on an island. People smile. Most of them women, widows, lonely of course, but the children smile, too. And they know my name as well as Coon Dog's. I wouldn't live here again. Hal never liked it, even in the old days. Didn't like highrises any more than I do, for himself anyway. I wonder when he lost those teeth. He never said a word about it. Such a vain man.

Ruth smiled.

Wait until Clara hears he had a bridge! And a third share in a beer parlor. "Hal talks a lot to keep from listening and to keep from answering questions." It's true, Clara, but it never would have occurred to me to ask him about his teeth.

She got off the bus and began to walk north toward the water and the mountains, but, when she crossed Fourth Avenue, she hesitated, uncertain suddenly of where she was.

"Excuse me," she said to a woman coming toward her, "but where am I?"

The woman gave her a puzzled look and then hurried by.

This isn't the place. This isn't the place I ought to have come. How could I have done this?

But she was still walking, and now she was beginning to be walled in by high construction fences, some of the plywood panels painted on: an ugly, realistic mural of the city and the mountains. It blocked her way and then forced her to look up. There above her head were giant legs of concrete growing up out of the soil that must have been her garden. The road would lift up on them and flow over the bulbs, the bones of birds, and Willard's blood, just as she had dreamed it, just as it had happened before.

It's your goddamned road, and it's broken your great big stupid heart. I didn't kill you, but what difference does it make? You're dead just the same.

"Hal! Hal!" Ruth shouted, but her voice stopped at the painted mountains, and there was no one this time to take the picture of Hal's wife, grieving like a stone, in her ordinary sorrow.

Ruth did not go on to the beach, nor did she buy anything for Clara. She took a bus to the terminal and sat there on a bench to wait the hours until she could catch a bus to the ferry.

When she was finally able to get on board, her seat companion was carrying a Siamese cat in a wooden cage. It called its distress rhythmically with every breath. Neither the reassuring nor the stern tones of its owner made the slightest difference. When the bus entered the Massey Tunnel, the animal howled. Ruth did not want it silenced. Instead everyone on the bus should take up that howl in protest against the speed and the echoing darkness. But the animal in them was so silenced that they were offended, cast disapproving looks at the owner, refusing to know that she was as helpless as the cat, as enclosed in this man-made cage of a bus, of a tunnel, roaring this time under the river.

Then Ruth was walking through the terminal, up into the covered walkway which would finger people onto the deck of the ferry, loudspeakers blaring above their heads. Finally she was on deck and could stand in the last light of evening and see the double hump of the southern tip of Galiano.

"Ruth?"

She turned to that light, young voice, and there was Gladys with Ruthie in her arms.

"It's April Fools' Day, did you know that?" Gladys asked, laughing in their crowded embrace. "I thought it was the right day to come home."

"Do they know you're coming? Did you tell them?"

"No. I've been enough nuisance, and anyway I wanted to surprise everyone. Oh, I've missed you so. It's so good to see you."

"She looks more like Tom than ever."

"She's begun to crawl. I don't think it's going to be very long before she walks. She's so strong, Ruth."

"So how did her granny like her?"

Gladys frowned. "We stayed long enough for them to get used to her. But they're still upset, ashamed somehow because the other one died. Mother kept talking about what strong and healthy ancestors we have, and she kept asking me what I knew about Tom's family. It took her a long time to see Ruthie as a person, you know, instead of something I'd half done. It shook me a little. A lot of things did."

Ruthie had gone to Ruth and was settled now on her lap in the lounge of the ferry.

"But I saw Boy," Gladys said, her face clearing.

"Boy?"

"Yes, he just phoned Mother one day to say he was a friend passing through, and she told him I was there; so he came out. His name is Luther Baldwin this time, and he said he'd write when he'd found a place. He said there must be other people like us somewhere in the Ontario bush."

"Will he ever be able to come back?"

"Someday, he said. Someday he would, and he told me to, for love's sake, go home while I could. Ruth, what's the matter?"

"Hal died this morning. Clara doesn't know yet."

"Oh, Ruth …"

"I should have telephoned. There won't be anyone to meet the ferry."

"I just wanted to walk to Jonah's anyway. How did he die?"

"An accident …on the road, his heart. He didn't make it through the operation."

"Will it be very hard for Clara?"

"For a while, but not as hard now that you and Ruthie are home."

A tall black man, as elegant as Boy had been outlandish, sitting right across from them, took a guitar out of its case and began to play. Ruthie's attention led Gladys and Ruth to listen. Then he began to sing in a voice at the same time powerful and sweet. Ruth didn't try to follow the words, wanted instead to be carried along with the melody, but fragments of statement kept lodging in her mind.

> "Don't want to be brave,
> Still don't want to be no slave …
>
> These chains, they are rusted and worn,
> It takes all this dying to be born.
>
> There's a light on the mountain for me …"

The deep voice lifted out of its register into a high treble, taking that refrain far off, until it faded from hearing.

"Most people don't understand," Gladys said.

Ruth gave her a questioning look.

"I don't think I did either until I was back there in the old way. I never wanted that: marriage, babies. I tried to tell my sisters about the politics of survival, about trying to be all right where you are …"

So Boy's and Tom's rhetoric had become Gladys' own.

"It's no easy thing," Ruth said, the words still there in her head. "It takes all this dying …"

The boat sounded for landing.

"We're home, Ruthie," Gladys said, taking her from Ruth. "We're nearly there."

They hurried off the boat and left their suitcases in the waiting room on the dock before they started up the road.

"Go along ahead," Ruth said. "I need a minute to myself."

She watched Gladys hurry along with Ruthie up the dark road toward the lights of Jonah's.

"*Every time I make it back, I'll know I'm about the Lord's business,*" she heard Boy say. It was not her vocabulary any more than it was Clara's. The world was in no one's hands. The baggage of death she was carrying could not even be put down in the little graveyard. It had to be taken home and spent, like all loss, like all death. "*It takes all this dying …*"

She would buy the house they lived in, and they could begin the spring ritual Clara had taught her, the digging up of the soil to plant the seed. One day, even nearer the end of the world, the road would inevitably lift and flow over the water, flow over them all, but, as she had known from childhood, anyone left would go right on planting, in the April Fool day.

"'Scuse me, lady."

The singer from the ferry stood at her side.

"Luther Baldwin, he said …"

"Come along," Ruth said. *Until I die, until I die.*

Appendices

From *The Body Politic*, April 1977
By Michael Lynch

There are lots of things Jane Rule's new novel is not. Historical, like *Patience and Sarah*. Zippy, like *Rubyfruit Jungle*. Unique, like *Nightwood*. Etc. It is not realistic either, though its setting in Vancouver and Galiano Island ground it in our geography.

Like Rule's earlier novels, *The Young in One Another's Arms* is a gentle, serious comedy. Like all comedy it relies on stereotype and artifice; but – also like all comedy – these artificialities have "real" effects on us "real" readers. (If these presuppositions seem silly now, please hear me out; I think Rule's novels ask us to grant them, and unless we do, we miss what she's up to.)

Plots have long been, for Rule, and artificial underpinning to allow her to get on with her subject. *Against the Season*, for example, transparently moves toward a simultaneous birth and death for its climax. *The Young* condenses this, incredibly, into one birth (of twins, one living and the other dead) against a whole series of deaths. It has the soap opera's – or the comic opera's – impossible density of individually possible events: an OD, an eviction, a murder, cops, cop evaders, and accidents so conveniently timed you'll wonder where the casual went.

Its characters appear as cartoon-types, at least from a distance. There's Clara, the dying but mellow old lady; Joanie, the man-chaser in hair rollers; Gladys the easy radical; Tom the easy countercultural-ist and draft evader; Willard the moron who can accept no change; Mavis the antipolitical (read *reactionary*) PhD candidate uptight over her lesbianism; and, most incredibly perhaps, Boy Wonder, the book-cooking, Bible-spouting, quick-tongued faggoty black. And others. Like her plots, Rule's characters are conventional underpinnings for her subject: her tone. Rule is a comic novelist, with all the artifice of a Jane Austen, say, or a Robertson Davies. To fault her for these artifices is like faulting Schubert because his structures aren't so tight as Beethoven's. No, if you want realism, read May Sarton.

What tone is her subject? If Austen's *Emma* is a comedy of manners, and Davies' *The Manticore* a comedy of the Jungian intellectual at play, Rule's new novel is a comedy of – I borrow a venerable four-letter Anglosaxon word – a comedy of *ruth*. Ruth is a kind of tough unsentimental mercy, and Jane Rule is our Portia. The quality of her mercy is as unstrained as the Vancouver climate.

The Young in One Another's Arms centers on a character whose name, in fact, is Ruth – one-armed Ruth Wheeler, whose boardinghouse houses all those typed characters in an "arbitrary family" that comes to span four generations. Like her Old Testament namesake, Ruth Wheeler is devoted to her mother-in-law, and the warmth of this relationship suffuses all the younger characters – those in and those out of one another's arms. Indeed, these young are sometimes at arms against each other, for Rule, if I may pun, tests her *ruth* mercilessly.

As in *Against the Season*, the comic diversity of types becomes a comedy of interchange and reciprocation. Clara can speak and be spoken to about old age and dying. Radical, sleep-around Gladys has to confront, and talk about, pregnancy. Boy Wonder (whose name tops even Davies' Boy Staunton) is a consummate self-parodist who can speak as easily of his book-cooking as of his quickies at the baths. And so on. Rule's comedy grants a language to her characters which we don't, yet, have: one for speaking with each other, warmly but fully, of drastic personal differences. Like Clara, looking through her opera glasses at the birds and the trees on Galiano, tenderly distinguishing each species from each, Rule looks into her characters not to control but to distinguish, deepen, and respect them.

It's a language where small images may resonate with implication: a dead bird under a lilac, a lungfish from Loren Eiseley, an electric cable to a neighbour's house, a mechanical "reel of events." These enable Rule to deal with questions of options, age, sex, and progress without pomposity or impersonality.

A scholar, some day, should show how this novel replies to the ageism and sexism of W.B. Yeats – the modern Irish poet from whose work Rule takes her title. Rule, like the lesbian-feminist poet Adrienne Rich, enhances her own meanings by "correcting" those of Yeats on women and old age.

Through all its artificiality, comedy (as I began by saying) impinges upon what we call the "real world." I think, in this respect, that even if Rule's new novel isn't "liberationist" in a direct sense, it's an important novel for the lesbian/gay movement(s). Not because it compels us to form café-operating communes on Galiano; it doesn't; besides, Ruth and her friends don't even choose to do it themselves, but go there only when all their other options are closed.

Its importance rather lies in its tone, in the quality of its *ruth*, when we set about to offer collective alternatives to exploitative family units. We need a language, a tone, which lets us be different by caring, to show anger (as these characters show) without hate. "If you start hating what hurts and breaks us," Boy says to Ruth, "you'll end up hating the waters of the earth. You'll end up hating the sky."

Not hate, but anger and action. And *Ruth*. It's a novel we're lucky to have.

From *The Ontarion*, Tuesday, November 1, 1977
The Young in One Another's Arms
Jane Rule, Doubleday, 1977, 204 pp., hardcover, $6.95

By D. Reid Powell

Jane Rule is a lesbian. That being said, it must also be said from the outset that this fact is no more significant than the fact that Jane Rule is American-born. In CanLit circles, too much is often made of these sorts of details, and too little of the literary merit of a given piece.

This is Rule's fifth volume of fiction, her fourth novel. As the title suggests, the book concerns itself with the dependencies that people create for one another. The W.B. Yeats quotation which forms the title is from the poem *Sailing to Byzantium*, a peon to the triumph of youth's holiness over the sin of aging.

In the broadest sense, *The Young in One Another's Arms* is a love story or rather a set of love stories stacked one in the other Chinese puzzle-box style. The setting is Vancouver, in a boardinghouse run by an expatriate American, Ruth Wheeler.

Ruth gathers to herself all manner of odd lodgers, in many cases those rejected by society or even themselves. To her home come draft dodgers, closet revolutionaries, grown infants, and more. The mix of persons who find themselves at the doorstep of the soon-to-be-demolished roominghouse is the most difficult aspect of the book for a reader to accept.

Each character, in some manner, leans upon another and is strengthened. Casual friends become lovers, creating jealousy and eventually tragedy, and lovers split apart to create stronger friendships. Love in this world has little to do with sex (perhaps this is the most valuable lesson of the author's own sexuality), and less to do with sexual activity.

A baby is born to one of the book's characters, but not as the culmination of any societal set of givens; rather the baby is a loving symbol of the interaction of love on this seemingly disparate group.

When Ruth Wheeler's roominghouse is taken from her, her 'family' persuades her to live with them on an offshore island, where they set up a small restaurant. Individual 'family' members are lost to the group, but always replaced by others.

The unit is always intact, as is their love. I found this book disturbing, in that it potentially threatens an entire set of conventions; in the author's obvious acceptance of clearly different conventions than most people, she populates the world with like personages.

Implicitly, this is revolutionary thinking, a challenge to the status quo. Explicitly, it will probably be glossed over by most readers. Some of Rule's conceptions stretch credibility, but others haunt the heart's complacency. The presentation of this in a readable, intelligent novel is a triumph of both skill and courage.

Editor's note: Whether this review speaks to the sexual politics of 1977, or simply the reviewer's somewhat square take on the book, it is helpful for contemporary readers to witness the atmosphere in which the book appeared. "Jane Rule is a lesbian": The reviewer makes this announcement as if to scandalize his readers. He then dismisses his lead-in as being a detail of no significance, but returns to the point when he has to dissect the politics presented within. Most telling is the statement, "in the author's acceptance of clearly different conventions than most people, she populates the world with like personages." Personages? In our current age of same-sex marriage and pop cultural embrace of homosexuality, it can be difficult to appreciate the unsubtle tone of prejudice with which the book (or at least its author) was received.

STAR STUFF

BOOKS

Jane Rule's new novel conveys the power of life itself

By Katherine Govier

've been a Jane Rule fan for two years now after having read her great short stories, which manage somehow to be simultaneously beautiful and blunt, in the little-circulated collection, *Theme For Diverse Instruments.* For years the victim of a media blackout because of her lesbianism, 45-year-old Rule has recently surfaced in *Content, Books In Canada* and even *The Canadian* as a literary martyr. She deserves to be better known, but the more important fact about Jane Rule is that she is simply one of our very best writers. However, after reading **The Young In One Another's Arms,** her third novel, I still prefer the stories for their purity and nerve.

In this novel, Rule's voice is subdued, reflective. She's chosen the novel's lyric title from that bitter moving poem by W. B. Yeats: *That is no country for old men. The young/ In one another's arms* . . . Yet it is used almost ironically. A place which can be home to both the arrogant young and the life-damaged old is the refuge sought by Rule's characters. She puts them in a boardinghouse near Vancouver's downtown beaches, where grad students, draft dodgers and other displaced persons rub shoulders with the old residents who refuse to be bumped out by development.

It's a house full of rambunctious, quarreling bed-hopping 20-year-olds, run by their surrogate mother, Ruth Wheeler, who has lost one arm and her only daughter in violent accidents. The house also contains her bedridden mother-in-law for a third generation. Ruth's doors are open to anyone on the lam, no questions asked. It's a challenging setting for a novel, and Rule handles it well, alternating contemporary dialogue with the

★★★★ DON'T MISS ★★★ PRETTY GOOD ★★ FAIR ★ LOUSY

consciousness and memories of Ruth, her central character. It is Ruth's solitude and watchfulness that give the novel its depth, and her madcap boarders who give it action.

There are new arrivals, like brush-cut Arthur, who escaped the U.S. army with nothing but his khaki, and the black Boy Wonder, who goes out to the steam baths every night to get picked up. There is Stew, the acid-head, who gets a hair cut and goes to law school after betraying Arthur to the police for the love of yet another resident, Gladys, the beautiful one with the bad mouth, whose gift and punishment to them all is her sexuality. And there is Joanie, the misfit wearing curlers at the dinner table and running out afterward into the waiting red Ford or blue Olds. Some stay and some go, escorted out by the police on their way to the border, by voluntary disappearance, by death. Their lives get tangled together in incidents like a police shooting after they've been evicted from the house, and although they take up other homes, they find it hard to live apart. Suffering various reverses and successes, the group reunites on Galiano Island, running a cafe, transforming itself into a true family—a family by choice, to which Gladys contributes a baby.

It's a short novel and a good read, partly for the villains, who are all very modern—police, bulldozers, hospital wards. In Hal Wheeler, "a bowlegged bully who works as an earth-mover on wilderness road gangs," Rule has created absolutely and realistically the worst husband in any book I've read in years. She also conveys the power of something more frightening than villains, and that is life itself—a brutish irrational force, smashing and destroying like Hal's machinery slashing trees off a mountainside,

taking in its careless course, pieces and whole lives of people, tearing at those who are left. What remains in the end is a fierce but not very hopeful protectiveness for youth and its hair-raising energy.

Reading Rule's novel, I feel that it comes out of a large love for young and old, and a wisdom that may see youthful mistakes but refuses to call them. These qualities give the book an urgency that is more compelling than the contrivances of plot. They draw the reader on through sometimes awkward dialogue and rapid changes of tone that can be confusing. Rule has that gift which, in this country, perhaps only Margaret Laurence has consistently shown: If she does not always have the power to make us laugh, she can certainly move us to grateful tears.□

★★★ **The Young In One Another's Arms** by Jane Rule (Doubleday Canada, $6.95)

POP: SEE PAGE 18

11

From *Miss Chatelaine*, Summer 1977
"Jane Rule's new novel conveys the power of life itself"
by Katherine Govier

I've been a Jane Rule fan for two years now after having read her great short stories, which manage somehow to be simultaneously beautiful and blunt, in the little-circulated collection, *Theme for Diverse Instruments*. For years the victim of a media blackout because of her lesbianism, 45-year-old Rule has recently surfaced in *Content, Books In Canada*, and even *The Canadian* as a literary martyr. She deserves to be better known, but the more important fact about Jane Rule is that she is simply one of our very best writers. However, after reading *The Young in One Another's Arms*, her third novel, I still prefer the stories for their purity and nerve.

In this novel, Rule's voice is subdued, reflective. She's chosen the novel's lyric title from that bitter moving poem by W.B. Yeats: *That is no country for old men. The young / In one another's arms...* Yet it is used almost ironically. A place which can be home to both the arrogant young and the life-damaged old is the refuge sought by Rule's characters. She puts them in a boardinghouse near Vancouver's downtown beaches, where grad students, draft dodgers and other displaced persons rub shoulders with the old residents who refuse to be bumped out by development.

It's a house full of rambunctious, quarreling bed-hopping 20-year-olds, run by their surrogate mother, Ruth Wheeler, who has lost one arm and her only daughter in violent accidents. The house also contains her bedridden mother-in-law for a third generation. Ruth's doors are open to anyone on the lam, no questions asked. It's a challenging setting for a novel, and Rule handles it well, alternating contemporary dialogue with the consciousness and memories of Ruth, her central character. It is Ruth's solitude and watchfulness that give the novel its depth, and her madcap boarders who give it action.

From *Essays on Canadian Writing,* **Spring 1977**
"The Dying Generations"
by Ken McLean

Jane Rule's fourth novel is an analysis of the establishing of "community", of the need for isolated men and women to enter into what she, in a recent interview (in *Canadian Fiction Magazine,* No. 23, Autumn, 1976, an issue devoted to her) calls "voluntary human relationships" based on love and understanding. The novel traces the growing together of 50-year-old Ruth Wheeler and the tenants of her Vancouver boardinghouse. Though in the *CFM* interview Rule insists that "there is no main character in the new book," Ruth is clearly the main character – most of the time the events and other characters are perceived from her point of view, and we experience her through interior monologues, in which she re-examines and re-lives her past, adapts to her present, and occasionally contemplates and plans her future.

As the book begins, the boarding-house has eight tenants: Clara, Ruth's mother-in-law, bedridden but actively involved in the boarding house life, sympathetic and knowing, a devotee of Ethel Wilson's novels; Willard, a mentally-retarded, uncomprehending middle-aged man, who has been with Ruth longest, and for whom she feels particularly responsible; Tom, an independent, confident, practical young man who works temporarily as a short-order cook; Mavis, intellectual, ascetic, just completing her PhD thesis on Dickens, seeking both a job and a family; Gladys, liberated, political, naturally sexy, teaching at a school for handicapped children; Joanie, a fashion-conscious, gold-digging secretary; Stew, who gets stoned and plays the clarinet; and Arthur, a recent American army deserter, hiding out in the basement, still recovering from the trauma of his flight. Ruth is occasionally visited by a ninth character, her husband Hal, a macho male chauvinist ("a woman's mind is a cunt"), who doesn't take kindly to Ruth's tenants nor they to him. Internal strife soon besets the boarding house: resentful of Arthur for taking Gladys from him, Stew comes out of his miasma to report Arthur to the police and flee.

But Stew is soon replaced by a somewhat unusual newcomer, a happy-go-lucky, self-mocking young black homosexual called Boy Wonder (an ironic echo of Richler's Boy Wonder?), who deliberately, but without bitterness, acts out the old "nigger" stereotypes, "guilt-tripping" everyone, as Gladys puts it. He describes himself thus soon after his arrival:

> I'm a sort of James Baldwin reactionary, born too late
> for my style, faggoty little nigger making up to white
> boys; so I got to come to a backward country like Canada
> where there's enough social lag for me to survive. I mean,
> you want to be *nice* to me, don't you? Tom here does,
> too. He wants to be my *friend*, and this here is a tree I
> can swing in. They cut all that kind down by now in my
> native land, and that's the truth. I mean, I've only been in
> Canada a week, and the guilt here is just unreal, and you
> hardly got no niggers to make up to. *(p.86)*

In the *CFM* interview, Rule said that Boy Wonder is "the best character for me," a representative of a recurrent type in her fiction, the "holiday character," "who can break the tension when everything gets very earnest and very uptight … who can cool it, can clown it … and restore a kind of sanity." Moreover, as Helen Sonthoff observes (in an article in the same *CFM* issue), Boy is not naïve – he realizes that to live in community one must take risks, risks that involve inevitable loss, loss that must be accepted and survived, a realization that is the central meaning of the book. But Boy is too good to be true – he is always loving, always making the peace between the others, always cool. Thus, unlike the other characters he must be taken on a nonrealistic, semi-allegorical level.

Crisis tends, of course, to knit a family together. When, soon after Boy's arrival, the land on which the boardinghouse stands is expropriated for development, the community is temporarily broken up. Clara seeks the refuge of a nursing home, Ruth shares an apartment with Willard (on a mother-child, not woman-man basis), and the "young" rent a farm-house, away from the evils of modern urban society. But the eruption of violence, all the more effective for being quite unexpected, brings the family to its senses, and both Ruth and Clara join the younger members on an island off the B.C. coast (Galiano, where Jane Rule herself lives with Helen Sonthoff). Here, away from city pressures, the family is able to grow into a close knit unit and develop (literally in that Gladys has a child whose parents are all of them). They still have their problems of course – police harassment, sexual rivalry as Tom and Mavis contend for Gladys' affection – but with Boy's help and in the island setting they survive.

The villains of the piece, the enemies of human community are obvious, perhaps too obvious: the developers and their henchmen the city politicians who expropriate the land on which the boardinghouse stands; the courts which extradite American draft dodgers and deserters; the men and machines who lay roads through the wilderness; and especially the police, who fit the fascist pig stereotype assigned them by Gladys, evicting the family from the boarding house, harassing them on the island, setting up roadblocks and wearing riot helmets, and shooting first and asking questions later.

Jane Rule told Geoffrey Hancock (in the *CFM* interview) that her publishers "loved" the title ("They think it will sell the book"). "But", she added, "most people who approve of it don't know the Yeats poem it comes from and how dark the implication is." It is taken from the opening stanza of Yeats' "Sailing to Byzantium":

> That is no country for old men. The young
> In one another's arms, birds in the trees

– Those dying generations – at their song,
The salmon-falls, the mackerel-crowded seas,
Fish, flesh, or fowl, commend all summer long
Whatever is begotten, born and dies.
Caught in that sensual music all neglect
Monuments of unageing intellect.

The dark implications, the awareness of mortality, are certainly present in the novel. Two people die, one is dying, and Gladys gives birth
to twins, one alive and healthy and one still-born. But Rule added that
"the thing I want a title to do is say something about the experience of
after you've read the book or story. So that you look back at the title
and say, 'Uh huh, that's right.'" And we do. For the dominant feeling of
the book is not of melancholic awareness of death, but of celebration of
life, of the "sensual music" and vitality of "the young in one another's
arms", of the joy of community. It is for this affirmation, and for the
novel's, to use Margaret Laurence's words quoted on the dustjacket,
"cool low key analysis" of human relationships, and for "the sensitive
artistry of [its] language" that it, despite its weaknesses (conventional
technique, some stereotyped or exaggerated characterization, too obvious villains) is well worth reading.

Jane Rule was interviewed by Larry Goldsmith for Boston's *Gay Community News*, November 17, 1984. What follows are excerpts from that issue's feature article.

"I suppose what I do is try to concentrate on relationships and community," says Jane Rule. "I think those are the things that I write about most. They're books about voluntary community, because I think most of us have moved away from our families. Not just gay people, I mean everyone. And I'm fascinated with the kinds of support groups we build around ourselves to make a community."

Rule's exploration of the interpersonal relationships among her characters never neglects the political context in which their lives are led. Novels such as *This Is Not For You* and *Contract with the World* guide the reader along the passionate and conflicted paths of lesbian and gay characters with the meditative eloquence of a writer familiar with the terrain. But these works are not merely stories of psychological journeys; the paths are lit in the harsh light of a political reality that's usually more blinding than it is illuminating.

The political sense in Rule's writing, however, is less didactic than it is simply revealing. "It does seem to be that literature is about what *is*," she explains, "and a lot of people in the movement would like literature to be about what ought to be or what we'd like it to be. So, you know, I do write about happy lesbians and I also write about unhappy lesbians, I write about very competent gay men and I write about gay men who kill themselves, because I think we have a great range of experiences, as anybody else does, and I think we're also people under pressure. So a gay character can give a kind of deeper vibration of those social pressures than perhaps some heterosexuals."

"My response to the whole role model thing," Rule says, "whether it's I who am to be a role model or the characters in my books who are to be role models, is nobody needs any, except bad ones. Those were the only role models that were ever any good for me. I'd think 'I'm never going to teach like that' or 'I'll never talk to people like that.' As long as you have those negative role model checks, I don't think you need heroes. Of course, all the heroes we have are those that we then want to tear down – set 'em up and bat 'em down – and that's certainly not of interest to me."

Similarly, Rule finds limitations in the idealized communities in which lesbians and gay men try to live. "None of my characters is ever totally sustained by the community," she says. "I don't think anybody ever is. I think there are times when you feel really involved with and sustained by your community, but – maybe this is partly the statement of an artist, too – you spend an awful lot of time alone."

"It would be, I think, totally false to say that the community hasn't done marvelous things for all of us. It also has its scary aspects. I sometimes worry about people who come out in the community and feel buoyed by it and get a false sense of what that world is out there and try to go back into it and get pretty badly hurt and troubled. I think communities can provide false senses of security, as families can provide false senses of security. My family always says, 'Why do you have to go out there in the world? It's safe here.' I think all of us have to go out there if we're going to grow and be. But I think in any community, there's that sense that we all want to protect each other… I think where you are inside your head has to be scary some of the time. And certainly the world is."

"I believe we learn more about a culture through our fiction writers than we do from anyone else. I think that's where case by case, individual experience by individual experience can add up to an understanding of the range of experience people are actually having, far more than any other sociological studies that are going on. And that's very exciting."

There are new arrivals, like brush-cut Arthur, who escaped the U.S. army with nothing but his khaki, and the black Boy Wonder, who goes out to the steam baths every night to get picked up. There is Stew, the acid-head, who gets a hair cut and goes to law school after betraying Arthur to the police for the love of yet another resident, Gladys, the beautiful one with the bad mouth, whose gift and punishment to them all is her sexuality. And there is Joanie, the misfit wearing curlers at the dinner table and running out afterward into the waiting red Ford or blue Olds. Some stay and some go, escorted out by the police on their way to the border, by voluntary disappearance, by death. Their lives get tangled together in incidents like a police shooting after they've been evicted from the house, and although they take up other homes, they find it hard to live apart. Suffering various reverses and successes, the group reunites on Galiano Island, running a café, transforming itself into a true family – a family by choice, to which Gladys contributes a baby.

It's a short novel and a good read, partly for the villains, who are all very modern – police, bulldozers, hospital wards. In Hal Wheeler, "a bowlegged bully who works as an earth-mover on wilderness road gangs," Rule has created absolutely and realistically the worst husband in any book I've read in years. She also conveys the power of something more frightening than villains, and that is life itself – a brutish irrational force, smashing and destroying like Hal's machinery slashing trees off a mountainside, taking in its careless course, pieces and whole lives of people, tearing at those who are left. What remains in the end is a fierce but not very hopeful protectiveness for youth and its hair-raising energy.

Reading Rule's novel, I feel that it comes out of a large love for young and old, and a wisdom that may see youthful mistakes but refuses to call them. These qualities give the book an urgency that is more compelling than the contrivances of plot. They draw the reader on through sometimes awkward dialogue and rapid changes of tone that can be confusing. Rule has that gift which, in this country, perhaps only Margaret Laurence has consistently shown: If she does not always have the power to make us laugh, she can certainly move us to grateful tears.

Doubleday US press release, 1977

"I enjoyed Rule's novel a lot. It has a rare human warmth about it, rare these days when fiction is apt to be sour in its view of the human race. Every one of her characters lives for me and I shall go on thinking about them, especially Ruth and her strange but totally believeable marriage."— May Sarton

". . . simply written . . . and genuinely touching."— The Kirkus Reviews

The traditional definitions of what makes up a family are blurry. The terms "nuclear family" and "extended family" represent only a head count, a sophisticated census; they do not make allowance for the non-traditional family embraced by Ruth Wheeler in THE YOUNG IN ONE ANOTHER'S ARMS. Ruth is a fifty-year-old woman for whom loss is more the rule than the exception— her arm and her daughter. And before the story is played out—her home and her occasional husband, Hal. "What you lose is what you survive with," says Ruth ironically. The insurance money for the loss of her arm has paid for her house, and her absent husband has been replaced by his mother, Clara.

Ruth Wheeler's boarding house on the Canadian West Coast is home to an assortment of people, many of them young and most of them disenfranchised. They include her ailing mother-in-law Clara who openly welcomes death, beautiful Gladys the

street radical, Mavis the conservative PhD candidate, American draft-dodger Tom, Boy Wonder, and others, all different.

At various times they are a band of refugees, soldiers, missionaries, and playmates. They bicker, tease, and even betray each other. But when Ruth is faced with giving up the house, and they must scatter, they finally realize that they have become a family, complete with all the dependencies the word implies. Together they move to isolated Galiano Island where they share responsibilities for the house, garden, restaurant and the neighbors. There they involve themselves in the politics of loving each other, children, old people, birds and gardens.

It is a fragile alliance, frightening in its brittleness. But, thanks in a large degree to Ruth's example, the members of the group find the love necessary to nurture each other. This is a delicately told tale that arouses real lump-in-the-throat concern for these lonely people, and real gratitude that they have found one another.

Jane Rule is the author of three novels, numerous short stories, and a work of nonfiction, LESBIAN IMAGES (Doubleday, 1975). She was born in New Jersey and travelled all over the U.S. as a child. After graduating from Mills College in 1952 she moved to London, England. She has been a teacher of everything from swimming to creative writing. She moved to Canada in 1956 and recently to Galiano Island, British Columbia, the island to which Ruth and the family also retreat.

Publication date:
                    March 4, 1977
Price: $6.95
Pages: 204

Review copies: Olivia Blumer (212) 953-4574
Author promotion: Andrea Granet (212) 953-4485
TV/Radio: Jean Booth (212) 953-4888

DOUBLEDAY & COMPANY, INC.
245 PARK AVENUE
NEW YORK, NEW YORK 10017

First page from the first draft of manuscript, with corrections in the author's hand.

Wheeler

In that darkened street, Ruth ~~Peters~~ might have been mistaken for a boy
of middle growth, spare bodied, light on her feet. She nearly always wore
trousers, and the empty right sleve of her windbreaker could seem a boy's
quirk of style. But if she stepped under a street light, looked up and sharply
beyond that illuminated space, her face redefined the first impression, ~~deeply~~
~~lined~~, the color of false pearl, dark eyes of remarkable size but limited by
aging lids, anchored by taut lines to her temples: the face of a seventy-year-
old woman. Ruth ~~Peters~~ Wheeler was, in fact, just over fifty.

"I looked older than my mother when I was born," she claimed.

Most new born do but outgrow it. She had not. She had lived with that
birth face until age became the excuse for it or was beginning to be. Her
body, ordinary enough in growing, had refused to age, small breasts still high,
belly firm as if it had never given room to the one child she had borne.

"I'll die in pieces," she said, her right arm the first sacrifice to that
process, an accident she didn't remember.

"I can only remember what's happened to other people."

Those accidents which she had not witnessed stayed vivid: her father crushed
under a redwood tree (it didn't matter that the report blamed a bull dozer),
her daughter falling like Icarus out of the sky (the late news invented an
automobile accident). She still dreamed occasionally of the falling tree
and the falling child (who was twenty-two when it happened). She dreamed as
well of the great six lane highway that flowed over the valley in which she had
grown up, a river of cars spawning to impossible cities, to be seen as broken
and battered as fish on its urban shores.

She had been part of the debris, carried along like an uprooted bush or
root-- or so she dreamed it, snagged her and there by a job that didn't last,
a man that didn't last.

"You're not a sort of woman to live with," her husband explained to her
when he left. But not the sort to leave behind entirely either. A memory
of her would catch him like the first breath of cold air in the lungs, and
he would go back to her for a day or a week.

First page from the second draft of manuscript, with corrections.

The *tame* in one *brother's* *Corner*

Chapter I

In the darkened street, Ruth Wheeler might have been mistaken for a boy of middle growth, spare bodied, light on her feet. Shewnearly always wore trousers, and the empty right sleeve of her windbreaker could seem a boy's quirk of style. But if she stepped under a street light, looked up and sharply beyond that illuminated space, her face redefined the first impression, the color of false pearl, dark eyes of remarkable size but limited by aging lids, anchored by taut lines to her temples: the face of a seventy-year-old woman. Ruth Wheeler was, in fact, just over fifty.

"I looked older than my mother when I was born," she claimed.

Most new born do but outgrow it. She had not. She had lived with that birth face until age became the excuse for it or was beginning to be. Her body, ordinary enough in growing, had refused to age, small breasts still high, belly firm as if it had never given room to the one child she had borne.

"I'll die in pieces," she said, her right arm the first sacrifice to that process, an accident she didn't remember.

"I can only remember what's happened to other people."

Those accidents which she had not witnessed stayed vivid: her father crushed under a redwood tree (it didn't matter that the report blamed a bull dozer), her daughter falling like *a spray of sparrows* ~~Icarus~~ out of the sky (the late news invented an automobile accident). ~~She~~ still dreamed occasionally of the falling tree and the falling child (who was twenty-two when it happened). She dreamed as well of the great six lane highway that flowed over the valley in which she had grown up, a river of cars spawning to impossible cities, to be seen as broken and battered as fish on its urban shores.

Ruth
~~She~~ had been part of the debris, carried along like an uprooted bush or root-- or so she dreamed it, snagged here and there by a job that didn't last, a man that didn't last.

"You're not a sort of woman to live with," her husband explained to her